Praise for Rosalind Stopps

'Cutting between past and present, Stopps has
written a tense page-turning thriller that is also
a powerful study of old age and disability.'
The Times

'At times both touching and darkly funny, *A Beginner's
Guide To Murder* explores the vital ways in which women
can support one another through their darkest hours.'
Anna Bailey, *Sunday Times* bestselling author of *Tall Bones*

'[An] excellent character-driven tale... by
turns amusing, sorrowful, and thrilling.
Stopps is definitely a writer to watch.'
Publishers Weekly

'A beguiling, beautifully crafted treat of a novel...
with dry humour, a great plot, exquisitely realised
characters, and more than a hint of feminist
sensibility... truly everything I want in a novel.'
Jessica Moor, bestselling author of *Keeper*

'Darkly comic and gripping.'
Woman's Own

'To weave these threads together in this way
is a masterful feat of storytelling.'
Tim Pears, author of The West Country trilogy

'A quirky, witty thriller that reminds us not
to underestimate the older generation.'
Best

Rosalind Stopps lives in a multi-generational, doggish household in South London. She dreams of escape to Margate, like the characters in her books. She has a weakness for reality TV, and for her grandchildren, not necessarily in that order. Rosalind has always been a passionate believer in social justice, particularly for the more vulnerable members of society.

Rosalind's debut novel, *The Stranger She Knew*, was shortlisted for the Paul Torday Memorial Prize, and her second novel, *A Beginner's Guide to Murder*, was longlisted for the CWA Gold Dagger Award. *Virginia Lane is Not a Hero* is her third novel.

Also by Rosalind Stopps

The Stranger She Knew
A Beginner's Guide to Murder

VIRGINIA LANE IS NOT A HERO

ROSALIND STOPPS

ONE PLACE. MANY STORIES

HQ
An imprint of HarperCollins*Publishers* Ltd
1 London Bridge Street
London SE1 9GF

www.harpercollins.co.uk

HarperCollins*Publishers*
Macken House, 39/40 Mayor Street Upper,
Dublin 1, D01 C9W8, Ireland

This edition 2024
1
First published in Great Britain by
HQ, an imprint of HarperCollins*Publishers* Ltd 2024

ISBN: 9780008599430
TPB: 9780008599447

This book contains FSC™ certified paper and other controlled sources to ensure responsible forest management.

For more information visit: www.harpercollins.co.uk/green

This book is set in 10.7/15.5 pt. Sabon by Type-it AS, Norway

Printed and Bound in the UK using 100% Renewable Electricity at CPI Group (UK) Ltd, Croydon, CR0 4YY

For the fam, with love

PART I

CHAPTER ONE

London

I didn't want to kidnap that baby, and if I could have helped her any other way I would have. I'm not a troublemaker and I don't relish confrontation. I prefer to keep my head down and go for the quiet life but I've always had limits. Morals even, and sometimes a person has to stand up and be counted, even when they'd rather sit the whole thing out. Anyone else would have done the same thing if they had seen what I saw and known what I knew, I'm sure of that.

I'd had a very bad year. It happens sometimes, to any and all of us, some years just stink. Things happen to a person one after the other, little things and big things until you're not rolling with the punches any more, you're lying on the floor curled up in a ball trying to protect yourself from whatever's coming next. I know there are good years too, golden years when everything goes well and babies are born and people fall in love and pass exams and get the jobs of their dreams but not everyone has those. And even if they do have a sparkling year it seems to be over very quickly. You don't notice time passing when the sun is shining on you but the spiteful years, they go slowly and they don't fade. They stay with a person until they're part of their body, like an extra arm that can do nothing but flail around and knock things over. That's what my year had been like, and I was looking forward to seeing the back of it. I didn't have anything to look forward to except the possibility of getting out, finishing myself off and closing the chapter and the book.

I spent a lot of time looking out of the window. I'm not particularly curious about people but I live in a flat in a Victorian house with big bay windows, and I have my desk in the biggest window so that I can catch the light. I wasn't writing much then, but it was a good place to sit and much less lonely than turning inwards and staring at the four walls. I saw it all, but not in a nosy way. I liked seeing other people have other lives. Going shopping, coming home again, taking dogs for a walk, I liked the fact that life was going on, and that people were doing things even if I wasn't. I collected them, all the little things I saw, and I wished that I could put them into an album so that I could flick through it when there wasn't much happening. When it was dark, for instance, or on rainy days. It would have been nice to look back on the time the woman from number ten slipped on the ice and the young man picked her up as though they were in a film, or the time that the little baby from number six noticed me in my window and smiled. She opened and closed her fist too and I was sure it was an attempt at a wave.

Most of my window memories involve Ocean. That was her name, the little girl with the sweet wave, although I didn't know that in the beginning.

I'd watched her a lot when she was tiny. I saw her mum

4

bring her home from hospital, all wrapped up in a car seat with just the smallest slice of her face showing. Her mum looked so proud, tired but triumphant as if she'd won a gold medal, which I guess she had. The baby was so little I had to catch my breath. I described her to Jed, I remember that. He couldn't see at all by then, just shapes, he said, and some light and dark. He lay there on the bed, listening to me prattle on.

'I think it's a girl,' I said, 'because I can see a lot of frilliness going on.'

He laughed at that, my Jed.

'Now I'm imagining the baby dressed like one of those toilet roll holders your mum used to have, V,' he said.

He was the only person who ever called me V. My name is Virginia, although it always seems too long for me. Too much to expect people to say, especially if they have a one syllable name like Joan, or Ruth.

I sent a card and I knitted a little cardigan for Ocean when she was born. It was the same pattern I'd made for William all those years ago and the feel of the soft wool made me want to cry. Jed said he liked listening to the click of the needles and so I clicked them for him even when I had finished making the little cardigan. He didn't know I wasn't really knitting, I'm sure he didn't. He asked me to describe what I was making and I loved that part.

'I'm making a shawl for myself in a lacy pattern, like the ones I used to wear in the Seventies,' I said. 'Rainbow colours.'

Sometimes I wonder how he could have believed that I had such a hidden talent, but it's a fact that good men will believe almost anything if it's told the right way. Bad men believe nothing but that's another story entirely.

5

Jed died round about Ocean's first birthday, so I stopped looking out of the window. I didn't see much of her for a while. I was busy trying to figure out who I was and how to go on living. William flew home for the funeral and stayed for the first month or so and that helped. There has always been a lovely, easy-going side to him, even when he was a baby. It wasn't always in the forefront, but this time he was really amazing. He brought me cups of tea without asking, and we spent hours going through old photographs and talking about Jed. He talked a lot about his life and how great it was and how he didn't really like England any more and the whole time, I knew I had to make it easy for him to leave again. That was the worst part. I could probably have kept him with me if I had told him how desperate I was feeling but I knew that wouldn't be right. He had a job and a sunny life in Australia with people he cared about. Maybe I could have gone with him if I'd really tried. He even pretended he wanted me to go out there and live with him and I appreciated that, although I didn't believe him. He made it sound wonderful, like some kind of Disneyland for grown-ups but I would have spoiled it all with my grief. Besides, I wasn't ready to leave the room with the bed where Jed had been, or the books we had read together, or the cups he had drunk from.

I couldn't even go to our little place in Margate. I needed the recent past all around me at that moment, and we hadn't been to the seaside flat for the last year. I needed to be in a place where I believed it possible that Jed would walk in, or call me from the next room, even though I knew that wouldn't happen. It was complicated, as the young people say.

So William flew away and I made myself smile while he

6

packed. I talked about getting back to work and writing an article about the cost of funerals. I told him he couldn't monopolise me for ever and I reminded him of all the people I needed to catch up with. When he still hesitated I told him I had made an appointment to get my hair cut. That was the clincher, I think. William doesn't know a great deal about women and he assumed that I must be fine to be left alone if I cared about my appearance again. So easy to fool a person who has been known to you since they were a foetus. He left and I waved at the door, then I came back inside and counted out my pills. I had done some research on the internet to find out how many it would take to finish me off, although I think I would have had to care a lot more about what was happening to me to go through with it right then. The fact was, I didn't. I didn't care about anything at all.

I don't remember what happened for a while after that, not in detail. Days and weeks went by and I kept the curtains closed. I lost a lot of weight because I didn't remember to eat. My phone still had alarm reminders for Jed's medication and his meals, and I didn't turn them off so I should have known when it was lunch or dinner time but I had a lot on my mind. Sorting memories, that was my job and it's a slow job if you do it on your own and do it properly. It's probably never finished. Some you've got to keep, in a compartment where you'll find them easily even if you lose some of your marbles, and some need to be archived. Never thrown away completely, not at my age. If you start doing that there's no knowing where it might end.

It's no wonder, with all that going on, that I stopped keeping an eye out for Ocean. I thought about her sometimes, calming thoughts with the whoosh of the waves in the background. Such a lovely name. I wasn't worried about her. If anything, she belonged to a different time, a time with Jed in it and quiet chats about how much she was growing, or what she was holding. She always liked to have a toy or an object in her hand when she went out, right from when she was tiny.

'It's the penguin today,' I used to say to Jed, or, 'my goodness, that giraffe is nearly as big as she is.'

Jed died in November, and after William left I kept the curtains closed until spring. Christmas nearly finished me off. All that time alone. I'm not saying I didn't see anyone because I did, friends and neighbours called and tried to chat. They brought cheese pies or robust cakes. I think that seeing how miserable I was made them feel better about themselves and the pies often had grey hairs in them so I was glad when they stopped. I waited until the food sprouted the first growth of mould before I put it in the compost bin. They came less and less as time went on. I must have looked OK. I had become skilled at putting a good face on and chatting a bit, even getting some safe Jed memories out on show but when the people stopped coming, that was a different story. I would literally lie on the floor sobbing until I frightened myself. I went into every room calling for him and once I even got down so that I could look under the bed, as if he might be there. That really did scare me and I decided to give it three months. If things didn't change in that time, I promised myself, if I still felt this bad, I would take the pills. I would finish things off and tidy it all away, my life. William would be OK without me. Anyone would agree that it's better to have a dead mum than a mad one. I argued it successfully to myself and then I circled the fifteenth of June on the calendar in the kitchen. Three months to save my own life.

I opened the curtains that day, all of them, and for the first time I changed the sheets on the bed where Jed had died. It was hard, and I cried as I buried my nose in the pillowcases but there was no part of him there, not even a molecule and I knew that. I even felt an unexpected relief as I turned the washing machine on. I imagined Jed applauding and I slept a little better in the clean bed.

The next day I put on different clothes as if I was going somewhere. A dress, one of the ones that Jed had liked and an almost new cardigan. A cardigan with no memories. I ate a bowl of limp cereal and I went to my desk. Nothing much had changed. The street was quiet. The new leaves were getting ready for their debut and the sun that had been shining in October was shining still, though through a different part of the window. I wished first for Jed to be alive and second for a job to go to. Something I needed to do that was bigger than me, whether it was selling sofas or writing about microwaves. It's weird, I thought, that young people never have enough time in their lives although they really have loads, and old people have too much time even though it's actually running out. It was the kind of observation that made Jed chuckle. I opened my mouth to speak and turned in my chair before I realised that there was no one there. It was as if he had died at that exact moment, that's how strongly I felt it. It was hard to bear. I would have loved someone to talk to, even for a minute. I could have rung or texted William but I knew that I might cry and sound like I was seeking attention and I didn't want that kind of fuss. Worse, I didn't want him to find me a nuisance.

I've seen that happen with other parents of adults, the balance can tip and once it does, it never goes back. Then you become a problem for them to solve, a weight they have to carry, that sort of thing. They come round to see you and they're sighing before you've even opened the door, thinking of all the jobs they have to do. Changing light bulbs that the old dears can't reach any more, that kind of thing. I'm not having any of that. I wouldn't, even if William lived in London instead of Sydney, although it would be lovely if he could pop round. I've had a flashlight in the toilet for ages because the bulb is too difficult to reach. William didn't even notice when he was over, he takes after me. He's got other things on his mind.

I opened my computer and scrolled past all the messages of sympathy and advertisements for sheltered flats. I knew I'd seen an email from the magazine that employed me sometimes, and I thought it would be good to read it and make a start on whatever work they were offering me. I was ready to roll up my sleeves and write about anything but it wasn't good news. I should have read it earlier, before I got my hopes up. They were sorry to hear about Jed, the email said, and they knew I'd need to take things easy, and they were sure I'd want to kick back a bit, so they wouldn't be expecting any more pieces from me for the time being. I knew what that meant. I was being put out to pasture with a subtext that I should be pleased they'd kept me on so long.

I stood up and walked around the room for a moment, trying to absorb the information. It shouldn't be a surprise, of course it shouldn't. No one wants to employ women over a certain age and I'd been lucky to sell them three pieces in the last year. None of my same age friends had jobs and there was no reason I should. I was aware of that but at the same time I wanted to cry like a small child. It's not fair, I wanted to say, I didn't do anything wrong except get old. I've still got things to write about. I didn't say any of that in my email, of course. I thanked them and said that I was doing fine and if they ever, blah blah blah.

I sat at my desk anyway and stared out onto the street. I thought I might write a poem about how it felt to be lonely, or about Jed and how much I missed him but one of the skills I have is that I can recognise a good poem when I see one. I can recognise a good poem at a hundred paces and it stands to reason that I can recognise a bad poem too. And mine were consistently terrible. They rhymed, for goodness' sake. Proper rhymes with the right number of syllables and everything, and they would tell no tale of how empty my life was. No one would read them and weep, not even me. So I sat there and stared at the street and thought about the three months I had to save my own life and as I was thinking I saw her again. Ocean, and she had grown a lot while I had been wintering in solitude. She was in her buggy, but sitting more upright and she was holding something pink but I couldn't quite see what it was. Her mum was pushing her and the pair of them looked about as miserable as could be. I stood up to lean over my desk towards the window so that I could wave and Ocean saw me and smiled but her mum kept looking down at the floor as if there was something there that she needed to keep track of.

I smiled and waved at Ocean until her mum turned in front of my house to walk up the left hand side of the crescent towards the main road. I could only see her back as she pushed the buggy but she looked absolutely defeated. I tried to think back to how she had been before, when Ocean was little and Jed was still alive but I couldn't remember her looking like that before, not ever. She had always been bouncy and cheerful and happy to smile or wave as she passed my flat. I guess everyone has bad days, I thought. I'd been engrossed in my own troubles and hardly thought about anyone else for months, and I was ashamed of myself. I'll go and knock when they're home, I thought, take something for the baby and stay for a cup of tea, if she asks me in. There was a problem, of course, in that if, when my three months were up, I decided to leave, I didn't want to have to worry about how anyone else might feel. I considered that for a moment or two but some things are too complicated to worry about. I'll think about that later, I thought.

I waited until Ocean and her mum had turned onto the main road before putting on my coat and leaving the house. I needed to help in some way and I had decided to get a present for Ocean, something that would cheer her up and put a smile back on her mum's face. Difficult to explain why it was so important but I think it was the link with Jed, and all the times we had enjoyed talking about her while he was so ill. He wasn't William's dad, that was the thing, so we had never had the delight of sharing a tiny baby. I was on my own when William was born but I imagine that for people in couples there must be a great deal of mutual cooing, counting fingers and toes and marvelling over how cute they were. And we never had that but we loved to talk about Ocean, so I was in her debt for giving us that chance.

I'd left the house before since Jed died, obviously I had. I'd put the bins out in the middle of the night when it was quiet, and I had scurried to the shops and back when there was absolutely nothing left to eat. This time felt different. I went out with my head held high, that was the difference. I had a job to do for somebody else, and it wasn't all about me. I tried to look at ease with myself as I sailed down the road, hoping that I wouldn't see anyone I knew.

The shops seemed a lot further away than they used to be and by the time I got there I was wishing myself back home and on the sofa, but I had a mission. Besides, I might have used up a whole hour without checking the clock by the time I got home and that had to be a plus.

I didn't see her again for a while after that. I sat her present, a cuddly avocado toy with a smiley face, on the windowsill. It was looking out so that Ocean could spot it and I spent longer than I should have each day at my desk doing nothing but waiting for her to leave the house, but she didn't. Or if she did, I didn't see her, which was odd. Maybe they were away, I thought, and I had missed their leaving. They might have left when it was dark, after all. Or maybe she was ill, little ones often got colds in the early spring. After five days I was worried, and I had convinced myself I should knock. I hoped the concern was for their sake, not mine, but it had been a long time since I spoke to another person face to face. In lots of ways I didn't want to. It was tempting to keep my door shut, read the paper and chat to Jed like I usually did, but the misery on Ocean's mum's face haunted me. I think it was because she had looked even more miserable than I felt, and I hadn't thought that was possible. I hadn't instigated any social contact with anyone since Jed died, and probably not for some time before that but this seemed like something I could do. Something I had to do, even.

I put the avocado toy and a packet of fancy biscuits some rubbernecker had given me into my shoulder bag and walked two doors along and up their front path. Between our two properties was a student house with several residents and it always tended to be a bit messy but I was shocked to see that Ocean's garden was even more so. There were bin liners full of rubbish where there had been bulbs and flowers, and potato peelings and other food debris were everywhere on the path. There was a picture of a fierce-looking dog on the door, warning callers to beware because he wasn't house trained. That stopped me in my tracks for a moment. I was sure it hadn't been there before. I couldn't believe they had a dog, though, even a non fierce one. I would surely have heard it bark, even little dogs make a noise sometimes. Or I would have seen them take it out for a walk.

I didn't believe it but still I was nervous. I had to steel myself. I sometimes like friendly dogs once I get to know them, but I'm terrified of strange dogs, especially the big ones. I could hear Ocean crying as I knocked on the door, so I knew that they were in. Quiet crying, more like a sad toddler than a stroppy one. I knocked again and I could hear muffled voices. Ocean and her mum lived alone as far as I knew, so I turned to walk back up the path, thinking that she wouldn't want me bothering her if she had friends round. I'd reached the gate and I was almost sighing with relief when the door was flung open.

'Can I help you?' the man said.

He said it in quite an ordinary way, but there was something about him that made my blood freeze. I knew he wasn't OK, that's the only way I could put it, although I didn't trust my judgement. Who would trust the judgement of a woman who still sometimes cooked meals for two and scraped one into the compost bin?

'Hi,' I said, 'I live two doors down and I've brought a little present for Ocean.'

He stared at me as if I was talking in another language and I was so unsure of myself that I wondered for a moment whether I had only spoken in my head. Like in those dreams where you think you're screaming and shouting but when you wake up you find you were only making small puffy noises. I busied myself with getting the cuddly avocado and the biscuits out of my bag and handing them to him.

'They're busy,' he said, 'you know how it is. Thank you.' He grabbed them and went inside in what appeared to be one swift movement.

I felt shaken. It was so not what I had been expecting. Ocean's mum and I had not been exactly friends, I didn't even know her name. Or maybe I did know and I couldn't remember, I wasn't sure which. Either way, we had always had nice chats on the street, and when Ocean was tiny and I took the little cardigan I had stopped for a cup of tea. I had only stayed for a few minutes because of Jed, and I hadn't seen her since he died. I know young people are surprised and frightened by death, so I wasn't expecting her to have called on me, but I thought she might have come to the door. Of course, I berated myself, I should have asked to speak to her. That could have worked. I should have said, can I give this to Ocean, or, how is she?

I could have done things really differently. He was probably shy. She had asked him to answer the door and he might be quite a new boyfriend. Maybe it was nice for her that he was helping out, especially if she was in the middle of a nappy change or something like that. My social skills were way off, I knew that. I was an old woman, out of touch with the way things were done these days and what's more I'd just spent the best part of three years either nursing a dying old man or grieving for him. What on earth did I know about anything? I had probably got everything wrong.

I felt so sad that evening. It shouldn't have mattered, I knew that. It wasn't important at all. The whole thing was stupid but I had so wanted to see the smile on Ocean's face when she saw the little toy. It might have made things better for a moment. I'll see them tomorrow, I told myself, I was making a mountain out of nothing at all. I put the TV on for company, although I have no idea at all of what I watched, and I decided to forget the whole thing.

It almost worked. It might have worked quite well if it hadn't been bin night, the night I needed to leave the house again to drag the bins to the kerb. There's a cat I see sometimes who lets me stroke her and I always have a look for her on bin night but that night I could see something else. It was the little avocado toy I had got for Ocean, either that or an astonishing coincidence and it was in the gutter outside my house, sur-rounded by the smashed remains of the fancy biscuits.

CHAPTER TWO

London

I brought the avocado toy indoors and tried not to think about it. There didn't seem much I could do, after all. Ocean had a mum, and I was sure I could remember a grandparent too, back in the days before Jed died. Jed had always been a little sad about our lack of grandchildren and he talked about it that day that we saw Ocean with the older couple.

'Imagine,' he said. 'Imagine how proud you'd be pushing a buggy again after all these years.'

'Hang on,' I said.

I rarely got cross with Jed, but there's no point pretending that just because someone has died, they're a saint. Jed could drive me mad sometimes and this was one of them. I had tried to explain to him that I didn't want to be the sort of person who talked endlessly about their grandchildren, but he didn't believe me.

'I honestly don't want a grandchild,' I said, 'so you can stop feeling sorry for me right now.'

'William isn't ruled out any more,' he said. 'Loads of gay couples have babies. You've got as much chance as anyone else of being a grandma.'

I left the room, pretending that I had heard the postman. As if I didn't know that William could have children. As if I was some silly old bat from the last century with antiquated views and prejudices you could cut with a knife. I wasn't and I didn't and if Jed hadn't been so ill I would have had a right old quarrel with him. Who do you think you've been living with all this time, I would have said, do you even know me? Do you know who I am? I would have asked him to get out of the house until he could come and apologise and talk it through. We always used to do that in the early days. One or the other of us would always be going to stay in a B and B in Brighton, or sleeping on a friend's floor while we recovered from whatever it was we'd been arguing about. Of course I always took William with me so I probably ended up having the better time because Jed always came back really sad and contrite and I tended to march in explaining how I had been right all along.

Obviously things were different now that he was so sick, so the farthest away I got was the hallway, where I stood thinking of all the things I would have said to him if he wasn't. It wasn't fair, that was what got to me. I had never had a problem with William being gay, and I had never longed for the patter of tiny feet on my parquet floors. And the bottom line, the killer argument, was that even if William did have a baby I wouldn't really get to see it. Not unless he moved back to London, which wasn't likely.

'The surfing, Mum,' he said whenever it came up, 'the sunshine and the surfing and the sheer joy of being alive.'

I nodded and agreed with him, of course I did. It's nice for a person to have what they want, exactly what they want, all the time and I'm not denying that. Life's not all beer and skittles, my mum would have said but even then, when I was fourteen, I used to think, why not? Why can't there be beer and skittles at all times and in all places, if that's what a person wants?

I would have loved more children but Jed and I had decided not to. So that we could give William everything. Everything we had, anyway. And he took it, and he's having a nice life, full of beer and skittles. So I didn't mind that I wasn't a grandmother, but I wasn't, and Ocean was no business of mine.

I looked out of the window most days, but I didn't see them even though the weather was getting more spring-like. Surely they would go to the park sometimes, I thought. I used to take William every day, and I would have gone mad if I hadn't done that but I know things change.

So although I was worried that I didn't see her, I had other things to think about. Counting down the days, for one, and Jed's things, for another. He wasn't a person who had loads of things, no ornaments or paintings or big items, but there was stuff. Stuff everywhere. Clothes, shoes that looked as if he might have just slipped them off, books and papers, letters. The letters were hard and I couldn't believe how many there were. Pen pals were his thing, his hobby. He wrote to prisoners on death row, and to lonely pensioners in Hull and Scotland and New Zealand. I'd been taking dictation and reading the letters out to him for a couple of years by the time he died, so I knew a lot of the regular people. Of course I was going to have to write to them all to explain why their letters weren't being answered. They should know, I mean they'd known he was unwell and couldn't see and they knew he was old but some of them persisted in writing and asking if he was OK.

I moved away from the window and sat at the dining table to write. I knew I had been spending far too much time looking out for Ocean, and it was time to stop. I got through several letters at the first go, but the last one I stumbled on. It was Jed's favourite correspondent, a lonely older woman who lived in Oban, up on the west coast of Scotland. She'd always wanted to be in the big city, but there were a whole load of reasons she had got stuck up there, I think family stuff mainly, she wasn't specific. Her letters were always a delight, even though she was so unhappy. She used to describe the scenery, and tell little stories about the other people in the town. Jed and I had always looked forward to her letters so that we could hear the next instalment.

Are you not jealous of her? Jed used to tease me, and the truth is I never was, because she seemed to be my friend too. She was always so nice and it was all so innocent. As if they were children corresponding, really. She had suffered a lot of loss, Jed thought and he talked about her often. I couldn't help thinking that for her at least, maybe he shouldn't be dead. Maybe it would be OK to keep him alive for a little longer, there was no need for her to find out yet. I wanted to have a few more of the letters, and I wanted to hear how the spring was turning out up there now that Jed wasn't in the world. I wanted someone not to feel sorry for me. I was fighting the denial that came with grief and sometimes I couldn't quite believe that he'd gone, or that the world would be able to carry on as normal. We had known he was dying for so long but it still seemed impossible.

I'd gone to make a cup of tea, that was the thing I found hard to bear. I'd gone to make a cup of tea and I'd seized the chance to stick the radio on for as long as it took the kettle to boil. He hadn't wanted it on in the bedroom that day and there was some damn stupid news story I was following for some reason. I wanted to hear how it turned out. Just while the kettle boiled. Maybe I stayed a tiny bit longer to get all the facts but it was partly so that I could tell him too, because he'd been following it with me. He'll never know how it turned out, that was the first thing I thought when I realised he had gone. I told him anyway, before I rang the ambulance. We'd agreed on no heroics, no CPR to bring him back for just another hour or another day, no matter how many of his brain cells had died off in the process.

It's strange because we all know that dying is a thing everyone does sooner or later. Everyone. No one gets out of here alive and yet it always seems like a tragedy. Even if the person dying was one hundred years old without a friend in the world, it would still be a sad thing. It's the missed opportunities, I guess, and the loss of all those memories, all those links. You take one person, any person, out of the network of life and all those links they have with other people, other things, animals, teapots, they all snap and then reattach themselves elsewhere.

Jed was my life, and the links between us were old and strongly attached so it hurt when they snapped. There was no way I could be philosophical about it. But some part of him lived on in those letters to Oban. Just while I got used to things and decided what to do. It might even be doing a kindness to Annie. She might find it difficult to process his death, I comforted myself with that. A good deed for me and for her.

I started the letter but I didn't have much to say and it was difficult to imagine what Jed might have said. Nothing had happened to me for ages except for the one thing I couldn't talk about. I explained my name, as if I was Jed, that was the only thing I could think of. It's a dull story and I tried to keep it in Jed's slightly plodding style.

Virginia's father was an American soldier, that's where it came from, I wrote. It wasn't even wartime and Virginia's mum was vague but she thought he'd been on the run for a few years in Britain and didn't want to go home to West Virginia. He didn't show up again after her mum told him about the baby but she always loved the names he had told her of places he knew. I think Virginia would have preferred Carolina.

I included some tosh about spring in the letter and something I hadn't watched on TV. It was difficult impersonating a dead person but I loved the fact that he was still with me. I even told Annie about Ocean, but it wasn't playing on my mind that much.

So Annie, I wrote, my wife Virginia is writing this down for me again because I still can't see too well. I can hear the birds singing though, and Virginia describes what's happening outside the window so I don't feel too bad. In fact it's quite cosy here compared with the kind of storms you describe in Oban. I'm a little worried about the baby who lives two doors down. I haven't seen her much and I can't quite shake a feeling that something bad may be happening.

I couldn't believe that had popped out of nowhere, as if my worry was just waiting for a chance to hijack me. I'm overcautious, though, I always have been, so I started the letter again and played that bit down. I talked more about the foxes instead, the scraggly old London foxes who foraged in our bins and sometimes slept on the roof of the garden shed in the sunshine. But I moved from the dining table back to my desk again, as a kind of acknowledgement that it would be nice to see her. Ocean. Just to put my mind at rest. I'd washed the cuddly avocado and it had taken up residence on my desk as a reminder.

I was coming back from the post office the next time I saw Ocean's mum. I'd been to buy stamps and post the letters, and I was feeling a little brighter. Not perky exactly, not happy but at peace. It's good to accomplish something, even if it's only posting a letter. She was dressed smartly, in a tailored jacket and high heels, but her hair was visibly dirty and hanging round her face as if she had forgotten to brush it. I smiled, although I was so out of practice it might have appeared more like a grimace, and I went right up to her so that she couldn't just walk on.

'Is everything OK?' I said. 'Only I called round the other day with a little present for Ocean.'

I didn't fill in the rest because it suddenly struck me that it would seem as if I was worried about the stupid toy, rather than the child. Or that she might think I was talking about myself, and I wasn't, I really wanted to know how they were.

'She's fine,' Ocean's mum said but she didn't look at me when she spoke.

She looked at the floor and kicked a stick with the toe of her shoe, as if she were a child being told off.

'They're lovely at that age, aren't they?' I said.

I wasn't sure why I said it and I still don't know, looking back, but I think it was some sort of impulse that I had to keep her talking. Whether that was for me or for her I'm not sure, but the urge was so strong I couldn't ignore it.

'Are they?' she said.

She sounded utterly defeated and completely different from the young woman who had seemed so joyful when Ocean was first born.

'I'm, erm, on my own now,' I said. 'You've probably got loads of people to help, grandparents and all that, but if you ever need a bit of time out or if you've got an errand to run or anything, I'd be happy to have her for a bit if it would be helpful.'

As soon as I'd said it, my offer seemed like the silliest and most attention-seeking thing, but I meant it. It didn't mean I was desperate for grandchildren or anything like that, I said to Jed in my head, I just wouldn't mind helping out, that's all.

'My partner is around a lot,' she said, 'but thank you.'

We must have been told each other's names way back in the time before Jed died but I had definitely forgotten hers so I introduced myself again.

'I'm Virginia,' I said. 'Like the state in America. I've never been there, and it's a long story.'

It was what I usually said to new people. Just enough information not to appear rude, but enough, I hoped, to close down the discussion so I didn't have to explain my name again. It worked most of the time, and I could see that she had no curiosity at all so I was quietly confident that I wouldn't have to say anything until she said, 'I'm Cate, but I spell it with a C because my mum thought it sounded a bit more fancy. If you're going to have a plain name, she used to say, you may as well spell it nicely. That's why I gave Ocean such a beautiful name, so that she would never feel plain and a plus is, no one can query the spelling.'

She seemed surprised afterwards, Cate, that she had made such a long speech. She pulled her jacket around her as if she was cold and turned away from me and towards her house.

'I can see you're busy now,' I said. 'But one name explanation deserves another, so next time we meet I'll tell you about Virginia. Why I got saddled with it, I mean.'

I think she smiled a little so I called after her, 'And Ocean is a lovely name,' but she didn't turn round, just hurried off.

I thought about her a lot that evening. Cate, as well as Ocean. The thing was, I didn't think I had ever seen her on her own before, without the baby. Jed had talked about it once, saying how difficult it must be to have to take a small person with you everywhere.

'Tell me what it was like for you, when William was really teeny,' he had said. 'I don't think we ever talked about that much and now when I think of you and William all alone in the world and him so small it seems very sad and worrying.'

Of course, I didn't tell him just how dreadful it had been. We got together when William was three, so I had had three years of hard times and loneliness but there was never any point rubbing his nose in that. It seemed like a criticism of him, as if he hadn't managed to find me in time or something. Also, and this is a weird thing, there was a part of me that was happy in those early days despite the difficult times. Me and William against the world, team us, no one to consult about the good or the bad. Sometimes we ate Weetabix for dinner, and sometimes, if he had had a bad run of sleepless nights, we would go to the playground in the evening when other two-year-olds were getting ready for bed. And when Jed and I got together I left William with him a few times, of course I did, I even did an adult education course in writing at the local college. But not in the initial period, not at all. I didn't make a thing of it, but I wanted them to take time to get to know each other, rather than be foisted on each other. I had watched some of the women at the playgroup telling their kids that a new boyfriend was an uncle or even a dad. Even in the Seventies I knew that was bad.

So I thought about Ocean and Cate and I wondered, was she sure that it was OK to leave the baby with the new guy? If she even did, I could hear Jed saying, it could have been her mum that Ocean was with, or an aunt. Or it could be that the partner wasn't new at all, could be Ocean's dad even, Cate isn't likely to spill the whole thing out straight away, not to you. Don't get carried away, Jed always used to say to me. That imagination of yours is going to get you into trouble.

I stopped looking out for her. I'm ashamed of that now and I would always be much more careful in future but I stopped looking out for her after the first couple of weeks. I got totally involved in my own misery, that's the only way I can put it. I couldn't see anything outside my own tiny circle of existence. The feelings swooped in from nowhere like an ambush and I didn't know how to fight them off. I couldn't wait for June. It seemed slow in coming even though it was less than two months now. I spent several days sitting in Jed's chair, even at night times, and I didn't answer the phone when my friends rang. I would have answered William's call, but he was very busy at that time with some kind of big deal at work, he told me later. I didn't mind that he didn't ring. It gave me one less obligation.

I might have stayed like that for longer, sitting in a chair wearing tracksuit pants and Jed's old sweatshirt. I might have stayed like that for ever, I guess, because there was no one checking in on me. At least until June. The letters piled up in the hallway and even if Annie wondered why I didn't write back I knew she wouldn't come from Oban to knock down the door. No, I could have safely stayed there in the chair until I rotted but there was a sound that shook me out of myself, made me stop obsessing and thinking about nothing but my own troubles.

It was Ocean, although I didn't know it at first. I thought it might be foxes screeching, or an animal that had been hurt. Perhaps a dog or a cat that had been run over. I heaved myself out of the chair and went to my desk in the window. He was pulling her along. Little Ocean, who clearly hadn't been walking that long. She couldn't keep up with his big strides so he was holding her by the upper arm and pulling, as if she was a rag doll. Her feet were dragging along the ground.

I acted before I could think it through. I charged outside in my socks, and I'm sure I was blinking in the sunlight after being inside for so long. The momentum that carried me out didn't stay with me, and I wasn't sure what to do. I looked around for moral support, but the other houses in the close were quiet. There were never usually many people around in the work hours.

'Hi,' I said.

I tried to sound friendly. I had read somewhere that friendliness is the best tactic for old or otherwise vulnerable people to adopt when faced with an aggressor. It takes them by surprise and they're less likely to attack. Ocean stopped screaming, probably because he relaxed his grip on her arm so that he could turn and glare at me.

'What,' he said and at the same time, Ocean held up her little arms towards me to be picked up. I could hardly bear it, and I stepped towards her.

'Hello, poppet,' I said and I picked her up.

It was an instinct, I think, not so much a maternal instinct as a human one. She had asked me for protection and I couldn't refuse. It was the first time I had hugged anyone in a long time, and it felt wonderful. She snuggled into me like a koala, still sobbing quietly and hiccupping.

'Could you put her down?' the man said. 'She's not in our good books today.'

He tried to smile as if he was being friendly and normal and it was the most grotesque thing I've ever seen. I had a problem. Ocean was clinging on to me as if letting go would mean dropping off a cliff into crashing waves. He was coming closer, the man, and holding out his arms to take her. I had no idea what to do and I could feel her shrinking further in to my body. I kissed her head, it was an automatic impulse and the smell took me back to William days. That generic baby smell must be one of the most powerful in the world. I held on tighter.

'Ooh,' I said. 'Isn't she gorgeous? I wonder whether she could come and play at my house for a while.'

I pointed back over my shoulder towards my house as if its whereabouts might be persuasive. I was stalling, really, playing for time in a battle I knew I couldn't win. Still, though, it surprised me when he acted as quickly as he did. He swooped, that's the only word for it, and grabbed her out of my arms, swinging her round and pulling her against his own chest. She didn't snuggle in like she had with me. I kept thinking of that all evening. She kept herself rigid and away from him, as if she was trying to keep as many parts of herself as she could from touching him.

'She's got plenty of toys at home,' he said. 'She doesn't like strangers.'

She looked back at me as he walked away with her, and she reached out one little hand as if she knew there was no point but she wanted to make a gesture anyway.

Sometimes I get a kind of hindsight feeling, even while things are happening. I got it on the day I married Jed, and that was a lovely feeling. I knew I would remember the day for ever and in a good way. The feeling I had as that man walked off with Ocean, though, that was something different. That felt more like the end of the world, and worse, that I had made a wrong choice. A terrible choice, and I was letting her down.

He walked off stiffly, as if he wasn't used to carrying her, and I was sure that he would put her down and drag her again as soon as he was out of my sight. I busied myself with tidying a straggly bush in my garden and picking up some flyers that had blown in. I didn't want to go indoors, that was the thing. I wanted to stay outside where I might be able to help her, or to make things turn out differently. And I was busy thinking about my three-month deadline, and my own misery. Less than two months to go.

I should have done something then.

CHAPTER THREE

London

I still didn't think it was any of my business. Seven weeks to go, that's what I held on to, forty-nine days and I could be out of there. I couldn't make myself forget her little face though, or the way she had clung on to me. I kept thinking, if he made me feel this shaky and unhappy after just an encounter in the street, what on earth must it be like to be in the same room with him if you're only a baby? Maybe it was my fault, that's one of the things I was worried about, maybe I was overreacting, maybe I'd lost my sense of proportion altogether. Perhaps lots of parents or carers get cross with dawdling children and end up pulling them a little more forcefully than they intended. I might be remembering William and his toddlerhood through ridiculous rose-tinted glasses. Maybe I might have dragged William if I was in a hurry, or if I didn't feel well. I tried to think about those days, the days of me and William against the world and our park visits, but I couldn't remember an angry one. I could remember sad times, me pushing William along and crying as we walked but babies faced outwards in their buggies then, not inwards, and I don't think he ever noticed.

I did remember one thing, though, and it was one of those memories that pushes its way to the surface even though you try to keep it down. William was about eighteen months old, probably about the same age as Ocean. He hadn't been sleeping well, I remember that and of course it's more difficult at that age because you can't just feed them off to sleep like you can when they're little. I used to dance him round the little flat, singing to him and patting his back so that he didn't feel lonely when he woke up, and looking back, that was a mad thing to do. He found it much more pleasant to dance with me than to lie in his cot all alone so we spent a good deal of the night doing it and I was exhausted.

One night we were negotiating his return to his cot. It's easy now to think, why on earth didn't I take him into bed with me if the poor little chap just wanted some company and warmth. That's what I'd do if I had my time again but back then there was so much talk of how bad it was for children to allow them to sleep in your bed, and how, at worst, they might easily die of cot death and at best you'd have a weird teenager on your hands who couldn't sleep unless they were in their mother's bed. And the negotiation thing – I knew it wasn't sensible to negotiate with someone so small. My own mum had been very clear about 'showing him who was boss' but the fact was, he was the boss at that time in our relationship and negotiation was our style. I was offering him various cuddly toys to go in the cot with him and he was chucking out the ones he didn't want. Finally only Trevor the sheep was left and he said something that sounded like 'Trev', held out his arms and settled down with him. I tucked him in and started to creep out of the room, still singing our song. He waited until I got to the doorway. I was thinking of the cup of tea I would make and the book I was going to get a chance to finish when clear as anything, William said, 'No Trev. No, no, no no Trev.' He pulled himself up to standing against the cot bars and threw Trevor to the floor. I stood in the doorway with my heart sinking as he proceeded to throw out his blanket and his dummy and then he rocked himself against the sides of the cot and shouting, 'No, no, no.'

This was the memory I'd been trying to find. I'd buried it deep, unable to bear the fact that I'd been so mean to William, but I'd marched in, scooped up all the toys from the floor and shouted, 'OK, no toys then.' He had reached out his little hands for them and I'd thrown them into a corner and said, 'Goodnight,' and left him to cry himself to sleep. OK, so I didn't physically hurt him but I'd scared him, made him unhappy and ignored him, and those were pretty bad things as well. I'd lost my temper, that was the point. I'd lost my temper and I'd been unkind to a tiny person who needed my protection. I sometimes wondered if he carried a memory of that somewhere inside his complex little brain. If that was maybe the reason he'd decided to go and live in a country on the other side of the world, far from me and Jed. It might not be, and it may never have registered on his subconscious but I remembered, and the memory made me think that I wasn't really any better than the man. Dragging, shouting, removing toys, they were all terrible things to do to small people so I wasn't sure I could claim the moral high ground here.

I know now that there's a huge difference between hurting and shouting and that although neither is OK, I can cut myself some slack about Trevorgate. There were good times too, loads of them, and I could still feel the weight of his little three-year-old body curling up against me while we watched *Sesame Street* and sang along. One evening of sheep throwing wasn't the same at all and the only thing I can say in my defence is, I'd lost a lot of confidence and I didn't know how bad people could be. I was still thinking in normal terms, in human terms.

I went back into the house after the incident. I mean really back into my house, hardly coming out at all and ordering my shopping online. It's not linear, grief, and anything can set a person back. When I should have been worrying about Ocean I was thinking about myself and how wretched I felt. That's how self-centred I'd become, but in my defence, grief does that. It twists up your head until you wonder who you are, until the person you're grieving for is almost lost in a sea of horror about the human condition.

I had nearly two months left before I gave up waiting and finished things off for good, and I thought about that a lot. I would have liked to do it then and there but I have always been stubborn and I had promised to wait. The sun continued to shine and my worries about Ocean never left, so after a while I ventured out again. I have always loved the spring.

I met Jed in the spring. He was sitting on a bench in the park, drawing daffodils. William was three and he was entranced at the idea of a grown-up drawing so he kept trying to get closer to him, despite my caution. I'd been trying to teach stranger danger because William was such a friendly soul, and I worried that he would seek out the company of strangers because we were such a small family.

He ran in front of me across the grass.

'Hello,' he said. 'I want to colour in too.'

'I'm sorry,' I said, puffing and panting behind him. 'William, what have I said?'

I knew that sounded like the most awful, nagging cliché but I really was worried. Jed could have been anyone.

'I'm very sorry, young man, but I'm not allowed to talk to strangers,' Jed said.

He winked at me and I noticed how twinkly his eyes were.

'If your mum says it's OK, you can colour in my daffodils but we have to be properly introduced.'

Of course, I introduced William and Jed introduced himself and then he asked William to tell him who I was, so that I wasn't a stranger. 'Lady is V mummy,' William said, which brightened the day no end and meant that I had to explain that he couldn't say my real name, which meant I had to tell him my name and then we stayed in that park for hours. Jed drew with William, and he pushed him on the swings, never seeming to tire of it. In terms of winning my heart that was the best thing he could have done. Forget roses and champagne, Jed swept me off my feet with a mediocre drawing of daffodils ('the trumpet bits are hard,' he said and William agreed) and the fact that he taught William how to push his legs out on the downward swoop of the swing to make it go higher.

I was thinking about that day the next time I saw Cate. It was the same sort of weather, all racing clouds and promise. I hadn't seen her for a week and I was so pleased. Maybe everything was fine, I thought and as soon as I thought it I realised how much I had been worrying underneath all the other stuff.

'Hi,' I said, 'isn't it a nice day? How's wee Ocean?'

I don't know whether it was because I used the word 'wee'

and that made her think of how little Ocean was, or just the fact that someone had asked after her, but Cate let out a kind of strangled sob and then looked back at the house, clearly scared.

I've had quite a boring life but I've watched a lot of TV in the last few years so I knew what to do.

'Keep walking,' I said. 'Don't look back, go round the corner and keep going. There's a café just down at the bottom, Gray's, it's called. Wait for me there. Go.'

She didn't even question me, the poor love, and I thought, that's because she's used to people telling her what to do. I didn't have time to explain but it didn't feel safe for us to walk along together in case he was watching her. I turned and went back into my house, counted to ten and then left again. It wouldn't be a trick I could use more than once or he'd be wise to it, but I was pretty sure that it was necessary then. I wouldn't be able to help her from the minute he was on to it, that's what I thought and what I knew. I turned a different way at the top of the crescent in case he was still looking out, and doubled back on myself to get to the café.

She was inside, tucked away at the back, nursing a glass of water and still crying. I picked up a couple of little boxes of fruit juice at the counter so that I wouldn't have to wait while they made a hot drink and I sat down opposite her.

'I want to help,' I said.

She shook her head and blew her nose.

'No one can help,' she said.

I let her cry for a moment, hoping that it was a companionable silence.

'It's Ocean,' she said after a while. 'She's so naughty and I try to tell her but she doesn't listen.'

I had a flash memory of crying when William had drawn a monkey with my lipstick on the white bedroom wall. It was not long after I'd met Jed and I worried that he would think we were lawless and hopeless, and that we lived in a hovel. I couldn't have been more wrong. He threw his head back and laughed when I showed him, and congratulated me on having such an artistic son. I tried to remember what he had said.

'She's much too little to be naughty, Cate,' I said. 'She's just trying to understand the world and how it works and the rules and where she is. She can't even speak the language here yet, it's a whole new place to her now that she's learned to get around.'

Cate sniffed and I knew that she was listening.

'He gets so cross, though, and I know it's Ocean's fault but I can't stop her. She cries, and she won't eat, and she spills stuff, and she puts her toys in her mouth and everything. Even if they've been on the floor.'

I tried to keep a poker face. I was shocked at what she had said, but I didn't think it would be any good for Ocean if I showed that.

'None of that is really naughty, though, is it? I mean it can be annoying and I get that but it's not bad behaviour, don't you think she's far too little for that?'

Cate looked at me as if I'd said something really strange.

'My mum says that,' she said. 'But he says my mum is trying to split us up, I'm not sure.'

'I don't know anything about your mum, or your relationship with her,' I said.

I was trying to choose my words carefully. 'But on the whole, mums want the best for their children and grandchildren. It might be worth listening to her.'

I knew it was a reckless thing to say. I knew that there are mums who don't want the best for their children, and mums who don't care but this young woman appeared to be in free fall and I wanted to give her a rough guide as to which way was up. Until she told me that her mum wasn't any good, I'd rather be pushing maternal advice than the advice of that man, whoever he was.

I had a flash memory of my own mum at the thought of mums. She had told me that William's biological dad was dangerous the first time she had met him.

'Virginia,' she said. 'I've made a lot of mistakes in my life, lord knows. And I would be a bad, bad mum if I didn't tell you to get the hell away from this horrible specimen while you can. No, don't shush me, he can't hear and I don't think I care if he can. He will lead you a merry dance, my girl, and you need to walk away.'

I was never sure whether it was a good thing or a bad one that I didn't listen to her straight away. On the plus side I wouldn't have William if I had, but on the minus I could have saved myself a whole heap of trouble and a couple of trips to A & E.

'He's going to try harder,' she said. 'You know, not get so angry and stuff. It's just, Ocean.' Cate shrugged. 'She makes things so difficult.'

I pictured Ocean's sweet little face, and the big smiles I used to describe to Jed.

'She used to be such a happy little thing,' I said. 'Children have reasons they do things too. Do you think there could be something that's upsetting her?'

Cate's mood switched as quickly as the sun going behind a cloud.

'He's right,' she said. 'You're an interfering old busybody and I don't need your help.'

I'd gone too far. I wanted to hit my head on the table in frustration. It was important for Ocean that I said the right thing, tried to help, and somehow important for Jed too. I'd let both of them down.

'Hang on,' I said. 'I'm sorry, I didn't mean to upset you, I was trying to help. Please let me know if I can do anything, I'd happily look after her.'

Cate pushed over the glass of water she'd been drinking so that it spilled into my lap. 'You're a paedophile,' she said. 'He told me you were. You should be ashamed of yourself.'

She stormed out. I was shaking, and all the people in the café stopped talking and looked at me. I wasn't sure whether I should say anything. Saying I'm not, to the room in general, seemed as sure a sign of guilt as saying, yep, that's me. I said nothing and I made myself sit still while I counted to one hundred. As I left I could definitely hear a couple of hostile tuts.

I was deeply shaken. It was my first foray into personal interaction since Jed had died, unless you counted the Pie People or phone calls with William. I was obviously unable to function any more. I should have been able to see that coming and sidestep it somehow, but instead I walked straight in with open arms. I hadn't helped Cate, and more importantly, I hadn't helped Ocean. In fact I had probably set things back enormously. One or both of them might take it out on her, and I would be responsible as surely as if I had hurt the little sweetheart myself. I paced up and down my living room trying to work out what to do next. If I went to see them, obviously things would get even worse, so that was a terrible idea. If

I stayed in my house with the curtains closed, which was what I wanted to do, it was like an admission of guilt. And I would become a prisoner, effectively, scared to go out. Staying in my house and not going out seemed like a good result in many ways, but it wasn't all about me. There was Ocean to think of. I was an old woman, not much use to anyone but that little girl had her whole life in front of her and I had a really bad feeling.

I tried to talk to William about it on the phone and to be fair, I think he tried to listen and comment but he was right in the middle of something at work.

'Other people's lives, Mum,' he said. 'Honestly you should just keep away from them, get on with your own life. People like that just aren't worth it. I'll have a word with them next time I come over if you like.'

I imagined for one moment what that would be like, and how it would go. Tanned, beautiful William and poor Cate, or worse, that man. I wasn't sure whether to laugh or cry.

William's first day at school, aged four. Because he was an only, we'd talked through lots of possible social situations with him. Only children were unusual then, and we worried whether he would know what to do and how to share. He had new shoes for school, Velcro trainers and he was very pleased with them. He loved making the unsticking noise with them.

'Listen, listen,' he kept saying to me that morning before squatting down and unsticking the Velcro again so that he could hear the noise. Every time it made him chortle with laughter. He did it when he got to school too, as a conversational opener but it didn't work so well.

'I showed this boy my trainers, Mum,' he said.

It was the first thing he said when he came out of school.

'I showed him my trainers and asked him to be my friend but he hit me. So I gave him a kiss.'

At this point William burst into tears and held his hands out, palms up to indicate how baffling the next piece of information was. 'And he hit me again,' he said, sobbing, 'right in the middle of my tummy.'

I thought of that while William was explaining to me that what those sort of people needed was someone to tell them about themselves. I knew better than to mention it. I'm not sure if other grown-up children like to hear stories about themselves when they were little but William did not. Especially ones where he seemed not to be in total control of the situation.

'I'm sure you're right,' I said and I continued pacing.

I think it was the next morning that I got a letter back from Annie in Oban. It was addressed to Jed and me this time, and I thought it was really nice of her to acknowledge me too. She wrote about the weather, and how most mornings it was so grey that they couldn't see the Isle of Mull. *People think it's picturesque here*, she wrote, *and it can be but today when the tide was out, the bay was full of plastic bottles, as if the fish had been having a drinks party the night before*. It was the last line of her letter that made me think.

I was thinking, she wrote, *about the little girl in your road. There's a saying, isn't there, about how all it takes for something terrible to happen is for good people to look the other way. Of course it may be nothing, or at least nowhere near as bad as you are thinking, but just in case, on the off chance, maybe you should report it to someone? Your local social services department? I think you don't have to say who you are, you can report things anonymously. And if they tell you everything is fine and you were wrong, what's the harm? You might feel a little bit silly but that's nothing compared to how you might feel if anything bad happened and you hadn't acted.*

She ended by sending lots of good wishes to Jed and reminding me that I should look after myself too, which could have reduced me to tears on a different day. Today was different. Today she made me feel as though I had someone on my side and a right to my opinion. Had I ever before worried about a child like I was worrying about Ocean? No, I had never knowingly obsessed like this over any of the children William had known, or the ones that I had known and seen in my daily life. And I had enough self-knowledge to realise that it had to be bad, for that little girl and her mum to haunt me quite so much despite my selfish preoccupation with the fifteenth of June.

Even so, it seemed like a big step, ringing social services. What would I actually have to go on? What would make them check her out, really check her out, not just go through the motions? Would they think I was being spiteful? And what if, this was the big one really, what if Cate and the man found out it was me who reported them and in retaliation told them I was a paedophile?

I felt ashamed of myself. Don't make it all about you. I remembered Jed saying that, don't make it all about you, when I was feeling so sad about him dying. I don't think he meant it spitefully, I genuinely think he wanted to help. Maybe he knew it would be a useful rule of thumb after he'd gone, I'm not sure. But it wasn't all about me now, it was about Ocean, and I saw her again that afternoon. I'm not brave, and I didn't leave my own flat, but I could see there was something

41

wrong. She was in her buggy, but she lolled to one side like a broken doll. I couldn't see her eyes and I presumed she was asleep but there was something terribly wrong with how she was positioned. I stood to the side of the window like they do in films, so that I couldn't be seen but I think he knew I was there. He waved towards where I was standing and Cate threw something at my window. I ducked instinctively and it bounced off with a bang and fell back into the garden. I waited ten minutes after they had gone round the corner before I went out to see what she had thrown. It was a stone, with a piece of paper wrapped round it. I straightened the paper out, my heart banging away like an accompaniment.

'PAEDOPHILE,' it said in big red letters.

I was shocked. I spent a minute or two feeling sorry for myself, then common sense kicked in. If they're doing this to me, when all I did was offer help, then what about Ocean? I suppose the thing I did that really upset them was to notice. I saw something, I wasn't sure what but I saw that something was wrong and that's what they couldn't forgive. And if they were this angry with me, how the hell angry must they be with Ocean?

I found the number of my local social services and I dialled.

CHAPTER FOUR

London

Making the phone call seemed like an important step. I was back engaging with the outside world, and I was going to have a stake in things. I had a reason to hang around, even if it was only for the next few weeks. There was still time, I thought, time to make sure she was OK and then check out. I had to try.

I wasn't sure who I should tell at social services but they make it quite easy these days. I looked online and there was a big orange alert sign for anyone wishing to report child abuse. The trouble was, nothing was clear enough with Ocean. I hadn't seen anyone hit her, I didn't know her well, all I had to go on was a gut feeling and a drag along the road and I suspected that wouldn't alarm anyone too much. There's a stereotype thing, that's why. An old lady, busybody stereotype where it's nothing unusual for us to be peering out of windows and imagining things because of our own sad pasts and empty lives. The trouble was, in my case I felt the stereotype was pretty accurate. I hadn't responded to any messages from friends for weeks now, and they'd understandably tailed off. I'd always had such a good relationship with Jed that I hadn't really needed anyone else, so I wasn't anyone's number one for book groups or cinema outings. So I did sit by the window, and I had been looking out for Ocean, and I wasn't sure whether I had got everything out of proportion but the website was reassuring. It said that I didn't have to be absolutely certain, and that it was fine to speak to someone if I only had a feeling that something wasn't right. It didn't say anywhere that I had the right to remain anonymous though, and that was a worry.

The woman on the other end of the line sounded friendly, which was a good start. She asked me some details about Ocean, but the only things I could be sure of were her first name and her address. They asked me if the people caring for her were drunk, and if I'd seen unexplained injuries, and I couldn't say yes to either of those things. I tried to explain how aggressive the man was, and that the baby looked wrong and unhappy. I could hear the woman sighing, and I could tell that I wasn't sounding like someone credible. I mentioned the avocado and I think that was where she lost patience. Looking back I can see why, but the website did say that even if you just had a feeling it should be reported. I was doing my best.

'We'll check everything out,' she said, 'but if you don't hear anything don't worry, we won't contact you unless we need more information.'

I thought it sounded as though she wasn't going to take any action, but I wasn't sure. I've done my bit, I thought, but it didn't really feel like that. What would Jed do, I wondered. Jed had been a forthright sort of person, calling out injustice where he saw it. It was one of the things I had loved most about him.

It was 1980 and we had been to the cinema in the West End. It was unusual for us to have a baby-sitter so it was a big deal and we had dressed up a bit, made a proper date of it. We hadn't known each other long so it was still a thrill to be sitting in the dark together holding hands and making sure that our bodies touched. I was relaxed and completely unprepared for the sight of at least twenty chanting skinheads when we left the building. I think they'd been on some kind of march against something or the other and it had finished so they were looking for a fight.

'Come on,' I said, my head down and ready to scoot away, 'come on, don't look at them, they'll only get worse.'

I could already hear the n word and the glee they obviously felt at finding a real live person of colour they could shout at.

'It's OK,' I said to Jed, pulling on his arm to make him walk the other way, away from the trouble.

I thought that was what he would want.

'You go,' he said. 'They won't follow you, it's me they're interested in.'

He was right, I could see that, and they were already making a beeline for him. He was beautiful, my Jed, dark-skinned and golden-hearted. His father came from Kenya, although he'd never been there. The skinheads clocked him straight away.

'I'm not going on my own,' I said to Jed. 'Let's run, come home with me.'

I felt suddenly and literally homesick, as if I'd been away from William for weeks. I couldn't bear the idea of being out one minute more than I had to. He might be hurt, or he might be missing me, anything could have happened. I think it was some kind of a displacement thing to worry about the one person in my life who was tucked up safe and sound in bed rather than the immediate and significant threat to us, and I put the thought away until later.

I can't even repeat the names they called us, and we never talked about it but they were bad, and accompanied by obscene gestures.

'Wait,' Jed said to me.

I could see the excitement in his eyes, which makes him sound like a fighter and he wasn't, generally, but he was hyped up and he definitely wasn't going to run away. He let go of my hand and I was terrified. I stood back and he absolutely charged into the middle of them and knocked a can of beer out of the hands of the loudest one.

'Excuse me, are you addressing my fiancée?' he said.

I didn't laugh then because I was too scared for him and for me, but I knew even through the fear that I was going to find it very funny at some point if we got out alive.

'That was the most middle-class opening to a fight I've ever heard,' I said to him later.

I was taping up the cut by his eye. Of course he should have gone to hospital and got it properly stitched but on the other hand, for the rest of his life I loved seeing the little scar and remembering how it had come to be part of him.

He was lucky that the police came along when they did. And I was lucky too, but I begged him not to ever do anything like that again.

'We've got William to think of,' I said.

Jed frowned and said that he had been thinking of William,

46

and he didn't want him to grow up in a world where people like that could be prejudiced to people he cared for. We didn't call it racist then, and prejudiced seems like such an old-fashioned word now.

'Sorry I said we were engaged,' he added, 'I hope that bit comes true.'

Jed wouldn't have let it lie, I thought that day after I'd spoken to the social worker. He hated injustice, he hated cruelty, and he loved children. So it was an easy guess that he would have tried to help Ocean and I wished he was here with me so that I could ask him what to do.

I started to keep a diary, to log when I'd seen her and how she was. It might help next time I rang social services. Borderline obsessive, I was aware, but I knew something was wrong and I couldn't stop thinking about how she'd pressed against me, thinking I was a safe place. I wished for someone, anyone to help me but the other people in my close didn't seem to have noticed. Mostly students and short-term renters, all too busy even to stop and chat. No one would be interested in Ocean, and probably no one had even noticed her. I was on my own.

The next morning, I went to knock on their door again. I hadn't slept, and I hadn't been able to eat anything, but I'd thought about it so hard that I knew I wasn't mistaken. Something bad was going on. I'd done what I could and called the authorities, and they might even follow it up, which would be great but it didn't mean that I could walk away from my personal responsibility to that little girl. I'd written that in a letter to Annie in Oban when I couldn't sleep and I had posted it first thing. I couldn't remember signing Jed's name though, which was worrying. It's so hard to keep a dead person alive, I thought, a bad joke that maybe only Jed would have appreciated.

I walked up their garden path again. It wasn't as messy this time, but still neglected. No more plastic tricycles but instead, several piles of dog poo. I was in the middle of processing this when I heard barking from inside the house. It's not a phobia, but I grew up on an estate in the middle of London where it was very sensible to have a healthy fear of dogs in the 1950s and '60s. The sound of a bark a few streets away can stop me in my tracks, that's how bad I am. So I stopped dead when I heard the dog bark inside the house. I wanted to go back so much that my head actually started to turn but somehow I couldn't, and my feet stayed where they were so I was totally caught off guard when the door opened. The man I'd seen before stood there holding a very fierce-looking, muscular dog on a short, thick chain. He smiled, but it was one of the least friendly smiles I had ever seen.

'Hi,' I said. 'I just came to say hello again. I'm your neighbour, remember? I hope that's OK.'

I hadn't planned what I was going to say and it showed, I'm afraid. I wished I could turn and go but I wanted to see that little girl with my own eyes, check that she was OK so that I could sleep at night.

'Oh I know who you are and where you live,' he said. 'Don't you worry about that.'

Something in his tone made the dog growl, but I stood my ground even though my legs were feeling distinctly jellyish.

'Is Cate there?' I said, trying to sound as casual as I could.

It was easier to feel brave when I remembered that I was

as good as done for anyway. I'd had my life, and I was probably going to leave the party soon, in a few weeks if all went
according to plan. It would be good to do something useful
first, leave a mark, help someone less fortunate.

I'd heard a local rumour about some women of my age who
had managed to kill a people trafficker recently, right here in
South East London and all by themselves. They'd made a good
job of it apparently, managed the whole thing without getting
the authorities involved. I knew that these kind of stories could
be massively exaggerated or even urban myths, but I loved this
one, nonetheless.

I stood a little straighter at the thought.

'Cate?' he said.

He said it as though I'd said something totally ridiculous,
asked to speak to the queen or something and that made me
feel angry.

'Yes,' I said. 'Cate. I've got some cuttings from my garden,
I think I spoke to her about it, and I've brought them with
me.' I gestured to the bag in my hand. It had seemed like
a marvellous excuse when I was in my own kitchen but out
here, it suddenly turned to dust. Clearly she wasn't interested
in gardening, I only had to look around me to see that.

'She's busy,' he said.

'Shall I leave them for her?' I said.

I held the bag out towards him and the dog looked at it
as though he would like to snap. It was horrible, what the
man did next. He took the bag from me and carefully turned
it upside down, so that the cuttings fell on to the concrete
path. He twisted his foot onto them as if he was putting out
a cigarette. I was so angry that I wasn't scared for myself at

all. I was not the person he was interested in terrorising at that time and I knew that, so I also realised that Cate must be watching somewhere. I looked towards the window and there was the slightest tremor of the curtain. I was sure I was right. I kept my voice steady.

'Tell her I said hello,' I said. 'Also I'd be happy to look after little Ocean any time, if you need a baby-sitter.'

I turned and walked slowly back towards my house. I didn't want to rush in case that gave him the satisfaction of knowing he'd scared me. He hadn't, in a way. I was surprised when I took stock of what I was feeling and realised that I wasn't scared so much as furious. Madly, rantingly furious. The kind of furious that makes a person pick up a pen and write a six-page letter in green ink to complain, if only there was anyone to complain to.

Instead, I picked up the phone. I rang the alert number again, to report that I still hadn't seen Ocean but this time they were a lot less interested.

'Is that the lady who already reported?'

It was the same woman I'd spoken to before. I could practically hear her examining her nails as she spoke, or raising her eyebrows to a colleague.

'We've visited, and it's all fine, thank you for your concern,' she said.

'It's not,' I said. 'It's not all fine, I've just been round there and I can tell you now it's far from fine. I never see the child, and the mum is scared, there's a dog and that man is a nasty piece of work.'

The woman sighed.

'Can I give you a bit of advice, dear,' she said. 'I'm very

sorry about your loss, your husband, they told me about that. And it can be very difficult to fill your time, I know that. My mum was the same. So maybe if you could do a class or something? They have some at the community centre. Silver surfers, ballroom dancing, writing a little bit about your life, those kind of things. Make some friends, stop worrying so much. They didn't mind, the baby's parents, they were quite worried about you in fact. Wanted our advice on how to help you, which I thought was really sweet. How does that sound like child abusers?'

I pressed the button to end the call. I felt absolutely stupid, and as if I should have known this would happen. Of course, I shouldn't have been surprised. I was an old woman without a partner so I must be mad or lonely or more dangerous still, both. I wanted to smash something. I knew Ocean wasn't OK, I knew it and I had no idea what to do about it. I didn't care what happened to me, but I wanted her to be OK. She was like a little piece of faith in the future, despite all the other things that were happening. I'd seen the babies and children who hit the news for the wrong reasons, and a lot of them didn't survive. I know Jed thought I always catastrophised the world and he was right, I did, but somehow I knew I was right this time.

I thought about it nonstop for the next couple of days. I tried ringing social services in other boroughs to see if anyone there would listen, but they had their boundaries. It was down to me to do something and I decided to wait until he left the house. He would have to go out at some point, and if I kept watch that would be my chance. I'd be able to talk to Cate and help her to get away. I couldn't believe she wouldn't want to go and I knew the perfect place. She could go to my little flat in Margate. He wouldn't find her there and what's more, I was sure that Ocean would love the ocean.

I checked my pill stock again and watched for three days solid, hardly leaving my post at the window except for quick drinks and essentials. It was horrible. I only left the house once to send a letter to Annie, and I didn't see anyone. In fact the house looked unoccupied. The curtains were closed and there was no sign of life.

I'm worried about you, Annie wrote. You're going to make yourself ill. And Virginia, another thing I've been wanting to say is, I do know about Jed. I don't know exactly when he died but I'm pretty sure he's passed away, because I have had this feeling for ages that I can't shake off. My mum was like this too, I don't think it's a psychic thing, more that I have the dubious gift of overthinking everything, and your last few letters haven't been the same. I could see the snow on top of the mountains on Mull this morning and that seemed like a good time to tell you that I know. And I want to thank you for trying to keep him alive for me for just a little bit longer, because I can imagine what an effort that must have been. Jed and I had been writing to each other since we met in a chat room somewhere around the year 2000. The internet was new to me then and it seemed like such an exciting thing that I could connect with a person whose life was so different from mine. I was so cut off. And I always thought it was wonderful how Jed spoke of you, he said you were the best thing in his life. I know you've been writing the letters for a while now, since his eyesight failed, and he wasn't so soppy about you when you were scribing but I thought you'd want to know just how much he loved you. It might help you do what you need to do about Ocean, to know that he would have thought you would make the right choice whatever you do, and to be honest I think so too. You know how these cases can end up, we all do. We've seen it in the news and read reports we wished we hadn't. But you know the down side too. There's a possibility, just a tiny smidgeon of a possibility, that you might be wrong. Or that you might not be able to prove it, that's the other thing. But for what it's worth, I think you should go with your gut feeling. And I'm happy for you to ring me any time, if it helps.

Love, Annie

I thought about the letter all day while I sat at the window looking out. I sat to the side so that I couldn't be seen and I felt very hopeless. I felt I had failed to keep Jed alive and that without him, I had no one to turn to. I had friends, but I had always been the sort of person that other people go to for help, and I wasn't sure how to change. I'd always had Jed, and no one else even came close. It was different when William was little. I made friends with the other mums and we watched the children play together and drank tea. I loved that bit, but without the children to anchor us a lot of those relationships changed. People became strangely competitive, firstly about their children's education and careers, and then about grandchildren. I couldn't join in and I didn't want to, but now I wished I'd kept up more with a couple of them, so that the silence didn't echo so much in the house.

I rang one of the ones who'd brought a pie after Jed died. She had two daughters and three grandchildren and I had often avoided her but she had been a teacher so she must know lots about safeguarding. I asked after her grandchildren and then set the timer on my phone. She talked for nine minutes and forty-three seconds, which wasn't too bad. The youngest was roughly the same age as Ocean so I used that as a way in to say what I'd wanted to say.

'I'm a bit worried about a little one in my street who is the same age as your Mariella,' I said.

It may have been a little abrupt but I had listened to a lot of talk about Mariella's mysterious rash. I felt I deserved a chance to have the floor, as it were.

'Oh,' she said.

I waited a beat or two but there was nothing more.

'There's a new boyfriend on the scene, mum seems withdrawn and I'm sure he's unkind to the little girl at best, and at worst, goodness knows.'

She didn't say anything for a while and I thought the line might have gone dead. When she did speak it was in a low, conspiratorial tone as if we were planning something together. I couldn't help holding the phone away from my ear.

'Virginia, darling,' she said.

That was a bad start. I hate being called darling.

'I can imagine how you're feeling,' she said. 'It must be so awful when you lose the love of your life, your best friend. I would be just the same if my Mike died. I'd be hopeless. Good for nothing. Luckily he's quite healthy.'

She gave a little nervous laugh and I realised that I was supposed to laugh with her at the audacity of the idea that her Mike would ever become unwell. I didn't laugh, and I only just stopped myself from saying, everyone's quite healthy until they're not healthy, you fuckwit. Do you really think your Mike will be spared the tragedy of the human condition?

'Why don't we go out for a coffee?' she said.

She had clearly decided there was no point in waiting for me to respond. 'I have Mariella three days a week and I said I'd go with Lil to an art exhibition up in town but I could do Friday at ten, as long as we're not out too long. I'm helping Jake with his maths homework straight after school and I have to get ready. Honestly, sometimes I envy you the freedom you've got, being a grandparent is hard work, let me tell you.'

I pressed the red button to end the call while she was still talking. I knew what would have come next, it would be something about William and how sorry she was about how far away he'd chosen to live, followed by an explanation that gay people could have children now, as if I hadn't heard. And nothing, nothing about Ocean. She thought the same as the woman at social services, I realised. She thought I was a lonely, grieving woman with no friends and nothing in her life except an only son who had chosen to live his life thousands of miles away, on the other side of the world. A woman who was giving her life purpose by fantasising about a child she could see from her window. Like that play by Alan Bennett.

Was she right? I wandered into the kitchen and looked around. Two mugs out ready for coffee, one with 'V' on and one with 'J'. When did I put them out? And why? I had just a few weeks left before I had to make my big decision but in a way it felt as though I had already made it. I wasn't functioning properly, and I had to admit it. There was no reason to continue. I sat at the kitchen table with my head in my hands, and I don't think I had ever felt more wretched. The light coming in through the kitchen window seemed to be fading faster than usual and everything seemed to point towards finishing myself off then and there. It would be so easy to go now, I thought.

I lined the pills up by the mugs and got out some paper to write to William. That's how close I was and I'd like to say it was something heroic or amazing that changed my mind that time but it was much more down to earth than that. It was spite. Pure spite. I could not bear that woman, Mariella's grandma, getting all the glory, that was the truth. She would love it. Adore the fact that she was the chosen one, she was the last person I had spoken to. She would probably squeeze out a little tear and tell everyone that she felt so guilty and she didn't know how to live with herself, and that she should have done something. And they would reply, her friends, they would say that she had enough to do with her grandchildren and that I had really been rather selfish to expect so much from her. I could have written the script, that's how well I knew what would be said. I felt far too cross to let it happen. Not yet, anyway.

It took me a while to realise that my doorbell was actually ringing, that I wasn't imagining the sound. I hadn't heard it for so long that I couldn't recognise it. The ring sounded urgent, abrupt and I wondered if that was how it had always sounded. I opened it and there was Cate and Ocean, as though I'd conjured them up by thinking about them. Cate had Ocean balanced on her hip, and she was snuggled into her mum with the sad face of a war baby. That wasn't all. She had a cut by her eye and her lips looked bigger than usual. I realised that they were swollen, and that Cate's were too. In fact Cate looked terrible, both eyes were blackened and she was thinner than ever. She thrust Ocean towards me.

'Here,' she said. 'Could you take her away somewhere safe?'

CHAPTER FIVE

London

Hang on, I thought, just wind back a little. Cate was clearly in no place to make rational decisions. I needed to be careful not to scare her away.

'Can you come in, so we can talk about it?' I said.

I knew I sounded dithery and old, but it was a cover because here's the thing, even though I knew I had to persuade Cate to go for a different solution, and even though I was planning how to do that successfully, my heart was soaring at the idea of being able to help that little girl. It was as though I had two brains. I thought of Margate first, of course I did. My beloved seaside on the edge of a sticky out bit of England. The beautiful thing is that there isn't anything special about it except for the sea and the sand, so that's what the eye catches on. Ocean's ocean. I could imagine her kneeling down and carefully shovelling sand into a bucket, then looking up at me with delight like William used to do.

Cate shook her head and winced at the pain.

'No,' she said. 'I can't come in, he'd kill me, please take her.'

'I can't,' I said. 'I mean, I wouldn't be able to look after her, and she'd miss her mummy. Look at her all snuggled into you.'

It was true, Ocean was burrowing into her mum as though her life depended on it. I could see that her little knuckles were white from holding on to Cate's jumper.

'He's not a bad man,' Cate said.

Her tone was almost conversational, as if his goodness or badness was already an open topic of conversation between us.

'He doesn't know much about kids, that's all. He doesn't understand.'

She buried her face in the top of Ocean's hair. She was gulping in air, trying to calm herself down and she was so sad I felt as if I was going to cry too.

'Cate,' I said.

I was trying to pick my words carefully.

'Cate, have you ever thought of reporting him? Or maybe even getting out, leaving and going somewhere he doesn't know about?'

She stopped sniffing and looked up at me.

'You don't understand,' she said. 'I've got nowhere to go and anyway, he'd find me. I know he'd find me, he said he would, it's only because he loves me but still, there isn't anywhere I could go.'

'What about your mum, or any family?' I said.

I could tell as soon as I'd said it that it was the wrong thing to say.

'Nah,' she said. 'My mum lives a long way away and she's cross with me and it wouldn't work. There isn't anyone. Don't worry, we'll manage.'

Cate turned as if she was going to go and I felt absolutely useless.

'Hang on,' I said. 'What about my other suggestion,

reporting him? I could come with you if you like, for a bit of support.'

'No,' she said. She looked terrified. 'We'll be fine, don't report us again, I'll sort things out, he's not too bad.'

Her words were tripping over each other on the way out of her mouth. I'd said the wrong thing and it was clear that Cate was very scared indeed.

'OK, I won't,' I said. 'But listen, I have a place, in Margate, if you need somewhere to go. It's a little flat on the seafront. I haven't been there for ages, since my husband was so unwell. But you are welcome to use it if you want to go, I can give you a key and directions and everything.'

'Oh,' Cate said. 'I went to Margate when I was little, on a school trip. It was beautiful.'

I waited to see what she decided. Come on, I thought, take my offer and get the hell out.

'Tell you what,' I said. 'I'll come with you. Help you with Ocean, keep you safe. We can go now, there's a train from Crofton Park and it's only ten minutes away.'

I could see she was really tempted. She wanted to leave, but there was something else I could see on her face. She was scared, that was clear, but it wasn't the whole story.

'It's not your fault, you know, how he is,' I said and I knew straight away that I'd hit the nail on the head. She thought it was something in her, or worse, that something in Ocean had brought out the badness in him.

'Trust me,' I said, 'I knew a man like that once. The only thing you can do is to get away. Let me help.'

It might have worked then, and I've thought about it a lot. They might have both been able to get away, to come with me and live a different sort of life but I saw him coming down the road and I knew it was hopeless.

'Hey, Cate darling,' he said and he hugged her. I could see both Cate and Ocean flinch.

'Who's a good little girl then,' he said to Ocean. He touched her under the chin and Ocean nearly fell backwards out of her mum's arms, that's how hard she was straining and pulling away.

'I just asked Cate to pop round,' I said. I knew I had to make things easier for her. 'I've been lonely recently.'

It was lame but it was the best I could do. I wished that Jed was there to tell me what to do and to add a little bit of moral support. I tried to think of Annie, and what she would say. Stand firm, I could hear her saying in a soft Scottish accent, bullies hate it when you face them down.

'Oh dear, that's sad,' he said.

There was a glint in his eye that made me realise again how scary he must be to Cate and Ocean. Something a bit wild about him, like a crazed baddie in one of the superhero films William and Jed used to watch. He nuzzled Ocean's neck and I swear I thought he was going to bite her. From the look on her little face I thought that she was thinking this too, and that made me mad.

'Perhaps you'd all like to come in for a cup of tea?' I said and I held my arms out towards Ocean. It was instinctive and she picked up my cue. She held her arms out right back to me, and Cate was so surprised she let go. Holding Ocean felt wonderful. Even under the circumstances, even with that badass man breathing down our necks, it felt good to cuddle her and I think she felt the same. I turned to go back into my flat with her but that was a step too far.

'Hang on a mo, Mrs P,' he said.

I opened my mouth to say that I wasn't Mrs P but one look at him showed me he wasn't saying it by accident. He meant p for paedophile, I was sure of it. He was miming something disgusting and seemed to find the whole thing hilarious.

'Come to Daddy,' he crooned, holding his arms out towards Ocean.

I felt the poor little mite stiffen. She didn't want to leave me but he took her anyway and while he was trying to settle her I tried to mouth the word 'police' to Cate and I was sure she understood.

'Bye,' said the man, 'be seeing you. Not.'

He found this very funny, and I realised he might be drunk. Cate gave the tiniest shake of her head, which I think was to indicate to me not to rock the boat in any way, and they went off together. Ocean looked back at me as they left and did a little wave.

It was the wave that finished me off. With all that she was going through, and even though she must be scared right now and I knew it, she managed a little wave, a skill she had learned only recently. The part of her that was just a baby learning new things and practising them was still functioning and I thought, you go, girl. Well done. I'm going to help you as much as I can.

I went back indoors and I rang the police. I rang before I'd even thought it through but I had to do something. I should have known it wouldn't go well.

To start off with, I tried to be anonymous and they clearly didn't like that. They didn't make it easy. They had so many questions and although I suppose they had to, they seemed as though they were much more interested in me than in the fact that I considered Ocean to be in danger.

'He's a psychopath,' I said. 'An actual bona fide psychopath and he's got a hold over the baby's mum, I'm sure he has.'

'Are you married?' the person on the other end asked.

I couldn't believe what I was hearing.

'What on earth has that got to do with anything?' I said.

'Calm down please, ma'am, we have certain things we need to ask before we can proceed. We have a lot of neighbourhood disputes, you'd be surprised.'

'Why do you think I'm a neighbour?' I said.

I was alarmed. The last thing I wanted was that man thinking I had reported him to the police. It wouldn't help Ocean, it wouldn't help me and it might mean I lost any chance I might have had of trying to help her.

'Like I say, ma'am,' he repeated, 'nothing we haven't heard before, nothing we won't hear again. You'd be surprised the lengths people go to.'

What people? I thought. The kind of people who terrify and hurt women and babies, or the kind of people who report something bad happening when they see it?

'Maybe we could concentrate on what's important here,' I said. 'You remember baby P? And all the other little souls who've been lost because nobody acted on information that was as plain as a pikestaff to anyone paying the slightest bit of attention?'

'Like I said before, ma'am,' he said. 'We won't get anywhere until you calm down. And maybe tell us a little bit more about yourself, and why you wanted to call us today.'

I slammed the phone down in the end. If they didn't have enough information by then, I reasoned, there was no point talking to them any more. I'd turned off my caller ID so that they didn't know who was ringing, although I wasn't sure whether the police had a way round that. I'm still not sure.

When I woke up the next morning and went out to 'PAEDOPHILE' written in dripping red letters across the front of my house, including the windows, I knew who'd done it. I knew who had done it and why, and I also knew that if I contacted the police again he would do something even worse. The flat upstairs is vacant so at least I didn't have close neighbours to deal with, but I knew the estate agents would be round soon to show prospective buyers. And also, and more important, was the fact that if he would do something as violent and aggressive as that, what else was he capable of? I wasn't so worried about myself, I had an easy way out in less than seven weeks, but Ocean? And Cate? And where on earth could I go for help for them next?

I rang the social services hotline again, but this time I couldn't even speak to a person. I could leave a voicemail and that was all, so I tried to make myself sound as rational and calm as I possibly could so that they would believe me. I was sure it wouldn't work, and for hours afterwards I could hear my voice echoing like a ludicrous character from a sitcom.

I kept my curtains drawn. I couldn't face going to wash the letters off and I wasn't even sure that I had the right equipment. I had a small bottle of white spirit and the thought of going out, getting on a bus and buying more seemed like a task for a person much stronger than me. I had never missed Jed as much as I did that morning. I lay on the bed cuddling his big cardigan, the one he had worn in bed whenever he was cold. I said his name, over and over again until I could hear myself and realise how stupid I sounded. Pull yourself together, Jed would have said, get dressed and make a plan. He had always hated lounging around in bed and that had been one of the ways I could tell when he was really unwell.

I couldn't stop thinking about that baby. I thought about her every moment, willing myself to come up with a solution but I was absolutely stuck. I almost took the pills then, I really did but at the last minute I realised, I didn't have to stay here. I could go to Margate. My little haven by the sea would still be there waiting for me and that man could paint his signs all he wanted and I wouldn't care. I'd done what I could, told social services and the police and I couldn't do any more. I couldn't help Ocean, I'd given it my best shot but there wasn't anything more I could do. And maybe, maybe I was wrong, maybe there was an explanation for it all. Or maybe the police or social services would see what I had seen, and they would take Ocean to a place where she could be safe with her mum. I hoped that would happen, but I couldn't help any more.

I packed a small backpack. I thought of the last time I went to Margate with Jed. He had been very unstable on his feet. I can still see the sea, he'd said as the tide came in, almost to our doorstep. He cried then, and we both knew it was his last time.

Remember the happy times, he had said before he died. Go to Margate and enjoy it. I like thinking of you down there.

I could already hear the seagulls and the waves banging as I packed and I felt a tiny glimmer of hope. It had always been a place of such joy. Canute Cottage, Jed used to call it because it was his attempt to turn back time. The place he'd bought when he already knew the cancer had spread but we had three fabulous years of going down nearly every weekend before it became impossible. I wondered for a moment whether

I should tell William that I was going away, but of course that was stupid. He wouldn't be interested. And he would worry, of course he would, about the man and the writing on the wall. Maybe he would even think there was something in it. He had always looked uncomfortable when I peeked in prams, and I had made sure not to do it when I was with him for a long time now. Perhaps if he had had little siblings he would have liked young humans more, but I wasn't sure. Sometimes I thought that he had got too used to being alone when he was little.

No, I would manage this on my own. I would go to Margate, clear my thoughts and try to decide which way my life would go next. Whether I would live on or die quietly. I'd read an article ages ago about how older couples shouldn't rely so much on each other, because one always dies first and the other one needs to have some definites to rely on. Thursdays at the wine bar with friends, or book group every Tuesday or even church on a Sunday but I didn't have any of those. I didn't like people much and I had always preferred to spend my time with Jed rather than with anyone else, especially when William wasn't around. I'll decide at the seaside, I thought. I don't have to think of it now.

I checked that all the windows were locked shut and in the spare bedroom I closed the curtains, taking care to keep out of view. That was when I saw him. The man, Cate's boyfriend, and he was walking fast and carrying a large bag. I thought for a moment. Would it be safe to go and check on them now that he was out of the way? I couldn't see how it could be. He might be hoping to trick me into going round, and he would hide out of sight for a minute and then come back and get angry. I didn't mind for myself, I felt so tired and miserable I thought I might enjoy trying to give him a punch on the nose. I wouldn't want it to rebound on Cate and Ocean though, so I decided to keep going, stay focused, catch the eleven fifty train.

I was downstairs putting my coat on when I realised that the noise of the seagulls wasn't just in my head. Shrill seagull noises, and they were definitely coming from my back garden. I didn't want to find out what was happening. Some poor bird or even animal was injured, I was sure of that, and I wouldn't be able to help. It would be distressing, I could already imagine phone calls to the vet who would tell me that they didn't treat wild animals. I might end up having to hit it on the head with a shoe, like Jed had done with the dying rat we had found. No, I would ignore it and catch the train. If my boots hadn't been so awkward to lace it might have worked, but as I straightened up with some difficulty after tying my laces, the cries were louder. Too loud to ignore.

She was in my little garden, in her buggy. Ocean, and her cries didn't sound like a baby at all. More like a sad, wounded old woman or a beaten animal. My garden is walled so it was difficult to work out how she'd got in there, especially as she was in her buggy, but there wasn't time to think about that. I wheeled it indoors and then I lifted her out of it and held her until she stopped crying. I sang to her, nonsense songs about little girls in gardens, happy songs with penguins and hedgehogs cooking porridge together. She seemed to like the sound of my voice so I told her a story about herself, a happy one where she could do anything she liked and all the animals and birds said she was the boss. It seemed ages before her breathing became regular and she leaned against me as if this was a normal day, and we were having a normal cuddle.

That was when I saw the note. It was in an envelope attached to a lanyard she had round her neck. Quite a high-risk strategy, I thought, given that Ocean could probably have taken it off and dropped it if she wanted to. The envelope had my name on.

I'm sorry, the note inside said. *I don't want to do this but she's hurt, and I never meant that to happen. Please could you take her to the seaside place you told me about and leave me the address. I will come and find you very soon. Steve doesn't mean it but he has issues. I'm going to help him. Her lamby and her dog are under the buggy, she needs them to sleep. She likes toast. There are some nappies I'm sorry I'll pay you for more when I see you. Please leave her light on at night*
See you soon
Tell her I love her and sing rockabye baby please.
Thank you
Cate
Ps he is out now and will be for a little while but don't come round it's better if you get going.

I didn't need telling twice. I wanted to go and grab her, make her come too but it was clear that she had made a decision, and that if I went round there I could mess up the whole thing and then anything might happen. It was best to do as she said, I reasoned. I'll always have to live with that.

There were bottles under the buggy, and a cup with a lid. Nappies, cuddly toys, a small bag of clothes. What more could we need? I felt excited, I'll admit it, despite the circumstances. As if we had both been given a second chance, me and Ocean together. I wasn't going to waste it, and we needed to go as soon as possible to catch the next train. The address, though. I needed to get the address to Cate before we left. I was going to have to take some risks, and my heart was hammering. I hoped the adrenaline wasn't going to trigger a heart attack.

'We're off on our holidays, Ocean,' I said. 'Just stay here for one moment. One, I promise.'

I looked around for something for her to play with and saw an unopened bag of pasta. She reached out for it happily and as she opened her little hands I saw that they were hurt. Concentrate, Virginia, I thought. Give her the pasta and sort everything else out later. But hospital, I thought, even as I left her in the hall, shut the door and ran, actually ran, from my house to hers. A distance of no more than five yards but I wasn't taking any chances. He might come back. I posted a piece of paper with my Margate address through the letterbox and sent a quick prayer that Cate would find it first. I heard footsteps coming towards the door and as I turned to run back home. I heard Cate call 'thank you', in a voice that sounded as if she had been crying. This was just what I needed. I'd been slightly worried that it might all be a terrible trick that he, Steve, was playing on me for some crazy reason but it wasn't, it was all true. Cate wanted me to take Ocean out of the danger zone, and I needed to shape up and do it.

Ocean was pleased to see me even though it had only been a few minutes.

'I won't leave you again,' I said. 'But your mummy has to know where you are.'

'Guh,' she said.

69

I grabbed ointment and plasters and bandages from the kitchen cupboard and stuffed them in my backpack, along with biscuits for the journey and my exit pills for fifteenth June.

I had never been as scared as I was on the way to the station. I went through the estate instead of along the street to lessen the chance that he'd see us but still, I was trembling so hard I could hardly push the buggy. My legs and feet felt as though they belonged to someone else, and not even a person I knew. With every step I thought I might fall and the station seemed much further away than usual. I carried the whole buggy, complete with Ocean, down the stairs to the platforms.

'Seventy, schmeventy, I'm not old,' I said to Ocean and she nodded wisely.

We had only one change to negotiate, and luckily she was so interested in everything going on around us that she didn't seem at all upset.

'I've got a granddaughter,' a woman across the carriage said, as we pulled into Faversham. 'They're marvellous, aren't they? All the fun in the world, and then you get to give them back.'

I opened my mouth to say I hadn't got any grandchildren but realised just in time what she meant. I nodded and smiled and tried it out.

'Shall Grandma read you a book?' I said.

'Book,' Ocean said, and it was settled.

Grandma. I loved the sound of it.

PART II

CHAPTER SIX

Margate

Jackson was coping. Just. Sure, he worried from morning to night about everything but he was definitely acing it, at least that was what Noah said and Noah was smart. Every morning he leapt out of bed with a lurch of panic in his stomach and checked not only that Panna was still breathing but that Noah was OK in his little box room. Watching Noah was good and sometimes it calmed Jackson down. He looked peaceful, and so young in his Tottenham pyjamas. He lay in a heap, quilt usually flung on the floor and his hand under his chin as if he was thinking. Jackson decided every morning afresh that he would never, ever have children. Having Noah for a little brother was enough and it hurt too much. Plus there was a lot to it, running a household, and by the time everything was up and running Jackson often felt as though he would like to go back to bed.

Jackson and Noah started every day with a little conference round Panna's bed, talking about what they would do. Jackson made brief notes about how Panna was, what subjects he and Noah were going to cover in home-school that day and what everyone wanted to eat. What Panna wanted to eat, really. He and Noah had decided early on that they would eat anything that she fancied so that they could try to build her up. The truth was, Panna didn't really fancy anything, and they all knew that. Her cancer was stage four and she had already lived longer than the doctors had predicted. She had come to the coast over a year ago saying that she needed to be near the sea for a while. It had been obvious to Jackson that she had come here to die, and to give the boys in London some space from that dying. It didn't work out that way and Jackson thought about that often, too often. She had wanted to be here on her own, to die on her own, and Jackson and his brother had put paid to that quickly when they moved in. He hoped she didn't mind. It was another thing to worry about, and Jackson had so many things. The only time he could switch off was when he was teaching Noah. For those few hours at least, he could think about something else.

Jackson and Noah had already established a routine. After breakfast and the morning briefing Noah would work on something by himself while Jackson washed Panna and got her settled for the day, and then they would work together, on a project or something that Noah suggested, like a tidal chart or why the Second World War started. Jackson was constantly astonished at how smart Noah was. He wondered how he had managed to miss it all this time and accept the view of the school that Noah was not very bright. He was better at maths than Jackson already, and eager to read whatever his brother suggested.

Today had been particularly taxing. Jackson sat at the table with his head in his hands. Just one more minute, he thought, one more minute like this and then I'll get up. Get up, stand up, put the kettle on, start making the dinner, talk to Noah about his schoolwork.

'I'm hungry, bro,' Noah said.

On cue, Jackson thought, and he tried to smile.

'Tell me something I don't know,' he said.

Noah grinned.

Noah hadn't been to school for two months now. At first Jackson hadn't wanted him to stay home in case Noah missed important things, not least the chance to be with his peers. Jackson had more than enough to do looking after Panna but it was clear that things were really bad at school and he had not been able to bear seeing Noah so sad.

'Spag bol,' he said to Noah, 'will that do you?'

'Spag bol, Panna,' he said again, more loudly this time, in the direction of the room at the back of the flat, near the front door.

'Lovely jubbly,' she called.

It was a charade. Jackson knew that she couldn't really eat it, and that even if she did manage a few spoonfuls it would make her sick, but he was so, so grateful to her for keeping up appearances. His grandmother had always understood him like no one else, and she had tried to make things easier for him whenever she could. She hated the fact that he was having to care for her, and more than once Jackson had lain awake at night thinking that if he wasn't careful, for example if he moaned, she might take too many of her pills. To make his life simpler.

It hadn't always been like this. Panna had made sure that Jackson and Noah lived a fairly ordinary life in South East

London until two years ago. OK, they were looked after by their grandmother instead of their mum, but that wasn't unusual and they had a good life on the whole. So much had happened since then that Jackson sometimes felt as though he was a different person. That he'd shed his skin like a snake or burst out of his cocoon or something and transformed into someone else. He could hardly remember the things he had been worried about back then. Schoolwork, that had definitely been a big stress. He couldn't think why he'd worried now. He had got good, maybe even great, GCSEs, and he would clearly have managed the A levels just as well. Schoolwork had never been a problem for Jackson. He'd be in his first year at uni now if things had gone to plan, he thought as he chopped an onion. In London or Leeds or Birmingham, a big city somewhere. Not some small seaside town where nearly everyone else was white, where he'd had to go and talk to Noah's class teacher three times this term about the racism he'd been getting from the other kids. Eleven-year-olds. No, he'd be in a student house somewhere, a noisy, messy place. He'd probably still be chopping an onion, but he'd be making dinner for a load of friends. They would all be laughing about something and berating the government, checking they had enough beer, making a house rota, that sort of thing.

'That's why you're pathetic,' Jackson muttered to himself, 'even in your fantasies you're still cooking for people, what the hell is wrong with you? Who the hell fantasises about house rotas?'

'Bro,' said Noah, 'what's that onion done to you? It's proper mangled.'

Jackson shook his head to clear the picture in it. Noah was

right. The onion had been chopped into tiny pieces and then some. He had to get a grip or he would be no use to anyone.

'I was just thinking, I guess,' he said.

Noah mooched around the kitchen area, picking things up and putting them down again. Jackson could tell that he wanted to say something.

'Jax,' he said, 'is it really serious, Panna's illness? I mean,' he lowered his voice to a whisper, 'is Panna going to die?'

Jackson wasn't sure what to say. I'm only eighteen, he thought, I'm not ready for the big parenting questions, the ones that people probably struggle with, even when they've been parenting for years, for the child's whole life. He knew for sure that he shouldn't promise anything, and that empty promises were definitely the worst thing a person could do to a child. He just couldn't figure out how people, real parents, managed that. How they managed to get across the knotty truths about what a terrible world we're living in without either telling a lie or frightening the child so much that they would never be able to put the lights out. Noah had not been able to sleep with the light off until recently, and depending on what Jackson said right now it could go straight back on again.

'We're going to try every way we can to keep her well, and make her happy, but you know there's a time for everyone, don't you? She really is very poorly, No. But she's happy here with us and we can look after her as well as we can for as long as we can, and that's something,' Jackson said. 'Is that OK?'

That's a fudge, Jackson, and you know it, he thought. Still, he hadn't promised anything, and with a bit of luck Noah might be able to concentrate on his schoolwork. He certainly hadn't been able to when he was attending.

'OK,' said Noah, 'don't call me No. Can I have my spag bol without the onions?'

He's a kid, Jackson thought, he really doesn't understand anything. For one moment Jackson wondered what his life might be like if he was a member of an ordinary family. One with a mum and a dad who sorted things out, did the shopping and cooked the meals. And cared for the grandmother, washed her and fed her and changed her bedding. What the hell would that be like? What would it be like if the biggest family problem they had was what to watch on the TV, everyone jostling to get their choice for the evening? If he was arguing with Noah over whose turn it was to use the dining table to work on, rather than Jackson trying to add Year 6 tutor to his growing list of unwanted skills?

'It's gonna be hard to pick them out, dude,' Jackson said, 'but I'm a nice guy, right? So I'm not going to look when you arrange the tiny pieces of onion in a ring round your plate, like you always do. And in return for my amazing and fantastic kindness, you are going to help me with the washing-up, afterwards. Is that a deal?'

Jackson held his fist out for Noah to bump.

'OK,' said Noah, 'and I don't really mind when you call me No. It sounds different when you say it compared with the guys in my class. They make it sound mean. They kind of sing it, like this.'

Noah threw his head back and yelled, 'Noooooooo,' as if something terrible had just happened.

'They say it like that?' Jackson said. 'Every time they say your name?'

Noah nodded. What kind of hell had Noah been living in,

Jackson thought. He'd talked about some of it, enough to make it clear that he had been really unhappy, but he'd kept a lot of things back. Since he'd been off school, though, bits and pieces kept coming up. The bleach thing, for example. Noah had come into the bathroom when Jackson was cleaning.

'One hundred per cent effective,' he read from the bleach bottle. He put it down again. 'Girls bleach their hair, right?'

'Some girls, I guess,' Jackson said, 'girls do a lot of funny things, Noah. I don't know exactly why.'

I don't know why because I haven't got time to meet anyone in this godforsaken seaside town, Jackson had thought. No girls, no boys. My social calendar is empty, and set to stay that way.

'Only I wondered,' Noah said, 'whether it would work on like, skin. You know, like make it a bit, like, lighter.'

Jackson had torn off his rubber gloves and held on to Noah. It wasn't something they usually did, hugging, but Jackson couldn't stop himself.

'Noah, little bro, what the fuck are you talking about? Pardon my French, little guy, but no, no, no, Noah. That is wrong in about a million different ways. You know that, don't you?'

'Yeah,' Noah said, 'I mean, I don't mind really, but sometimes it would be nice just to fit in, you know? To go to school and be one of the ordinary boys, the white boys.'

'They are not ordinary,' Jackson said, 'they are the majority here, that's all, and it doesn't mean a damn thing. You are you, Noah, and you are the most beautiful boy this side of . . . of . . . of anywhere, I guess. It's one little school, No, and in September you'll be in with a whole new crowd of kids and you won't think about this at all.'

Jackson crossed his fingers as he remembered. He stirred the onions with vigour. He knew that secondary school might be just as bad as primary, maybe even worse. Kids could be bullies all their lives, they didn't suddenly grow out of it. And the whole thing about being the only Black kid in the class, was that how it would always be in this town?

'I've found a meditation app, Noah,' Jackson said. 'If you listen before bed it might help you to sleep better.'

'Yeah but I'm used to being awake now,' Noah said. 'I do my best thinking at night, you worry too much.'

Jackson realised he had set the gas too high. He scraped the mince from the bottom of the pan.

'Keep an eye on that for a minute, No, I'm just going to check on Panna.'

Noah jumped up, happy to help. That was one of the things Jackson couldn't understand about Noah being bullied, because he was such a nice boy. A damned nice boy, and Jackson could not see why the other kids couldn't see that. Or maybe they did see that, and his niceness made it even worse. Even in the twenty-first century.

Jackson knocked on Panna's bedroom door before he went in.

'Come in, lovely boy,' she said, 'I'm sorry, I'm rather indisposed today.'

She always talked like that, as though it was a temporary thing. Jackson wasn't sure whether she actually believed it or whether she was doing it for him, but he was happy to go along with it.

'I just wanted to check whether there's anything you need before dinner,' Jackson said, 'let me help you get to the bathroom.'

'Oh you do spoil me,' Panna said, as if he had offered her a chocolate rather than a hand to the toilet.

By the time they all sat down to dinner it was overdone, but no one complained.

'We're lucky we've got so much food,' Noah said. 'Maybe we could give some away. To poor people. I saw a man sleeping under the bridge in the mini golf today. Imagine that. I didn't go out on my own, I promise, before you say anything.'

Jackson was sceptical.

'How the hell can you see the mini golf without going out?' he said.

'If I hang over the balcony and kind of twist,' Noah said.

Panna had a coughing fit at that point so Jackson had to help her back to bed but later on, after washing up and settling Panna for the night, Jackson tried again.

'It's not OK to go out on your own without telling me, little No, not in school time. You're still only eleven and while you're not in school we've got to be even more careful than anyone else to make sure we don't only home-school you, but that we're seen to home-school you. They'd love a chance to stick you with a foster family but we're not going to give them a teeny, tiny sliver of a chance. OK, buddy? We will be able to walk down the beach and stuff, especially if we can point to what part of the curriculum we're following, just give me a little bit more time to make a plan and we'll be off. Weekends is different and we'll negotiate that too. In the meantime, if you feel like going anywhere, run it past me first, OK?'

'OK,' said Noah, 'OK, I'm sorry. I just wanted to see how far the sea got up the steps at high tide, you know, like I sometimes used to do when we visited Panna before.'

Jackson felt like the worst brother ever. How could he have forgotten how much Noah liked to do that? To walk along the prom with his grandma at weekends and scribble down each day how far the tide came up? They even used to do a seaweed check every day.

'You and Panna were always talking about making a big graph for the wall, weren't you?' Jackson said. 'Maybe I could help you with that.'

'Really?' said Noah.

His eyes were so full of delight Jackson could hardly bear it.

'I've got lots of ideas,' Noah said. 'I think it could be more like a flow chart, you know, with different colours and everything. And maybe the seaweed could be on a different graph, like a bar chart, in green. It will be something for Panna to look at when she's lying on the sofa, won't it?'

'It will,' Jackson said, 'come on, let's go out on to the balcony for five minutes. It's cold, but it'll be nice to be outside.'

Jackson knew that when Noah had anything on his mind he was more likely to talk when they were outside looking at the sea, so they stood out there for a while, watching the rain and the waves. The sand hurtled along the promenade below the balcony as if it had a pressing engagement, and there were hardly any people around. Jackson was about to go in for the night when Noah spoke up.

'What happens,' he said, 'if it never stops? If everywhere I go people think I'm odd, or different, or whatever it is they think? And what would I do if anything happened to you, and I'm the grown-up?'

'You won't be,' Jackson said, 'it's all fine. This is just a blip, I promise.' Jackson fought a desire to cross his fingers. 'There's nothing to worry about, I promise.'

'Hmmm,' Noah said.

Jackson suddenly got a glimpse of the man that Noah would be in twenty years' time. Thoughtful and kind, and not taking any nonsense.

'What does, "hmm" mean?' he asked.

'Jackson, sometimes you are a great big brother. Not so good at cooking, but OK at other stuff. But sometimes, and now is one of those times, you don't know shit, if you don't mind me saying that. I'm eleven, you know, and I'm not stupid. Or a baby. Some people just never fit in. They never get the hang of all the stuff other people find easy. Mum, for example.'

Jackson felt winded. 'That's not you, No,' he said.

'I'm not gonna lie,' Noah said. 'I hated the school in London too. Maybe me and school just don't fit together, I'm too thick or something. I've been reading about various mental health conditions and I guess I've got one of those like Mum but I'm damned if I can work out which one. Some of the greatest philosophers and politicians didn't fit in too well at school though, so I'm not giving up yet.'

Jackson was glad it was dark so that Noah didn't see the surprise on his brother's face. Was this the same boy who didn't manage very well academically? Who still played with Lego and watched cartoons meant for much younger children, sometimes with his thumb creeping towards his mouth?

83

'I didn't know you were unhappy there too,' Jackson said, 'at least that's one thing I don't have to worry about any more.'

Noah laughed, and Jackson thought it sounded like the laugh of a much older person. A tired person.

'Don't forget, bro, you don't have to have all the answers just because I have all the questions,' Noah said.

Jackson laughed and raised his hand for a high-five.

CHAPTER SEVEN

Margate

Making sure they had everything they needed in the cupboards was fiendishly difficult for Jackson. Noah would have been happy to help out but Jackson had to be careful. Careful and strict. No matter how much Noah pleaded to be allowed to go to the shops on his own, Jackson was worried that he might meet some of the kids who had been bullying him, or worse, grown-ups who didn't think he ought to be out. It was completely possible, Jackson thought, that they would be reported. All those kids had parents.

The truth was, Jackson had to admit that he had developed an irrational anxiety about leaving the house. On a bad day it could make him feel as though his legs were trembling too much to hold him up, although he thought he'd managed to keep that from Panna and Noah. Some kind of agoraphobia he guessed, and yet another thing to be afraid of given their mother's history of mental illness.

This morning he couldn't put off shopping any longer. There were things they needed, and he had to pull himself together and get out there.

'Noah,' he said, 'I've got to go shopping and you can't come. You know the score. When I come back you can go up and down a bit on the beach, get some fresh air. Any requests?'

Jackson hoped that Noah hadn't noticed anything weird about his behaviour. The last thing he needed right now was to see how crazy his big brother was. Noah needed a big brother he could count on, however hard that might be for Jackson.

'KitKats,' Noah said. 'And popcorn and crumpets and that peppermint chocolate in little balls.'

'I'll try to get some actual food as well,' Jackson said.

'Counting on you, bro,' Noah said. 'And maybe we could work on your sarcasm game, because it's not really a good look at the moment.'

Jackson saluted and left. He had to keep clear of germs and get some food, that was all. Panna had more or less no immune system left so even a cold could make her very unwell. Or worse. Such a simple task, and yet Jackson felt completely unequal to it. The streets seemed full of danger and by the time Jackson got to the shop he had all the symptoms of a heart attack. His pulse was racing, he was panting and he couldn't think straight. He fumbled in his pocket for the list and tried to make sense of it as he concentrated on putting one foot in front of the other. 'Milk, yogurt, fruit, vegetables, popcorn,' he muttered to himself, the list back in his pocket now as he focused on selecting the right products.

Several items he'd missed occurred to him as he was paying but the idea of going back was out of the question. As soon as he left the shop Jackson broke into a run, not stopping until he was back at the flat. The relief was tremendous. Running, he thought, I could run again, keep myself sane that way. He felt like a conquering hero as he went in, and whooped loudly enough to wake Panna.

Noah watched, his graph on the table in front of him.

'Are you OK, bro? And did you get the oranges, so we can make fresh juice for Panna?'

Jackson's elation disappeared in an instant.

'You had one job,' Noah said gleefully, 'one job, bro.'

The biggest compensation of home-schooling Noah was the chance to get to know his little brother in a whole new way. To get to know him as a real person, not just a kid. It was easy for Jackson to imagine the two of them as grown men thirty years from now, walking by the sea and chatting about cars, football and their jobs.

'Stereotype city,' Noah said when Jackson told him about this fantasy. 'I can't believe you're so cheesy, bro. Why are we gonna to be talking about cars? Are you interested in cars now?'

'Well no,' Jackson said, laughing, 'but it might be different when I've got one.'

Noah shook his head. 'Self-knowledge, J, it's a powerful thing. You should try getting some.'

Noah aimed a fake punch at Jackson's torso.

'I mean, how we are now,' Noah said, 'I reckon we're not going to change that much. You like books, right?'

'You know I do,' said Jackson.

'Well, let's talk about books then, when we're old and past it and maybe trying to get away from our wives, or husbands, Jax, we might have husbands, did you think of that? And we can talk about when you were home-schooling me, and politics, and how you were such a scaredy cat.'

Noah held up his hand to high-five his brother and Jackson couldn't help laughing.

'I guess you're right,' he said, 'I don't know where the cars bit came from. Maybe I watch too much TV.'

'No,' Noah said, bouncing on his heels, 'I know what it is, I know exactly. It's called unconscious bias.'

He pronounced the words carefully. It was clear he was very proud of knowing them. 'It means when you make a judgement about something based on a person's race or age or gender without even realising it. I've been reading about it because of those kids in my school, you know, the ones who kept asking me where I kept my drugs. Because I'm black.'

'They did what?' Jackson said. 'Noah, that is another thing you didn't tell me. How am I going to help you sort things out if you don't tell me anything?'

Noah hung his head.

Jackson went in to see Panna once Noah was busy again.

'If you're scared sometimes, it's OK to admit it,' Panna said.

Jackson shook his head, amazed that she had seen through him again. How did she know?

'Don't worry,' she said, 'the little lad doesn't know every-thing, not yet. But he'll pick it up sooner or later, he's quick, that one.'

Jackson wasn't sure what he could say that wouldn't leave him blubbing like a baby. It seemed safer to say nothing.

'Did you think I was going to be cross with you for feeling scared?' she said. 'Hell no. That fear shows that you're very responsible, you want to do right by me and your little brother. I'm lucky that you're in my corner. It's just—'

Panna stopped and wiped her mouth with a tissue. It was

the longest speech Jackson had heard her make for a month or two. Maybe even since Christmas.

'It's just that when things get really scary, you can't let it take you over completely. You've got to keep a little bit back, like a sourdough starter.'

'Like a what?' Jackson immediately thought that his grandmother must have lost her mind. Brain tumour, he thought, stroke, possibly virus attacking the brain, maybe dementia, probably imminent death. Ambulance, should he go or stay, will Noah be OK on his own, what about Panna? He swallowed.

'Like a sourdough starter, you keep a bit back and add to it each day. So what I'm saying is, you keep a bit of yourself back when the fear takes you, and add to it every day. It's a work in progress, Jackson.'

Panna lay back on the pillows and Jackson could see that she was exhausted. So many words and so much effort. He felt ashamed.

'I get it,' he said, 'and I promise I'll try to keep something back. I'm just sorry for you that you've got me for a looker-afterer but I'll try and do better. And I'm sorry I forgot the oranges you wanted, too.'

Panna laughed. For a moment she sounded like her old, bouncy self and Jackson smiled.

'You're the best looker-afterer I've ever had. And bear this in mind – no one chooses when they get to come and go,' she said, 'and for me, I'd rather leave the party when there's a lot going on, when it's in full swing. I don't want to stay and be the last person standing. One thing though, I do want to make sure you're OK. And I'm grateful that we get to spend this time together, I am. But I'm tired now, so clear off and go out for a run or have a nap. I'll get up for dinner, oranges or no oranges, and maybe we can play Scrabble after. Go on, get.'

Jackson saluted and left. He wanted to hug her, but he couldn't quite get over the feeling that he might hurt her in some way, or introduce germs. He could feel himself straighten up. Panna seemed to be almost back to her real self, and somehow that made everything feel better. He lay on the sofa and drifted off to sleep.

When he woke up, Panna was out of bed and teaching Noah to knit.

'Pull it round, then through,' she said, several times.

She undid the mess Noah made and set it up again, over and over. Jackson marvelled at her patience.

'I remember teaching your mum to knit,' Panna said.

Jackson could see that the painkillers were starting to wear off and she was uncomfortable.

'Did you?' Noah said. 'Was she good at it? Was she better than me?'

Jackson always forgot how little Noah knew about their mum, and how eager he was for any snippet of knowledge.

'She was impatient,' Panna said, 'always wanted to be on to the next thing. But she's good with her hands, if she'd just sit still and concentrate for ten minutes.'

Noah redoubled his efforts, but Panna looked sad, Jackson thought. He noticed how she used a weird mixture of past and present when she was talking about their mother, her daughter, and he realised that he and Noah did the same. She wasn't actually dead, just in hospital, but she might as well be dead for all the contact they had. They used to go to visit her sometimes during earlier stays. Jackson had memories of scratchy, uncomfortable clothing, long waits in rooms that smelled of toilet cleaner and often going home without even seeing her because she wasn't well enough. That's what they had said to Jackson, she isn't well enough today, but he had been a snoopy sort of child. A listening outside the door boy. And he had heard one time that she didn't want to see them. That she'd changed her name and announced that she had no children, she had no mother.

'That's it,' Panna said, holding up a mangled piece of knitting. There was a definite air of triumph in her voice and Noah was grinning like a happy boy.

'Look at this, Jackson, your brother is a home craft genius.'

Jackson smiled, then saw that more was needed and whooped.

'Way to go, bro,' he said. 'Panna is a good teacher. Do you remember when you taught me to swim, Panna?'

She laughed. Such a great sound, Jackson thought, the sound of his childhood.

'Noah, I never saw anyone splash so much in my life,' Panna said. 'He was terrified, but he was so brave. So determined, everyone at the pool clapped when he finally did a stroke.'

Jackson knew there was a message in there for him, and he smiled at her despite his anxiety. Panna must be incredibly tired, he thought. She hadn't been out of bed for this long in a while. They were putting on a show for him, to cheer him up. He was sure of it.

'Hey,' he said, 'maybe we can have a trickle-down effect here. Maybe Noah can teach me. How would that work?'

Noah's eyes sparkled.

'Really?' he said. 'I reckon I've got the hang of it now. We're making a patchwork blanket, aren't we, Panna?'

Panna laughed.

'Hey, my work is done,' she said, 'I'm going back to bed and I'm going to leave you two boys to do your boys' work. Noah – you call me if you get in trouble. I've tried to teach Jackson other things as well as swimming and he doesn't always listen straight. It goes in one ear, twirls around while he makes it into something else, then it comes out the other. I'm warning you.'

'Do you think she's feeling better?' Noah said as soon as Panna had gone. 'She looks better, doesn't she? Like her old self. Right, loop the wool round like this, then move the needle so that it kind of tucks into the other loop, see?'

Jackson found Noah's chatter soothing. He enjoyed the repetitive nature of the knitting and soon he felt better.

'You need to go for a run, bro, like you used to. All this sitting around isn't good for you,' Noah said.

'Rubbish,' Jackson said. 'I'm happy here with you.'

A run would be nice though, Jackson thought. Uncomplicated and wholesome. It would get him out of the house with minimum anxiety. And the best thing was, he could pretend that he could keep going. Not that he wanted to run away, not that at all but what Jackson missed more than anything else were the possibilities.

'Are you sure you don't mind?' Jackson asked.

There was no mistaking the twinkle in Noah's eye.

'Yes!' Noah said and he high-fived his brother.

*

Jackson thudded along the promenade, thinking with each step how unfit he had become. How housebound. He promised himself that he would try to change that. What's more, for the rest of today, he would be grateful that he was able to look after Noah and Panna. The running felt cleansing, as if he was running towards a future.

By the time he got to the harbour arm Jackson had to stop. His feet and legs felt like ghost limbs and his lungs as though they were full of barbecue coals. He bent over to stretch and catch his breath, then did some gentle exercises. Touching his toes, twisting from the waist. The run back home had better be easier, he thought.

He didn't notice the police officers until they were really close. Probably closer than they should be, but Jackson didn't say anything. He stood where he was and held himself still. One of the police officers stood in front of him and the other one circled round, looking him up and down as if there was something to check out. Jackson remembered what Panna had taught him.

'Good afternoon, officers,' he said, 'can I help you?'

Neither of them spoke for what seemed like a long time, although Jackson thought later that it might have been no more than a minute or two.

'I'm wondering, sir,' said the first policeman, 'what you're doing today. And why.'

He peered at Jackson as if there was something very strange about him. Peered right up close. Jackson held his breath and tried to think of all the reasons the officer would not necessarily have any germs. Why the tiny particles would not be transferring themselves right now from Officer A, the peering, weird one, onto Jackson's face, hair or skin. Jackson pulled back. He couldn't help it.

'Excuse me,' Jackson said, 'I'm looking after my grandmother who is sick and I'm trying not to have close contact, in case of germs. No disrespect, sir.'

The second police officer, shorter and with kinder eyes, pretended to search the ground near to Jackson.

'Grandma, Grandma,' he called in a silly voice, 'no, I can't see her anywhere.'

Jackson ran through what Panna had always told him, since he was little enough to think that it was a joke. Be polite, she had always said, no matter what nonsense they throw at you, you can't join in. Stay calm, stay sensible, keep your hands in sight and stay alive. He had often thought that she was exaggerating, that she was thinking about the bad old days when things were much worse than they were now, but she had always been calm and convincing and Jackson was glad of that now.

'Sorry, sir,' he said, 'she's not able to come out. She's home with my brother and I'm taking a quick break. Exercise.'

'All the answers,' said Officer A.

'All the answers,' said Officer B.

Jackson decided that Officer B's eyes weren't any kinder at all. It was an illusion. He kept quiet.

'Look at that,' Officer A said. 'You thinking what I'm thinking?'

Jackson thought they must have used this script before, it came so easily, sounded so well rehearsed.

'He's not so eager to speak now, is he?' said Officer B.

'Exercise,' said Officer A thoughtfully.

'Exercise,' said Officer B as if it was a ridiculous word.

Jackson stayed still and quiet.

They stood there for another endless minute. The two police officers stared at Jackson, who tried to maintain a balance between staring back and looking away, both of which he thought would be inflammatory. He knew it probably made him look as shifty as hell, but he couldn't at that moment think of an alternative. Finally, the two officers turned as if they were leaving. Jackson stood still, even though his instinct was to run as fast as he could in the opposite direction. It might be a trick.

Sure enough, after the two men had walked away for a few seconds, they both stopped, as if the same idea had occurred to them at exactly the same time.

'You're not a local lad, are you? Where would you be from, then?' Officer A said.

'We've just got to ask,' said Officer B, 'don't worry, no one is doubting that you're taking your "exercise".'

He really said exercise with inverted commas, Jackson thought. He wished he could find it comical.

Jackson held his hands together in front of himself.

'Originally South East London, sir, but I've been living down here for just over a year.'

He hoped that would be enough, and that they wouldn't want to come to his house and frighten Panna and Noah. He pointed along the sea front in the direction of the flats.

'Funny we haven't seen you before, that's all, isn't it?' Officer A said.

Jackson kept quiet. Because I don't go out much, you fucking morons, he thought, because I'm stuck at home looking after an old woman and home-schooling a boy.

'One more thing,' said Officer B, whose eyes were getting less and less kind by the minute. Jackson realised that he knew what the one more thing would be.

'Where are you actually from, like originally?' Officer B said.

Jackson wondered how many times he had been asked this question since he moved to Margate. Too damn many, that was for sure.

'Oh, originally?' he said, knowing that his anger would show in his voice if he wasn't very careful, 'originally, I'm from North London. My mum moved to Lewisham when I was six months old though, so I don't really count it.'

Both policemen moved so that they were close to Jackson. So close that he could smell their breath. He stood his ground and imagined scrubbing himself as soon as he got in, letting the soap and water wash away every trace of these two clowns.

'Very droll,' said Officer A, 'off you go now, better get back. Let's hope we meet again soon.'

Jackson did not need telling twice. He forgot how stiff and tired he had been just minutes earlier, and raced off in the direction of home. He felt his feet pounding the pavement, thud after thud, and the rhythm drowned out the voices of the policemen for a while. The running, that's what he needed to focus on. One foot after the other until he could get home. He shouldn't have come out. Jackson's head filled with images of things that might have happened while he wasn't there. Choking, that was one of the ones he often worried about. Panna or Noah choking and him not being there to perform the Heimlich manoeuvre. Or someone breaking and entering, and hurting them. Or an accidental fire or a knitting needle in the eye or any number of household accidents. Anything could have happened. He didn't time the run, and he wasn't aware of Noah watching from the balcony.

Jackson was terrified as he went into the flat.

'Hello, everyone OK?' he called.

'Usain Bolt, bro,' Noah said, 'you were fast. Look.' He held out a piece of paper towards his brother. 'I did a drawing.'

Jackson stepped back and held his hands up as if the piece of paper was a gun. 'Don't come any closer,' he shouted, 'I've got to shower. I'm not clean.'

'OK, OK,' said Noah. He scrumpled the paper up and shoved it in his pocket.

'What's going on?' Panna called from her room. 'Is everyone OK, are you boys fighting?'

Jackson asked Noah to please go and tell Panna that everything was OK, and to see if she wanted a drink.

'I'll be five minutes,' he said, 'just five.'

Half an hour later Jackson emerged. He had scrubbed until he was sore, but he could still feel bugs crawling on his skin. He couldn't stop hearing the police officers and their sneering voices, and he couldn't stop imagining what might have happened if he had spoken up for himself, or if the police hadn't let him go. He had been so close to something terrible, that was the feeling that he couldn't shake.

Noah had peeled potatoes and set the table but Jackson hardly noticed. He made the dinner on auto pilot and afterwards he wasn't sure what they had talked about at the table. He was aware of Noah and Panna looking at him as if they were worried and he tried to smile but he knew his mouth didn't move properly.

It wasn't until they were watching TV that Jackson cracked. Jackson was hoping that TV would block out the difficult stuff and he needed to get those policemen out of his head. Noah clapped with delight when it was suggested. He loved them all watching things together. He said it made him feel as though he lived in a storybook family and Jackson and Panna smiled at each other over his head about what kind of story that might be. They all watched a detective series about an abducted baby. Jackson tried to let it wash over him and he was doing well with this tactic until the story showed an interview with the parents. The mum looked hardly older than Jackson as she pleaded with whoever had him to let him go home. He couldn't sleep without his bear, she said and Jackson couldn't keep it in any more. He started to cry, and once he started he found that he couldn't stop.

'Bro,' said Noah. 'It's fiction, bro.'

Jackson could hear that he was scared. This was the last thing Noah needed, the worst way for Jackson to look after his brother.

'I'm OK,' he said, 'I'm OK, honest. It's just, you know, sometimes stories can be powerful.'

He knew he was scaring Noah but he couldn't do anything about it, couldn't stop right now. Those policemen. And what could have happened.

'OK,' Panna said, 'I'm going to give you some instructions now and you're going to do what I say, right? Like when you were little? I want you to take three deep breaths, in through your nose and out through your mouth. Don't think about anything else, concentrate on that.'

Jackson felt as if he was three years old again, with a cut knee. It had always been Panna he wanted when he was hurt, Panna he had run to. She had always been the person who knew what to do whether the problem was a wasp sting or a broken heart. She was too weak to do much now, but she still had a presence, and her voice broke through Jackson's hysteria. He took the deep breaths she suggested and felt himself start to calm down.

'I'm so sorry,' he said as soon as he was sure his voice wouldn't let him down. Noah and Panna burst out laughing.

'Your little brother is smart,' Panna said, 'he just whispered to me that those would be the first words out of your mouth and he was damn right. And there's no need to apologise for anything. You're allowed a moment, we all are. Is your moment over now?'

Jackson knew she was pulling him together for his own sake as well as Noah's and he was grateful.

It wasn't until later that night that he had time to think again about what had happened. And about how frightened he was. Scared of everything. He felt ashamed. Noah had been so brave at that school, going off every day to face whatever was waiting for him. And Panna was coping with all kinds of pain that she hardly ever mentioned, plus she was probably terrified of dying and leaving the boys behind. The two of them were making such an effort, and Jackson felt as though he was no use to them at all. Just a big, blubbering, useless wreck dragging them down, that's what he was. He wished that there was someone he could ask for help. He wasn't sure what help would look like, but he knew that he needed something. In the meantime, he thought, the only thing that made any sense at all would be to redouble his efforts. To make sure that he concentrated on Noah and Panna and to stop thinking about his own stupid self.

CHAPTER EIGHT

Margate

Noah had become obsessed with a little dog who walked on the beach every day. He watched it carefully and every day he became increasingly concerned. He was convinced that the owner was cruel.

'He doesn't deserve to keep that dog, Jax,' Noah said.

Jackson was worried.

'You're not in charge, No,' he said, 'you don't get to decide who has a dog and who doesn't. There is so much trouble waiting for you out there if you start believing that.'

'But bro, he's mean. He's actually totally mean to that little dog and it's such a nice dog. He hit it the other day because it was too slow up the steps, but those steps are steep. And the dog is small. And he's often drunk, the owner, he falls asleep by the rocks and the dog just has to wait there, even if it's cold and rainy.'

Jackson sighed.

'I get it,' he said, 'and it's horrible, but what are we going to actually do? Kidnap his dog and keep it?'

'Yes!' said Noah. 'That's exactly what I was thinking. We

could wait till he's asleep, then bring the dog back here. I think he calls him Bill, but we can find a better name than that. And I'm sure he doesn't eat much, he's really very little and skinny.'

Jackson realised that Noah was deadly serious.

'No,' he said, 'that is not going to happen. Number one, we've got enough to do here without a dog. Number two, it's not our dog. What do you think that guy would do if we took his dog? He'd go to the police. Or he'd look for it himself. Either way, we would be in trouble. And we'd have to take it out for a walk at some point and someone would spot it and then we'd be in trouble. So no, no dognapping, thank you Noah.'

The boy looked sad and Jackson wished he had been a little more tactful.

'Just think about it, No,' he said, 'if we took all the dogs away from bad owners, and all the kids away from bad parents . . .' Jackson was going to say that the flat would be too crowded for them to fit in but a look at Noah's serious face told him that would be too flippant. This was serious to the boy, no matter what Jackson thought.

'You can't rescue all the dogs,' Noah said, 'but you can change the whole world for one dog. And we could hide him, bro, keep him in my bedroom.'

Jackson kept his expression firm and walked away. Jeez, he thought, who would be a parent? What a miserable, joyless task. A few years ago he would have loved to kidnap the dog along with Noah. Maybe even steal a car and drive off on a road trip as though they were in a film. Now here he was, Mr Sensible, Mr Responsible.

The up side was, Noah was a great companion. There

was a lot of laughter in the flat, and Noah was happy to help Jackson with the tasks involved in looking after Panna. It was Panna that Jackson was most worried about. He was sure that she was deteriorating. She kept up a good front, and Jackson thought that Noah was probably fooled, but he had found uneaten food under her bed when he was cleaning. Panna knew he had found it.

'I'm sorry, Jack,' she said, 'only I didn't want the baby to know.'

Jackson assumed she meant Noah. She hadn't called him the baby for years, though, and it niggled him.

'Will you tell me,' he said to Panna, 'if you feel worse? If you feel worried, or think you may need to up the pain meds? We can speak to the nurse any time on the phone, she promised.'

'Bless you,' Panna said, 'you don't need to be worrying about that. And nor does she, she has enough to do with the folk who are really sick. I'll tell you anything you need to know, you know I will.'

Jackson was not convinced. The doctor hadn't visited so much recently, but Jackson was sure that Panna had got worse. She tried to get out of bed at least once a day, and some days the effort this took was tremendous. Noah would notice that something was wrong soon if he didn't know already, Jackson was sure of that. The boy liked to spend as much time as possible with his grandmother while he was writing essays or doing sums, asking her for help that he probably didn't need.

There hadn't been any mention of the dog for a few days. Jackson hoped that it had been forgotten, in fact he had more or less forgotten about it himself until the day of the storm. It was a hailstorm, as full of drama as a whole box set, Noah said, and Jackson had to agree. The sky was dark even though it was ten o'clock in the morning and the hail crashed down onto the balcony like an aerial bombardment. Noah capered around the flat making shooting noises until Jackson had to cover his ears.

'OK, OK, enough now,' he said, 'do you want to go out in it for five minutes? I'm not coming, I don't want to leave Panna when it's this noisy. You'll have to go by yourself, and don't stay out long.'

'Oh can I?' Noah said. 'Yes, yes, yes. I love it.'

Jackson went to talk to Panna while Noah was out.

'Imagine being that excited,' she said, 'to go out and get beaten up by frozen rocks.' Jackson laughed. He agreed with her even though that put him firmly in the old people bracket.

'I always thought snow would be soft and fluffy,' Panna said, 'until my first hailstorm. It's vicious. Like a punishment.'

Jackson laughed.

'Noah doesn't see it that way,' he said. 'Noah is in his very own drama movie right now, killing icy dragons, I reckon.'

Jackson was still with Panna when Noah came in.

'Hi,' Noah called, 'I'm going straight to the shower, OK, bro?'

Jackson left Panna tucked up and comfortable, with her pillows rearranged. She might even have looked a little better today, he thought as he peeled the potatoes. Sausage and mash tonight, and he knew that Noah, at least, would be glad that the sausages were vegetarian. Dinner was almost on the table when Jackson became aware that Noah was in the kitchen, staring at him.

'Can I help?' Noah said.

Jackson tried not to feel suspicious but there was something about Noah's eyes. They were too bright, and he was holding himself very tensely.

'Are you OK?' Jackson said.

'Yes,' said Noah.

The word came out high-pitched and squeaky.

Jackson looked up from the saucepan. He could tell that Noah was surprised at the sound he'd just made, and he looked shifty as hell.

'I'm fine, bro,' Noah said.

Jackson noticed that he couldn't quite look him in the eye and also that he kept looking over at his bedroom door.

'Anything you want to tell me?' Jackson said. He had forgotten the conversation about the dog. He didn't remember it until he had taken Panna her dinner in bed and was sitting down with Noah at the table. He wouldn't have remembered it then if the dog hadn't smelled the sausages and whined at the thought of them being eaten without him, meat or no meat.

It was a little whine at first, more like a clearing of the throat. Noah coughed to cover it until he was almost sick but Jackson still knew what he had heard the minute he heard it.

'You all right, darling?' Panna called from her bedroom.

Jackson gave Noah his sternest, crossest look. 'He's OK, Panna,' he said, 'he just choked on a piece of sausage.' He turned to Noah. 'Right,' he said in a quiet voice, 'spill.'

Noah put his knife and fork down. He looked terrified, and Jackson's heart went out to him.

'It's not like you think,' Noah said, 'I mean I wasn't going to, after you said no and everything, it's just that, man, he really is bad, you know. He's awful. He was actually hitting him, proper hitting him with a stone, not even a stick. And it was storming too. And the dog, he was just sitting there, he didn't even try to run or anything, as if he didn't know anything else was possible. As if he didn't even expect anything nice to happen. He was drunk, the man, I'm sure he was drunk and he went to sleep then, even though it was raining and hailing and everything, he went to sleep in a little sort of cave in the rocks and Phil just sat there looking at him and shaking.'

Jackson felt a familiar surge of terror. Noah was so vulnerable. Anything could have happened to him, and still could.

'What have you done, Noah?' Jackson asked.

Noah bit his lip. His eyes were full of tears as he turned to Jackson.

'I'm sorry, bro. I really am. I totally didn't want to upset you.'

Jackson waited for the 'but'.

'But I couldn't leave him with that man. Poor little Phil.'

'Phil?' Jackson said.

'I wanted a new name for him, because Bill has like, bad memories for him. But I wanted something similar, something he would recognise. I chose Phil, and he totally gets it. It works well.'

Noah's tears stopped and Jackson could see how pleased he was that he had made a difference. He felt out of his depth and despite his panic he had to focus all his attention on maintaining a stern face.

'But Noah,' he said, 'he's not our dog. And how would we walk him when that man, or his friends, are probably local? And what if he barks? I don't even know if dogs are allowed here. I've never asked. Because I don't need to know, we do not have a dog.'

'And Panna will like him,' Noah said.

Jackson realised that they were having two entirely separate conversations.

'He's got to go,' Jackson said, 'maybe not right now but we have to think of something else, No.'

Noah sniffed and Jackson could see tears welling up again in his eyes.

'Please, bro,' he said, 'please, could you just meet him, then you'll see.'

Jackson had never been good with tears. And it was a right-eous crime to take the dog, Jackson had no doubt that Noah was telling the truth. I'll just meet the dog, he thought, take a bit of time to explain more clearly to Noah why it won't work. Help him to think of another solution.

Noah went to his room and came back leading the sorriest scrap of a dog Jackson had ever seen. He looked like a small terrier, but with long, black matted hair and sad eyes. His tail started to wag as soon as he saw Jackson.

'See, bro,' Noah said, 'he likes you, he knows you're not going to hurt him. Look at that tail!'

Great, Jackson thought, now there's a small dog who thinks I'm going to save him. Just what I need. He cut off a piece of sausage and held it out to the dog, who took it politely and carefully. Noah thrust his fist in the air, barely able to contain his excitement.

'See that,' he said, 'see that? Some dogs would grab and bite the food, but he's a good boy. We could train him to do anything. And Jack, I've been reading about dogs, on the internet and did you know that they often can't find homes for black dogs? Imagine that. People don't want them just because they're black. You wouldn't think that, would you? Look, I've taught him something already.'

Noah knelt down next to the dog.

'Who's a good boy, who's a good little Phil,' he said. 'Look, Jack, I've taught him a trick.'

Noah held his hand out to shake and the little dog gave him his paw. Jackson could feel the cuteness overload rising. Threatening to overwhelm him, in fact. He shook himself and tried to remember that he was the grown-up.

'Noah,' he said, 'you know, don't you, that this is impossible? We can't just steal someone's dog.'

'Listen to me a minute,' Noah said, 'if anyone asks, if we get rumbled, I'll say that he was walking on his own, down the beach. The guy was asleep so he could have been, for all he knew. And we can take photos, of the wounds he's got. So they can see that we are the good owners, we can clean him up and everything. I mean, look at this, bro.'

Noah lifted up Phil's right ear. He was so gentle, talking to him softly and holding him against his body, that Jackson felt an alarming swerve away from the path of sensible thinking. He crouched down next to them and he could see a big lump behind Phil's ear. There was no fur there, and the skin was bright red.

'There's more,' Noah said.

He took Jackson through an entire inventory of lumps, bumps, cuts, scratches and even some parts that looked as if they had been burnt. The dog stood there letting him lift and touch and stroke and photograph, even though it must have been difficult for him. At one point Noah went to get him a dish of water and Jackson watched as Phil's eyes followed Noah across the room and back, full of something that looked like devotion.

'Give me a minute, No,' he said.

Jackson went on to the balcony and scanned the beach. No sign of a man looking for a dog. Perhaps it wouldn't hurt to shelter him for a few days, he thought, Noah's idea of saying they found the dog on its own was a good one. The heart of it was, Jackson had had enough of making the right choices. And he couldn't bear to make Noah sad. Or Phil. Phil looked so much like a canine version of Noah. Jackson forced himself to think of the cons. There was dog food, they'd need that, but Jackson was good at managing money and there wouldn't be a problem. The main worries were, one, Panna and how she would react and, two, how would they walk Phil when his owner could be on the beach at any time? Even if they went farther, to a beach a few minutes' walk away, there was no guarantee that he wouldn't be there. Easy enough to walk him in the dark now, in spring, but the days were getting longer all the time. Jackson rehearsed all the reasons why not as he went inside, although he couldn't help feeling a crazy hope that it could work out.

No, Jackson thought, don't even think of it. Your job is to talk some sense into Noah. The scene that he saw when he got inside, however, reminded him of a scene from a book, maybe a Dickens novel. Panna was out of bed, that was the most unusual thing. She hadn't got up for days apart from meals, had felt too weak, but there she was, on the sofa in her nightdress with Phil in a large bowl of warm water at her feet.

She was washing him and singing, a lilting song that Jackson remembered from his childhood, and Phil was sitting still and letting it happen, even though he must be scared.

'This dog,' said Panna, 'has not been treated right. But he still knows how to love, isn't that amazing? Imagine if a human was treated like that. Hit and kicked, and probably worse, all their life. Some of these scars are old. I'm not sure the human would still be trusting. Chances are, they'd be meaner than a snake.'

Jackson could see, now that Panna was lifting up pieces of fur and washing underneath them, that the scarring was much worse than he had thought at first. Noah had been right to rescue the dog and Jackson had been unobservant, caught up in petty concerns. That would never happen again, he had learned a lesson. Jackson rubbed his eyes.

'Cigarette burns, some of them,' Panna said.

Noah gasped, and kissed the dog on the nose.

'I'm sorry, mate,' he said, 'but no one else is going to hurt you, ever.'

Jackson could see that Noah's eyes were glistening. He sniffed and coughed to cover up his own reaction, and Panna did the same.

'Who would do that?' Jackson said.

'Someone evil,' Panna said, 'we need to help out here.'

They sat quietly, Noah and Panna stroking the dog and talking to him, and Jackson watching them.

Jackson noticed that the dog looked at Noah all the time, and wagged his tail whenever Noah touched him.

'I can help,' Jackson said, 'Panna, you should get back to bed.'

'Jackson,' said Panna, 'you are a lovely boy, but not a very smart one, despite your certificates. I have spent a lot of time in bed recently, and we all know I may be going to spend a lot more there soon. But right now this little guy needs me, and I've got a job to do. I've been talking to Noah and this is our plan.' Panna broke off to cough, and signalled to Noah that he should take over explaining things to his brother.

'She's going to groom him, bro,' said Noah, bouncing with excitement. 'She's going to clip his fur and everything, make him look like a different dog. And then we're just going to make out that he's our dog.'

'Oh lord,' said Jackson, 'there's a few problems with that. What if he's microchipped?'

Panna and Noah stared at Jackson.

'What?' Noah said.

'It's what people do nowadays,' Jackson said, 'they chip their dog. Then if it gets lost, any vet can see who it belongs to.'

'Oh for goodness' sake,' Panna said. 'Top grades in every exam and the common sense of a small cooking hen. No one is going to be checking this poor mutt for chips of any kind. The kind of lowlife who's been looking after this little lamb, you think he's going to be the kind of responsible pet owner who pays up for a chip? I tell you now, the nearest this boy has been to a chip is hanging around outside the fish shop.'

Jackson looked at Noah, who seemed likely to burst with excitement, pride and admiration for his grandmother. Jackson wished for one small and disloyal moment that Noah would look at him with that kind of adoration.

'Good points,' he said, 'I know when I'm beat. How different can we make him look?'

Noah clapped and danced an honorary lap of the whole flat, a dripping Phil at his heels.

'Thanks,' Panna said to Jackson, 'sorry to outrank you. I know how dreadful it can be when someone does that.'

She looked thoughtful for a moment and then she burst out laughing.

'Yeah, I'm sorry but that was fun!' Panna said. 'D'you know for once in my life I got to feel like a man, like the father in the relationship, waltzing in with treats. And you, poor you, had to be the mum, the sensible one. Oh my. That was worth something, I can tell you.'

Jackson laughed with her. It was funny, he could see that. It was funny but it still made him feel weird.

They got to work on the dog after the victory lap. He was the most patient dog Jackson had ever seen. He let them wash him, put antiseptic on the sore parts and groom him. Panna did the grooming with Jackson's beard trimmer and a pair of nail scissors and Phil just stood there, letting them do it. Jackson couldn't believe the transformation.

'He looks like a different dog,' Noah said, 'he's not even properly black any more, more like a kind of brown. He's probably never even been washed before, have you, Philip? And can he sleep in with me?'

Jackson shrugged. 'On matters of dog business,' he said, 'I defer to higher authority. Panna? What do you think?'

'I think yes, that is certainly good for both parties. And I also think when you take him out for a last toilet stop, go in the other direction. Away from the beach. In the daytime he'll look more like a different dog because of all the grooming, but at night I reckon he'll look the same. And Jackson, you should go with him. Just in case.'

Great, Jackson thought, another thing to worry about.

Later, Panna and Jackson stood in the doorway watching Noah and Phil sleep. It seemed worth it then, and Jackson was glad that he had given in.

'Look at that,' he whispered to Panna, 'Noah looks about five.'

He was sleeping on his side, with one hand on the dog's head. It was hard to tear themselves away.

'I used to have a dog,' Panna said, 'when your mum was little, and we lived in North London. The signs in the boarding houses then, they used to say, "No Blacks, no dogs, no Irish," so when I found this dog on the street, a poor little scrap a bit like this one, I felt like we were connected in some way. And I called him Irish.'

'No,' Jackson said, 'I do not believe you. I would have heard about that, I swear I would. Mum never said, and you never said. Why the big secret?'

'Jackson,' Panna said, 'you really think I'm going to tell you every single thing that ever happened to me? The name of every friend, the content of every dinner? And do you think you would find that interesting?'

'Well, no,' Jackson said, 'but a dog, that's quite a thing not to know. A dog called Irish.'

He shook his head. It really was a most surprising thing. He had always thought his family didn't like animals, full stop. A lot of people didn't, it was perfectly normal not to.

'Did I ever meet Irish?' he asked.

'Long ago and far away,' Panna said, 'a story for another day.'

She put her hand on Jackson's arm.

'I know how hard it's been for you, all this,' she said.

Jackson felt terrible. He should have been able to keep it to himself, his misery. He had never meant it to be so obvious to Panna. She had enough to cope with.

'No,' he said, 'it's not been that bad at all. Noah is a good boy and you're always lovely to have around.'

'Oh Jackson,' Panna said. She shook her head and smiled. 'You've done so well. At least let me tell you that. And you wait, everything is better with a dog, I promise you. Phil is going to make all the difference, I can feel it in my bones.'

Jackson wasn't sure about that, but he couldn't deny that it was the first time he'd gone to sleep easily in weeks. His dreams were full of dogs instead of police officers, games on the beach rather than death. There might be something in what his grandmother had said.

CHAPTER NINE

Margate

Noah and Panna bonded with Phil in the blink of an eye, but Jackson couldn't help keeping his distance. He watched as the others pandered to Phil's every need and worried about what would happen if they were discovered. It was a few days before Jackson was alone with the dog.

'I suppose you want some breakfast,' he said.

Noah had slept in, which was unusual. He had been totally engrossed in feeding and training schedules and Jackson didn't want to wake him. He deserved a break. He bent to scratch behind Phil's ears as he had seen Noah do. Phil's tail started to wag.

'Wow,' Jackson said, 'is that for me?'

He was amazed at how happy it made him feel.

'One hundred grams, that's how much Noah says you have to have, right?' he said to the little dog as he weighed out the kibble, 'and one thing you can be sure of, Noah will have researched this, and he will have got it right. And little and often, so you're not sick, OK?' The dog wagged his tail even harder.

'He's technically a rescue dog,' Noah had said.

Jackson loved how serious and committed he was, how much his eyes shone as he leaned forward to make his point. 'And as such he needs extra care, doesn't he? I mean, living with that man was probably worse than living on the street.'

Noah had bent towards Phil, and Phil licked his face and then leaned against his leg as he stood up.

Jackson poured the kibble into Phil's bowl and added some wet food.

'Here you are, boy,' he said as he put the dish down.

Phil looked at him before he ate and Jackson thought he was getting as daft as Noah, because the look seemed like a thank you to him.

'No one could possibly recognise you,' he said to the dog. He was sure that was true. His coat was short and curly now that it had been clipped, and he looked several shades lighter. His old injuries were healing and he really did look like a different, happier and fluffier dog. They had been very careful every time they took him out, keeping away from the main beach and only taking him for short walks but this morning, Jackson thought that he could risk it. The beach was more or less empty and it was early enough to avoid most of the regular dog walkers.

Jackson scanned the beach from the top of the ramp. There were a couple of women walking back down the beach towards him with a greyhound and a tiny pocket-sized dog, plus a few people in the distance, but that was all. He unclipped Phil's leash and let him off. They'd ordered a new lead, a pink one.

'Phil doesn't mind pink,' Noah said, 'it's just a colour. And it will be another thing that stops that man from noticing him, his subconscious will be sure it's a girl dog because we are so used to assigning gender by colour.'

Jackson chuckled as he thought of that. He had no idea where Noah had picked that up, or even whether he had thought of it himself. Nothing would surprise him where his brother was concerned, he thought.

Phil ran towards the sea. He didn't swim, but seemed to enjoy rolling around and splashing at the edge. The sea was at its best point, Jackson thought. In the middle of tides, when the sand looked more golden and the sea more blue. Jackson walked farther down the beach and called the dog to follow him. Noah had spent ages training the dog to answer to the name Philip, rather than Phil, because it was a better cover. He wanted to add a last name too, Jackson had counselled against it.

'The last thing we want to do is make people notice us, even in a friendly way. Wouldn't you look up if someone on the beach shouted, "Philip Watkins or Philip Jenkinson"?'

It was when Phil came out of the shallows and ran in circles round Jackson that he saw him. Out of the corner of his eye as he turned with the dog, and sitting on the rocks at the end of the beach nearest their flat. He looked as Noah had described, old, unkempt and with a big beard. Jackson hoped that the man hadn't noticed him looking. He tried to keep on playing with the dog while moving as fast as he could away down the beach, trying to put as much distance as possible between the two of them. He couldn't even risk looking back to see if the man had clocked them, or if he was walking in the same direction. Jackson was terrified. He remembered the police officers who had stopped him when he was out running. He could still see every detail of their faces, and he had to stop himself from turning round every couple of steps to see if they were there. It was the terror of thinking that his life was actually in danger, that was the familiar and grim feeling he had. Only this time it was Phil's life he was worried about. From everything Noah had said and from the old injuries clearly visible on the little dog, it seemed like a real possibility that he would hurt him more, next time.

Jackson kept on running down the beach with the dog until he got to the big disused concrete café on the promenade. He stood by the public toilets and put Phil back on his lead before leaving the beach and walking up to the back streets behind the flat. It was only when he got to the top, overlooking the beach, that Jackson thought he could risk a look back. The man was still there, but he had turned so that instead of facing the sea, he was facing up towards the incline beyond the promenade. The same incline where Jackson was now standing with the dog.

Jackson picked the little dog up and ran for home, going in the back way. Noah was up and making toast for Panna when he got in.

'Did you like it, taking him out?' he asked.

Jackson could see that it was very important to him, that he had been waiting for some sign from Jackson that he was happy with the dog and enjoyed having him around.

'It was great,' he said, 'I reckon we've bonded now, haven't we, little guy?' Jackson bent to stroke Phil's head.

'Yes,' Noah shouted, punching the air, 'we've done it, Phil.'

Jackson knew he should tell him that he'd seen the man, that they were going to have to try even harder to keep it quiet, but he decided to wait until later. In the meantime, there was Noah's schooling to think about and today it was maths. Never Jackson's strong point, but he kept that quiet and the two of them worked together. It was fractions, and something about the order of operations that Jackson was sure had never been mentioned when he was at school. They had their heads down and were calculating away, 'calculating like beasts', as Noah put it, when there was a noise from Panna's room. Jackson looked at the clock on the wall, the one that Panna loved with the numbers round the wrong way. Still only ten o'clock, and early for her to be out of bed.

'See if you can finish three more before I come back,' Jackson said.

He took a glass of water through to Panna and shut the door behind him. He was glad that he had. Panna had been sick, and she was trying to clean it up.

'Panna,' Jackson said, trying to sound as gentle as he could, without leaving room for argument, 'stop that. Sit down there, in the chair, and I'll sort it out in a jiffy. It's no problem.'

Panna sat down heavily in the chair, but Jackson could see that she was crying.

'Oh Jack,' she said, 'oh my god, Jack, this disease is bad, no lie.'

He wanted to give in and cry with her. She was right, this was bad and she looked dreadful.

'It's a blip,' he said, trying to keep his voice steady, 'nothing but a blip. It'll take me no time at all to clear it up, then I'll make your bed nice and cosy and you can get back in.'

Jackson went on talking, keeping up what he hoped was a comforting noise. He tried to look as though he was coping with ease, not bothered by what he was doing. Breathing through his mouth helped. He knew that if he gagged, Panna would feel terrible. It was difficult, and on top of that, Jackson had to clear his head constantly of the picture of himself, strolling in a sunny university quad with a pile of books under his arm. Get over yourself, he thought.

By the time Jackson had finished cleaning, Panna had fallen asleep in her chair. Jackson wished he could leave her to sleep, but he could see that she needed cleaning up so he set to with a bowl of warm water and a cloth. She woke as he gently washed her face.

'I'm so sorry for all this trouble, Jack,' she said, 'I wish I could help you with the boy.'

'You do,' Jackson said, 'you help me every single day. And that's enough of that sort of talk, thank you. I can cope with vomit, that's easily cleaned, but when it comes to slushy talk you know I'm way out of my depth.'

He said it to make her laugh, and it worked. Panna brightened as Jackson had hoped that she would, and she laughed loudly enough for Noah to hear.

'What?' he said from outside the closed door to her room, 'what's funny? What are you laughing about? I'm doing maths and there's no laughs in it at all, can I come in?'

Jackson looked around the room. There wasn't anything out of place that he could see, nothing that would upset Noah. All the dirty water and the cloths were in Panna's en suite bathroom.

'Is that OK with you?' Jackson asked Panna. She nodded and smiled, and Jackson could see that she was trying to straighten herself in her chair and push her hair out of her eyes for the boy.

Noah came into the room like a spring breeze, the dog about an inch behind him.

'I've got it,' he announced, 'while you two were lazing about in here and doing nothing useful, I was applying myself. Like you're always telling me, Jackson, like everyone is always telling me. And I've got it. Maths is mine, mine.' Noah clapped his hands and jumped up, punching the air. 'I'm so great, I'm so cool, I don't need, to go to school,' he sang as he danced around.

Panna laughed. 'You're a tonic, boy, you know that? A pure tonic.'

Jackson watched them both. He felt as if Noah and Panna were in a room that he couldn't enter, and however much he wanted to join in he couldn't. He should be happy that Panna was happy, that Noah could cheer her up like this. If only, though, if only Noah was a grown-up and they could share the work. Or if Panna was fit and well. Or if their mother was here and able to help, or Jackson was . . .

He took a deep breath.

'Right,' he said, 'I'm going to make everyone some tea and brunch. Noah, it's your favourite thing, second breakfast. Whatever either of you want, as long as it's in the cupboard.'

Noah groaned. 'Bro, that means some kind of sensible healthy stuff. I want a doughnut.'

Jackson felt back on familiar bantering ground. 'Nothing wrong with lentils for breakfast,' he said.

Even Panna managed to eat a tiny amount of scrambled eggs. She seemed calm but it was obvious that she was struggling and Jackson wished he could help more. Panna had been such a big presence in both of their lives. It had been Jackson who had picked the name Panna, back when he was little and grandma was too difficult to say. He didn't realise until he went to school that not everyone had a Panna who brought them up and a mum who visited from time to time. The arrangement seemed perfect to him.

When Noah was born Jackson was eight, and without warning he went from living with Panna to living with his mum in a flat on the same estate. It was an awful time. Any chance he got, Jackson would get out of the front door and run to what he thought of as home, Panna's flat. His mother tried hiding the key, putting a bolt at the top of the door, double locking, everything, but nothing could keep Jackson in. He got out of windows, balanced on chairs to reach up high and he hunted down keys with ferocious intent. Finally, Jackson did what he should have done all along. He told Panna why he didn't want to stay at home. He explained about the boyfriend that his mum had asked him not to tell anyone about.

'You're my big boy, Jackson,' his mother had said, 'you understand things. Anyhow my mum hears about Paul, she ain't gonna approve. Because he's been in prison. But sometimes good people go to prison, Jack, you're big enough to understand that. Shit happens. And you want Noah to have a dad, don't you?'

He was torn about that. He remembered thinking that perhaps no dad was better, and then deciding that he was definitely right the day he caught Paul slapping Noah's little face, over and over, while his mum snored in the chair. He had tried to wake her up, but her head just lolled to one side when he shook her arm, so Jackson had taken matters into his own hands. He waited until Paul was looking at his phone, grabbed

Noah and left. The strange thing was, the key hadn't even been hidden that day. For one day only, it had been right there in the door and Jackson had been thankful to see it.

Jackson could still remember the feeling of holding Noah in his arms. In fact, he had suffered from pains in his arms for a year or two after the event, and the doctor could never find anything wrong.

'You're carrying your broken heart in your arms,' Panna used to say, 'let it go, you're safe now.'

He had been safe, she was right. Safe most of the way through until the previous year, when the world had scrambled again as Panna became unwell. Jackson wasn't sure if the news that Paul had been released from prison came before or after Panna found out that she had cancer, but it had been near enough to the same time for him to think that his life had been jinxed. There was no way that he could walk away, either to have a gap year of sorts or try to finish his studies and go to uni, so Jackson had chosen to stay and to help his brother and his grandmother. After all, Panna had literally saved their lives, for sure.

'I think I'll go back to bed now, if that's OK by you boys,' Panna said now, 'I just need a little rest and I'll be back for my dinner. You know how I love my food.'

Jackson put his arm round her to help her back to bed, but as they took the first step he felt her sag and crumple. Jackson bent and swept her up into his arms.

'That's how a young man should carry a lady,' Panna said, 'you remember that, Jackson.'

Noah laughed, and Jackson was glad that he didn't realise how serious the situation was. Panna would never ever have let him carry her unless she had no choice. She had always been so strong, so powerful. Jackson knew that his good exam grades were due almost entirely to Panna and her tough regime. She wasn't a person that you could ignore. Every evening after school, Jackson had had to show her what his homework was, and then again when he had finished it. She didn't always understand it, especially as he got older, but she always made an attempt to be aware of what he was doing and how long it ought to take him. If the homework was just to revise a particular thing, Panna would try to interrogate him afterwards to make sure he had learned it properly. Jackson had realised over time that she had left school at fourteen, and that she had always been sorry about it.

'I would have been a doctor, if that was a thing girls could do then. And when I came to England, I saw that there were some lady doctors, and I thought, this is a fine place, but I realised after a while that none of those ladies were Black, and that I had missed that boat anyway, old lady of twenty-five with mouths to feed. But you, Jackson, you're smart, and if you think I'm gonna let you go out on the streets and get yourself in trouble while you're causing trouble? You need to think again, boy. You're gonna keep your nose in those books and be grateful for it.'

Jackson had done as she said. Sometimes he thought that it was because he was so lazy, lazy and unsure of himself, and that if he had been stronger he would have gone out with the boys from the estate anyway, regardless of the trouble it would have caused. He was never sorry, though. Even if he couldn't go to uni now, he still knew he had gained something important because of Panna and her insistence, some kind of educational capital that no one could ever take away from him.

Jackson tucked Panna up in bed, making sure the pillows were puffed up in the way she liked.

'Shut the door,' she said in a whisper, 'I need to tell you something.'

Jackson shut the door.

'I know I'm not going to get through this, Jack, and I'm sorry I have to leave everything for you to do.'

'Panna,' Jackson said, 'don't say that, you'll be fine.'

Panna struggled to sit up a little. 'Don't say that,' she said, and Jackson could hear that she was really angry, 'that's not fair. I've got to tell someone in case, and make sure of my business, and you're the only person I can ask. I'm sorry for that, Jack, and I wish it wasn't so. But wishing never made anything true.'

Jackson waited.

'This flat,' Panna said, 'I've left it to you. Just you, because I reckon Noah is too young. He hasn't gone through his rebellious time yet but if and when he does, you'll be glad the place is in your name. When he comes out the other end, though, you make sure he gets his share. Even if you've got a wife and a pack of kids in every room, the boy has to have his share, you get me?'

Jackson nodded and Panna laughed, a weak laugh but a genuine one.

'You should see your face,' she said, 'when I said you might have a wife.'

Panna broke off to cough. Jackson thought that the cough went on for a really long time.

'It's not the wife that worries me,' he said, when Panna had finished, 'it's the bloody kids.'

He should have known that would make Panna laugh and set her off coughing again. She looked grey when she had finished, and she lay back against the pillows as if she had run a marathon. Her voice was quiet now, and Jackson had to strain to hear her.

'Seriously,' she said, 'you can do it, Jackson. You can do whatever you set your mind to. Go back to school. Get a good job. Keep the boy close.'

Jackson tried to stop her.

'Panna, he said, 'there's no need, we can talk about this another day. You felt like this on the last round of chemo, remember, and then things got better. Noah will be fine, I'll be fine, don't worry. Let's just concentrate on getting you well.'

It was after dinner that he saw the woman upstairs. Jackson and Noah were on the balcony, enjoying the last bit of the day. She was old, and pushing a buggy laden with bags and containing a sleeping baby. They could hear her singing softly as she walked along the prom and went into the doorway of the flats.

'Hey,' Noah said, 'another person under the age of ninety. Welcome, baby.'

PART III

CHAPTER TEN

Margate

Kidnapping a baby, even with the mother's consent, is terrifying. And complicated, especially for a person who was counting down to a personal exit strategy. What about my three-month plan, I kept thinking, only seven weeks to go. I missed the security of having my plan in the background, although every time I looked at her sweet little face I was ashamed. In my defence it was a lot, as people seem to say now. A lot to take on, a lot to process, a lot of worries. So many worries, in fact, that I didn't know which one to think about first.

It seemed important to know how old Ocean was, so I started with that. I tried to remember exactly when she was born. Jed was still well enough to chat, I remembered that because we talked about her and imagined what job she might do in the future, with such an auspicious name. Marine biologist, that's what we settled on, and I think Jed was up and at the table eating dinner when we said it so she must be eighteen months old by now. It was difficult to remember when babies turn into grown-up people but to me she seemed the size of a six-month-old compared with William. It was only her eyes that looked older. Her eyes looked like those of an old person, someone who's seen a lot and knows they won't see much more.

I picked her out of the buggy and held her on my lap so that she could see out of the train window. 'Sheep,' I said, then I pointed to her lamby. I pointed every time we saw one but Ocean didn't seem impressed. She preferred to look at her hands.

'Hands,' I said.

I turned her right hand palm side up so that I could trace my fingers round for 'Round and Round the Garden' but she flinched. I stopped, but not before I saw at least three round, red marks. I'd never seen them in real life, but I was pretty sure I knew what they were straight away. Cigarette burns, on her tiny, perfect hands. I couldn't help it, the thought of someone doing that to her made me so sad and furious I had to take deep breaths so that I didn't cry. I've cried very easily since Jed died. The slightest little thing sets me off and this was not a slight thing, but it was important that from now on if I could arrange it, Ocean's life would be full of smiles and happiness. I thought I was hiding it in a series of sniffs and nose-blowing but when the woman seated across the aisle from us said, 'Are you OK, dear?' I realised I had not been successful.

'Allergies,' I called back and that seemed to satisfy her.

I was going to have to be more sneaky, start thinking more like a criminal, I realised. I made sure the lanyard her mum had left was tucked down into one of the bags, in case it was noticed. He might even report me to the police, I thought, I wouldn't put anything past that man. The last thing I needed to do was to stand out, so that if anyone was looking for a suspicious old woman with a baby in tow, I would automatically spring to their mind. I cuddled Ocean and pointed out another sheep.

'Look, O—' I stopped in my tracks. Ocean. Such a sweet name, and the name she was used to but it was so distinctive. I didn't think it was just because I was old. I thought Ocean would be memorable for everyone. Growing up with Virginia as a name had been bad enough. It had always seemed unnecessarily long in a class where everyone else was called Sue or Ann. Teachers had learned my name first out of everyone when I was at school, so I was always asked more questions in class. Boys especially loved the 'virgin' part of my name and even ones I didn't know would stop to point and make unfunny comments. I had to help Ocean out here. Help us both out, keep her name quiet as if she was in witness protection, which she more or less was. I looked out of the window.

'Sheep,' I said again, and she definitely looked in the direction of my pointing finger. I hugged her.

'No need to say your name unless we're alone,' I whispered in her ear.

I wanted her to know what I was doing, even if she couldn't understand, and I know that sounds whimsical. She smiled, and it was the first smile I had seen since I found her in the garden.

I was quite sorry when we got to Margate. Trains are such complete little worlds, full of luck and forward movement. Just the place for a baby and an old woman. I didn't know if Ocean had seen the sea, so I got her out of her buggy and held her up so that she could see the full majesty of it.

'High tide, just for us,' I said. 'You're always allowed to make a wish, the first time in any calendar year that you catch a glimpse of the sea. I guess you're too small to do that now, so I'm going to make a wish for you.'

One more special thing about that darling child was, she had a way of looking at me as if she understood perfectly what I was trying to say to her. I haven't seen it in other children, and I'm sure it's because she's got buckets of empathy as well as being bright as a button. I wished for her, but I wasn't sure what to wish. Small children need their mums and I truly believe that but in this case there were circumstances to take into account. If her mum got away from that man, would she go back to him? Or would she choose another one just as bad? I've been around long enough to know that there were complicated forces at play here, and common sense is often at the bottom of the list. So I couldn't exactly wish for her to go home to her mum. Not until I knew what that might look like, and how safe she would be. I closed my eyes, hedged my bets and wished that she would have a happy and safe life. With me, I wished I could add.

We walked along the prom like a tiny team until we got to my block. The light was fading enough for me to feel anonymous, not an old woman at all but a grey blur. I hadn't been back for so long that everything seemed fresh and new. Was the flat really so close to the sea? It had been Jed's delight, not mine but I had grown to love it. We had talked of it often when he was dying. At first he liked to pretend that he would be going back there when he was better, but as he got more tired and sick he stopped that. I wondered for a long time whether I should have kept it up for him, kept the faith and gone on pretending. I'm still not sure. Just one time, I think the day before he died, he held my hand when I was washing his face.

'Can you hear it?' he said.

I stopped for a moment and listened, but I couldn't hear anything and I had no idea what he was talking about.

He suddenly looked embarrassed.

'I'm sorry,' he said. 'It's the drugs. I thought I could hear the sea. You know, the swooshing sound it makes when it hits the sand? I think I love that noise more than any other.'

His eyes were wet when he said it, I remember that.

I held Ocean tight in one arm while I pushed the buggy with the other.

'Welcome home,' I whispered in her ear.

'Sheep,' she said, pointing to a small dog on a lead, out for its nighttime walk.

I put her down and clapped my hands. 'Good girl,' I said. 'It's a sheep.'

There are two schools of thought on this, and maybe I should have corrected her, said, 'Dog,' but I wanted to have something to celebrate, something to show her that she was good and clever and valued. I had taught her that animals with four legs and fluffy bodies were called sheep, and she had learned her lesson well.

She walked the last bit of the way. We went slowly, but she was steadier than I remembered William being at that age. He always wanted to dart off, pick things up, look in other directions. Ocean kept her eyes firmly on her feet as if her life depended on it. She held my hand and muttered as she walked, as if she was counting. I picked her up to go up the stairs to the entrance.

'One, two, three,' I said.

'Bad girl,' she said and slapped her own little face.

I was shocked. It was real, what they had done to her, and she was going to need a lot of help. I caught her little hand before she could do it again, and I kissed it.

'Good girl,' I said. 'Lovely girl, special girl. Special person,' I added so that she didn't think it was the fact that she was a girl I was praising.

I hoped that my words could reach her in some way, but to be honest she just looked baffled.

The flat was homely and lovely from the minute we got indoors, and just as I remembered. Time really had stood still. On the arm of the sofa was the book of short stories Jed and I had been reading aloud together the last time we came, and our coffee cups were stuck in perpetual drying mode on the drainer. I was glad to have Ocean with me, not to be alone.

'I don't think I could have come here on my own,' I said to her. 'Too many ghosts.'

'Sheep,' she said.

I looked where she was looking, and sure enough, I had forgotten that there was a little ornamental sheep on the bookshelf. William had brought it back from a school journey to Scotland many years ago.

'Sheep,' I said. 'So clever.'

I held the sheep out to her. One hand came forward slightly to take it, but then she flinched. I wondered whether she had been offered things and then hurt for taking them, and I couldn't bear the idea. I opened her little hand and popped the sheep into it. She smiled and sat on the floor crooning to Lamby and the little sheep while I went round turning on heating and hot water and feeling something a little like happy. One day at a time, I thought, I can do this, I can keep her safe. I can work it out. I inflated the air mattress we used to keep for visitors and put it by my bed.

It was when I was washing her little face for bed that I realised. The flannel I was using came away a beigey grey colour, and her face was different underneath. It must have been make-up. Someone had slathered the little tot in face make-up and underneath she was bruised. Blue, green and pinky grey, all the colours of bruises on one tiny face. How on earth could he have done that to someone so small and perfect? And how could Cate have let him? And how could I keep her safe and make it all better and give her a happy ending?

My confidence dropped like a theme park ride and I forced myself to breathe in and out slowly. I think the excitement of the train and the thrill of the rescue had stopped me from seeing what a predicament I was in. We were in, not just me, because Ocean was the important one here. She was one and a half years old though, and I was seventy-something going on a hundred, so it was my responsibility to sort things out for her. I sat down next to where she was playing on the floor and tried to make sense of it all.

One, she had bruises and burns on the parts of her body I could see, and I hadn't even taken her clothes off yet. There were bound to be more.

Two, I'm not a doctor. I'm not even an experienced mum. One child who grew up long ago and lived as far away from me as he could. How could I tell when she needed to see a doctor?

And, above all, how could we see a doctor? Without the doctor realising that she wasn't my child, and that I'd effectively stolen her?

I put my head in my hands. I couldn't see a way out for either of us, not without putting Ocean at risk. There were computerised records to think about, and the hospital would be sure to send a social worker to investigate. At best, Ocean would never be able to go back to live with her mum because they wouldn't trust her. At worst, her mum would surely never be able to admit that she had asked me to take her. That would put her at far too much risk from him. I'd got the lanyard that had been round Ocean's neck, but it was typed. I could have made that myself if I'd wanted to. No, the chances were they would easily slither out of it. I'd given them the perfect alibi after all. The mad old woman who stole our baby and hurt her. I didn't care about any of that for myself, but for Ocean it would be catastrophic. She might not survive whatever they did next. I think I might have groaned at that point. I've got far too used to living on my own and talking to myself without anyone to shut me up. Something alerted Ocean though, and she looked up at me from her game with the sheep. She held it out to me.

'Sheep,' she said, for all the world as though she was trying to make me feel better. Of course I could have been wrong but that's what it seemed like, I swear. I scooped her up, kissed her and made my mind up.

'I'm not giving you up without an almighty fight, and not until it's the right place for you,' I said. 'And I won't be able to be with you for ever, but we are going to have nothing but nice times while we're together. Nice memories for your little memory bank and nothing sad, I promise.'

Two heads are almost always better than one, so the first thing I did was ring Annie. It might sound mad, because we'd never met and she was hundreds of miles away, but she knew. She knew all my worries about Ocean, and she had consistently taken them seriously. She seemed like a sensible and a trustworthy choice, and as soon as I heard her voice on the other end I knew I was right. She listened while I poured the whole thing out, and I had an increasing sense of calm. I still had no idea what we were going to do but it was so good to share it with someone who cared. We moved the call on to FaceTime so that Annie could see the bruises.

'Hello, little one,' she said.

I wasn't sure whether I needed to point the bruises out.

'Look,' I said.

Annie stopped me. 'I can see,' she said.

She sang a lullaby to Ocean in a language I thought was Gaelic, and I knew she was noticing everything, she understood.

'Such a good girl,' she said in a voice so gentle I could feel Ocean relax. 'And you're doing well too, Virginia.'

Ocean smiled and reached out to touch the screen and I wanted to do the same. It was wonderful to know that someone was with me, that I hadn't seen this on my own.

'I've seen as much as I need to and I've had an idea,' Annie said. 'I think you could do with some help. Maybe I'm wrong, but I don't think so. And I haven't got anything in my diary right now, and I've always wanted to see the sea down south. A beach where you don't always have to be wrapped in a blanket, what's not to like? I've been looking at trains, and I'll get the first one I can. I'll be there in a couple of days if you would like some help. It's a long haul, to Glasgow and then to London but I've got a good book or two. Also, and I don't want to blow my own trumpet too much but, long story short, I was a paramedic for most of my working life. I'd like to take a closer look at that lovely wee lassie. If there's anything broken or missing she'll have to go to hospital, I'm not taking chances, but I'll be able to tell. Is that OK?'

For once I couldn't think of anything to say. I hadn't thought of her like that at all. She had such a soft west-coast accent and she seemed so gentle. Even now I'd seen what she looked like that hadn't changed. If I had had to guess what her career had been, I think I would have said librarian, or maybe a person who ran a tea shop, one with nice cakes. I trusted her though, and it would be wonderful to have someone with me, someone I could talk to. I didn't regret anything I'd done, it wasn't that, but I knew the decisions might get more difficult from here, and having someone I could trust by my side seemed glorious. And a paramedic to boot.

'Ha,' she said. 'Or lol, as the kids would say. I've surprised you, haven't I? I don't think I ever told Jed that, we mainly used to talk about books and scenery.'

'Did you drive the ambulance as well?'

I could have bitten my tongue off the minute I'd said it. What a stupid, stupid thing to say, I thought. As if I was doubting her or worse, as if I hadn't heard the news that women could drive. I blushed, but it probably didn't show on FaceTime.

Annie laughed. It was a surprising laugh, kind of earthy and full.

'Do you know, I was actually the best driver in the whole district?' she said. 'I'm not being boastful, I actually got an award once, kind of a joke thing but everyone took it quite seriously. I'm retired now, of course, and I don't even have a car but I can be with you by bedtime tomorrow if you keep her up a wee bit late. And if she needs hospital treatment, I'll know. Meanwhile, if she's in any pain or anything . . .'

'Yes please,' I said. 'I'd love you to come, if you're sure. Take your time, we will be here. And don't worry. I wasn't the best mum, and it was a long time ago, but I still definitely know when to panic. And she seems happy at the moment, I think it would be more obvious if something was hurting.'

'Sheep,' said Ocean, holding the sheep out towards Annie's picture on the iPhone.

'Good girl, Ocean,' Annie said. 'Are you finding it difficult not to cry all the time?'

I was, and I was very glad that Annie had asked. It made me feel less freakish, more normal. I should have told her how pleased I was that she was coming, how relieved I felt and even a little bit excited that I would meet her but I was shy, so I just nodded.

'I'm not surprised,' she said.

Putting Ocean to bed that first night was wonderful even though I was so worried and full of unfamiliar emotions. I sat her in a big washing-up bowl filled with warm water and just a few of my lavender bubbles. The sheep had a bath too, and her lamby and dog from home. She washed them with care, saying, 'Sheep,' to herself every minute or two. I patted her dry with the softest towel I had, being careful with her poor little bruised and battered body. There were bruises everywhere, bruises on top of bruises and more of the little round burn marks as well, all in various stages of healing. I knew there would be other things, things that I didn't know how to look for but as I washed and splashed and played and sang, she seemed very calm. No flinching and no tears. I dressed her in the little pyjamas her mum had packed and heated up some milk. The cup with a lid was dirty but she seemed to drink well from a mug I had with a picture of a dog on it. I popped her under the duvet on the air mattress, which I had wedged between my bed and the wall. It was very snug. I didn't have any children's books, and I decided that would be a priority in the morning, but meanwhile I had a book of seabirds. Jed used to love identifying them when they sat on our balcony, even though I thought they all looked more or less the same. Different sizes, same basic equipment, I used to say to wind him up.

I could see the differences now, looking at the book with Ocean. We gave them all names, although most of them went by the name of sheep. I told her stories about all the things they'd done, all the babies they'd rescued and how whole flocks of them would get together to guide little boats safely into harbour. By the time I'd finished she was asleep, and I wondered why I'd only ever read existing books to William. Making up stories was so much more fun. Not for the first time, I wished I could ring William and tell him what was happening.

I pushed the thought away, but not before wondering what it would be like to have a grown child who thought you were funny and clever. Who marvelled at your exploits, and genuinely thought you were a great person. Does anyone think that of their parents, I wondered? Sporting heroes, people who wrote books and won prizes – did their children line up with bunting when they got home? If so, it must be the best part of the whole thing.

Before I went to sleep, I imagined a news conference.

'What inspired you to rescue this baby?' the reporter asked. He had his collar turned up against the wind, I always liked it when they did that.

I shrugged. 'Every baby should have the chance to be happy, like my son William was,' I said.

In the fantasy, William was standing behind the reporter and he gave me a thumbs up and blew me a kiss. I wondered if I could imagine that he held a greetings card in his pocket, saying, 'Best mum ever' and bought for the occasion, but that was over the top even for a dream, so I settled for the thumbs up and added a wink.

I slept better that night than I had since before Jed died. I woke up fully dressed and still on the floor with Ocean, only there seemed to be a very uneven distribution of room in the bed. She looked happy and relaxed, spreadeagled on the air bed and I was somehow wedged into an impossibly small dip between the edge of the mattress and the double bed. It was worth it a hundred times over when she smiled at me and said, 'Sheep.' Even without William's affirmation, I knew I had done the right thing.

There were oats in the cupboard so I made us some porridge. I wasn't sure what stage of feeding Ocean was at, so I made it quite solid in case she wanted to feed herself with her hands. She seemed surprised at the whole thing. The idea that someone would put food out for her in a little dish was clearly unusual in her life but she adapted to it quickly, and shovelled the porridge in. I noticed that Ocean had a way of studying what I was doing, for all the world as if she was swotting for an exam. After a couple of handfuls of porridge, she pointed at my spoon so I gave her a spoon of her own. She turned it over and examined it, then lined it up alongside mine to check they were the same. The spoon passed the check and she set about learning how to use it. I think that was when I was sure that she would be OK. That whatever had been done to her, however she had been treated, there was still hope for her. There were times afterwards when I would question that, times when everything would seem hopeless, but I tried to remember the porridge moment each time.

'Porridge,' I said.

'Podge,' she said. She licked the spoon first and then tried biting it.

I had forgotten how glorious it was to help a tiny person who has no idea what to do with a spoon. I felt so angry with her family, even with her poor mum. I knew in my heart that she meant the best for her baby. I remembered how she had been in those early days. So proud of her, so delighted. It was hard to comprehend how she could have allowed that man to become involved, that was all, even though I knew deep inside that it could have been me.

Once I had got rid of William's controlling father, and before I met Jed, while William was still tiny, I met a man. Looking back on it, he targeted me precisely because I had all the signs of a single mother. No ring, that was a dead giveaway in those days. No ring and probably a frazzled expression and the fact that I went on a protest march against the National Front with a little William in a buggy. That was probably enough to mark me out, but I'll never be sure. I was on the bus provided for mums and babies, and he was there helping. I don't know what made me suspicious, but I didn't take to him, even though he seemed to be so helpful. It was the way he looked at William, I think that was it. When Jed looked at William, there was a bit of admiration, a bit of curiosity, somehow a little recognition that they were a similar species, something like that. But this guy, he smiled at William but it was a cold smile, even perhaps a smirk. He turned his attentions to another mum on the bus quite quickly when I didn't respond, and I wasn't sure whether I'd imagined the whole thing. I kept in touch with her for a while, though, long enough to see the sorry arse mess he made of her life. Eventually he didn't even allow her to talk to me so we lost touch and I was glad.

But I remembered the attraction I had felt for him initially. If I was honest, it was there for a while and if he had been just a tad better at pretending he was interested in my son, I would have been happy to fall in love. I know I would. That's what no one tells you about looking after tiny humans on your own. It can be so lonely that falling in love with another grown-up, any grown-up, is a really good option. And there are a lot of men out there who know that.

So I couldn't think badly of Cate, but I sure as hell did not want Ocean to go back there. I worried constantly about what would happen if we were actually in the news, an enticing story for the public about bad grannies and stolen babies. I didn't dare to turn the TV on. Instead I made my own books for Ocean with no words and a series of terrible pictures that she seemed to enjoy. I showed her pictures on my phone too, although I worried that she would be damaged from exposure to screens so I found some more paper and went back to drawing. I drew her a sheep. Many sheep, in fact, because they seemed to be a never-ending source of joy to her.

I was drawing a herd of sheep at an elaborate dinner party with huge piles of grass on their plates when the doorbell rang. I had relaxed while we were playing but I still jumped like a cartoon villain caught robbing a safe. I didn't know anyone in Margate, so I imagined the absolute worst.

'Sshh, sshh,' I said to Ocean.

It was a totally pointless shush. She had been spooked by me being startled and now she cried properly, as if all the difficult things she had experienced in the last couple of days were crowding in on her and she was missing whatever bits of home she had found comfort in. The doorbell rang again and her cries went up a notch. I considered not answering the door, but when I followed that through to its conclusion, I could see it was just plain daft. What would I do, threaten to shoot if they took her back to her mum? Where on earth could I find a gun? How could I even be thinking about it?

'Hang on,' I said to the closed door. 'Come on, sweetie,' I said to Ocean, 'everything is OK.'

'Sheep,' she said, snuffling and I realised she had dropped it. In fact that might have been what she was crying about all along.

I picked it up, gave it to her, lifted her up and looked through the little spyglass in the door. There was a young boy standing there. He looked about ten, so I was fairly sure he wasn't working for the police. He smiled at the spyglass, as if he knew I was looking, and held something up. I opened the door.

'Tara,' he said, blowing an imaginary trumpet. 'I knew there was a baby here, hello baby. I saw you come last night and I thought, oh, a baby in the house, in the flats even. How nice.'

He was holding a soft black cat toy with a long tail and he held it out to Ocean.

'Sheep,' she said and she took it, which surprised me.

She buried her face in its fur.

'See,' the little boy said. 'I knew she would like it. What happened to her face? You might be wondering how I know she's a she? I'll tell you. The percentage of people who dress their baby boys in pink dresses is very, very low. This society is all about gender conformity, did you know that?'

I liked him straight away. It would have been hard not to. There was something about him that reminded me of William at that age. They even looked similar, which might sound like a ridiculous thing to say because William was pale and blonde-haired at this age and this little fellow was Black with black curly hair but there was something, nonetheless. Maybe their eyes.

'Would you like to come in?' I said.

'I'm Noah,' the boy said. 'I'm good with babies. I don't meet many but I think they're a bit like dogs, don't you?'

I was trying to think of a reply to this when Noah held his arms out and to my amazement, Ocean held hers out too and leaned forward towards Noah.

'She's a sociable little frog, aren't you, baby?' he said. 'My brother would like to meet you, baby, and it would give him something new to worry about. Do you know, he was talking to himself in the mirror when I was downstairs just now. He thinks I don't notice.'

He shook his head and carried her gently into the living

room and sat down, making sure that the black cat was sitting comfortably next to them.

'Is she always this friendly to strangers?' Noah asked.

I was stumped. I had no idea, but I couldn't let this rather observant little boy know that. For the moment, I'd have to stick to the cover story. The cover story I hadn't actually thought through yet.

'She varies,' I said. 'It can go either way.'

'Maybe she recognises that I'm a child, so I'm no threat to her,' he said.

I thought that was a smart observation.

'I reckon you might be right,' I said.

'High-five,' Noah said, holding up her little hand for a tap. 'What's her name?' he said. 'And would it be rude if I ask how she hurt herself?'

Noah pointed to Ocean's face.

'She's called Ocean,' I said.

I realised immediately that I shouldn't have told him her name.

'I'm her grandma,' I said, 'and she, she sort of falls over a lot. We're having a rest down here, so that she can get better and have some sea air.'

Noah and Ocean both looked at me without smiling. For a second it felt as if they both knew I was lying, that's how intense their stares were. Only for a second and then Ocean changed her mind about sitting with Noah and held her arms out to me again.

'That's it, go to Grandma,' Noah said. 'Grandmas rock. My grandma is called Panna, because my brother couldn't say her name when he was little. We live with her downstairs, but she's not very well. I don't think she's going to die but life has no certainties, does it?'

I wasn't sure what to say to this extraordinary child. The platitudes grown-ups normally fall back on when talking to children didn't seem to be enough for him.

'And another thing,' Noah said, 'I don't think grandmas would ever hurt anyone but I might be wrong, I know I'm only young and I don't know everything. You're OK though, I can tell that.'

'I'm going to keep her safe,' I said.

For a moment I could see my pills lined up neatly and waiting for me to swallow them. My one-way ticket. Every promise I made, every link I forged, that possibility was retreating.

'Babies should always be safe,' Noah said. 'It's nice to meet you.'

He put Ocean down on the floor and shook her hand and mine.

CHAPTER ELEVEN

Margate

'Today is going to be a good day,' Jackson said, speaking to the mirror in the bathroom.

He had decided to make a plan, take some positive steps to make his life better. It was an idea he had picked up from a women's magazine. Panna was an avid reader of women's magazines, and Jackson had always liked reading the odd one for light relief. His reading was normally the opposite of light. He had written himself a hit list of notable books that he reckoned a well-educated person should have read by the time they got to twenty, and he was going to have to read a little faster if he wanted to get them covered in the next year. He was making some headway on Dickens but it was heavy going and he loved curling up with a ridiculous article when Panna and Noah weren't around.

'Six steps to a positive you,' the latest was called.

He wondered why they never had articles like that in magazines for young men. Something to discuss with Noah, he thought. Just thinking of that made him laugh. His baby brother, transforming into the fount of all wisdom in front of his nose.

'Number one,' the article read. 'Speak to yourself as if you are your own best friend. Try talking to your reflection in the mirror, and always speak with positivity in mind. Things are going to be good, remember, because you're in the right space and doing the right things.

'You're doing pretty well, mate,' Jackson tried.

It didn't seem to be working. He could see that he looked scared and embarrassed in the mirror, a far cry from the young woman in the magazine illustration. She was standing with her hand on her hip in front of a full-length mirror and it was clear that she liked what she saw very much. Jackson only had a small mirror, and he was sure that the whole hip thrust full-length stuff wouldn't work anyway. He started to get ready for step two, have fun with your face, but he wasn't at all sorry to hear Noah whistling outside the door. He rolled the magazine up and stuffed it into the laundry basket.

'Hey, bro,' Noah said. 'I'm thinking of going to see the lady upstairs. The one we saw from the balcony, just to say welcome and hi. Do you want to come?'

Jackson didn't, but as soon as Noah had gone, the anxieties started to pile in. What if the woman upstairs wasn't alone? What if she wasn't even a woman? He remembered a story he had read, probably when he should have been revising, about a shapeshifting, undead thing that had assumed the form of an old woman to capture and eat children. It was nonsense, of course. Absolute nonsense, but Jackson was curious and worried, and it was rare these days that he got to speak to anyone outside the family. Noah was right, it would be nice to have someone occupying one of the other flats. He had felt isolated sometimes, especially when Panna was having a bad day. And there was always Noah to think of. It would be nice for Noah to have more people in his life. And the policemen, he thought, the policemen could be outside. He pushed the thought away. He'd been pushing it away at least seven times a day since it happened, but when he was alone it was difficult to deny how much the police who had stopped him the other day had shaken him up. What if they'd come back home with him? If they saw Noah and thought he needed to go into care? Or if they had arrested him for nothing but being Black in a white area and therefore suspicious? They might have locked him up and Noah would have had to look after Panna. Whoever this woman was, Jackson was glad to have her there. Safety in numbers. She had a baby with her, that was a good sign, plus Noah had said she looked nice. He needed to check, that was all.

She took a long time to answer the door, and Jackson was thinking of shouting out to Noah inside when he heard the sound of the door opening.

'Hi,' the woman said.

She had only opened her door just enough for him to see the small child in her arms, and he smiled and waved at her. Ocean considered him for a moment then waved back.

'Sorry,' he said. 'I didn't mean to disturb you, only I think my brother is here and I wanted to make sure that he wasn't bothering you.'

'Jackson,' she said. 'Glad to meet you. I'm Virginia. Your brother is quite something, isn't he? And, I hate to be so sexist, especially after what Noah was saying, but do you by any chance know how the heating works? I can't seem to make a damn bit of difference and it's cold in here. This is Ocean, my granddaughter.'

'Sheep,' Ocean said.

Jackson had a quick moment of panic about going into the flat. Several 'what ifs' flickered through his head and he pushed them aside. Whoever had heard of an old lady serial killer with a little baby? There was something wrong though, he was sure it wasn't just his usual jumpiness that was at work. She didn't put the baby down, that was one thing, although Jackson thought that might be normal with babies. He tried to remember whether Panna had attached Noah so firmly to her hip but all he could think of was Noah running away all the time on his chubby little legs while Jackson and Panna ran after him.

'Hey, bro,' Noah called. 'Come and see how good I am with Ocean. She really likes me and the Virginia Panna says I've got skills, come and see. There's nothing wrong with boys being good at babies, is there?'

Jackson groaned, and Virginia giggled. It wasn't usual for old ladies to giggle, Jackson thought and the sound made him like her more.

'I'm sorry about my brother,' Jackson said.

Virginia laughed again.

'Don't be,' she said. 'I'm finding him charming and helpful. And I'm sorry to hear about your grandma and Noah's difficulties at school, I really am.'

Jackson found himself in the kitchen looking at the boiler before he'd decided whether it was a sensible thing to do. He realised almost immediately why the heating switch wasn't working.

'This is marvellous,' Virginia said when he'd finished. 'Your brother said that you could do anything and that you knew nearly everything worth knowing, but I must admit I didn't totally believe him.'

Jackson could feel a blush spreading from below the collar of his T-shirt to the top of his head.

'My brother is a believer,' he said. 'He believes in everything, really hard, like he actually concentrates on believing things. I just worry.'

Virginia nodded as if she knew exactly what he meant, which was a good thing, Jackson thought, because he wasn't sure that he did, or why he'd said it.

'I think it goes with his age,' Virginia said. 'I think that when you start to change from a child to a young person, you either have something to hold on to or you don't. And if you don't, you can get very lost. So your brother is doing well, and I hope for that for this little one as well.'

Virginia looked twitchy and uncomfortable, and Jackson wondered if she felt as exposed as he did by their conversation. Or maybe it was because she must realise that he had seen all the bruises and bumps, and the little burn marks he recognised from when Noah was a baby.

'How old is she?' he asked, pointing at the baby.

He was hoping to ease the conversation into calmer waters but the question seemed to alarm Virginia.

'Ha!' she said as if Jackson had made a rather unfunny joke. 'Age again. She's about eighteen months, aren't you, sweetie?'

That was the second thing that Jackson thought was weird. He'd noticed that people in charge of babies and small children always gave their age in very precise terms when they were asked. Three weeks, four days, for example, or, she'll be two in seven weeks. Still, Virginia was obviously not your normal grandma. For example, when she finally put Ocean down on the floor, it was to play with a set of plastic glasses, an empty washing-up bowl and some spoons. Jackson thought that Noah would have something to say about giving girls domestic items to play with. He felt proud that he had noticed this and resolved to tell his brother later.

'We haven't got many toys with us,' Virginia said, as if she could read Jackson's thoughts. 'But at this age, everything is new, everything is remarkable. Would you like a cup of tea?'

'I think we've got some old toys and books of Noah's downstairs, do you think Ocean would like to play with them?' Jackson said.

There had to be a possibility that this woman was some kind of monster, Jackson knew that but he couldn't believe it, even for a moment. He simply knew it wasn't her who had hurt that little girl. She was one of the good ones, a helper, and he was willing to bet everything on it. Whoever had done this to Ocean, Jackson knew it wasn't her.

'If anything, bro,' Noah said when they were back downstairs, 'she's the safe place for that child, I reckon. Don't you think?'

They were in Panna's bedroom with her, telling her about the new arrivals.

'I don't know,' Panna said. 'I get that you want to help, and give the toys to the baby and all of that, but you can't tell a bad apple from the outside, can you? I think I need to check this lady out for myself.'

'I don't think she's a bad apple, Panna,' Jackson said. 'I'd say she's much more scared of us than we are of her.'

'Honest, Panna, she's a proper Panna,' Noah said.

Panna shooed him out to get on with his schoolwork.

'I'd rather see the shape of trouble before it climbs into my arms,' she said. 'I want to meet her.'

'Plus you're the nosiest neighbour on the block,' Jackson said.

Panna's laugh cheered him up, and they made plans to call together another day.

They were deep in an episode of an Agatha Christie serial they were watching together when Noah heard a knock on the door. A little knock, as if the person knocking was hoping to tiptoe away again without anyone hearing.

'I'm sorry,' Virginia said as soon as Jackson opened the door. 'I'm sorry and I won't stay long but your brother left this book.'

She handed Jackson Noah's battered notebook.

'Come in,' Jackson said. 'It's nice to see you.'

He wasn't sure what else to say, she was so nervous he was sure she would vanish upstairs as quickly as she'd come. And she probably would have done if Noah hadn't come to the door with his arms outstretched. Ocean leaned so far out of Virginia's grip that she had to let her go to Noah.

Jackson could see how reluctant she was to come in. Why are people so weird, he thought, and he was sure that Noah was thinking the same thing.

Virginia came in, looking over her shoulder as she walked. She jumped at the sight of Philip, so Noah shut him in the bedroom.

'I'll get him out later, on a lead, when Ocean is feeling more at home,' he said.

It was obvious that it was Virginia who was scared, not Ocean, but Jackson could see that Noah wanted to save her any embarrassment. Noah couldn't contain his excitement and hopped from one foot to the other, narrating events in case the others weren't paying attention. Virginia seemed nervous even when the dog had gone, jumping at noises and looking around a lot, but Jackson thought maybe that's what old white ladies were like in someone else's home. He hoped she would calm down.

'She likes the fire engine, look, she's turning the wheels. That's clever, isn't it, Jack, to know that the wheels turn? It's like she's inventing the wheel for herself. Do you think some people are so old-fashioned that they wouldn't let a little girl play with a fire engine?'

Jackson and Virginia both opened their mouths to speak but Noah couldn't wait for an answer.

'Because they need to stop that patriarchal nonsense, don't they?' Noah knelt down and patted Ocean as if she was a puppy.

'Is this a private party or can anyone join?' Panna said.

She had put some jeans and a jumper on and it was the first time Jackson had seen her dressed in regular clothes for ages. He was surprised by how much better she looked.

'Oh Panna, I thought you'd gone for a nap, I didn't want to disturb you. Sorry,' Jackson said.

Panna laughed.

'Meet my grandson, Jackson,' she said. 'Although it looks as though you already have. He's quite the apologiser, especially when it's unnecessary.'

Jackson thought that was slightly unfair, but he was glad to see Panna on such good form.

'I'm Juliana,' she said. 'But everyone calls me Panna these days. Pleased to meet you.'

Panna stuck out her hand and Virginia shook it, but there was something about the exchange that felt off key to Jackson. His grandmother sounded, not cross, exactly, but as if she was being very careful. As if anything she said could be misinterpreted. Virginia noticed it too, Jackson was sure she did. He looked at her when Panna spoke and she looked actually scared. She was finding it hard to walk away from the door and into the living room with Ocean and Noah. Why on earth would she be scared of Panna, he wondered. Perhaps it was an old lady thing, sort of vying to be top old-lady dog, that sort of thing. He wondered if he could ask Noah what he thought, but as far as he could see Noah was completely engrossed in his role of teaching Ocean.

'Fire engine,' he said.

'Fah,' she repeated and Noah clapped and danced around as if it was the best thing he had ever heard.

'Did you hear that, Pannas?' Noah said.

'Pannas?' Panna said. 'It's not a generic term for the older woman, you know.'

She laughed, and so did Virginia, but it was still there, that reserve, whether Noah could see it or not.

'Boys,' Panna said. 'There's a few toys and books on top of my wardrobe, if you want to have a look.'

Noah raced off to look and Jackson followed behind. Panna didn't usually talk to him like this, he was used to being treated like an adult and he felt most uncomfortable at his relegation.

He paused inside Panna's room, just long enough to hear her say, 'We really don't need trouble. I'd like to help, but—'

Jackson could almost hear Panna shrugging.

'Of course,' Virginia said.

She was gone by the time the boys came back with the toys.

CHAPTER TWELVE

Margate

I should never have gone to see them. I could have posted Noah's notebook through the letterbox, or left it on the doormat. Knocking on the door was foolish at best, and at worst, downright dangerous for them. But I was so lonely, and we had made a connection, me and the boys. A proper human connection and that can be as clear and as sudden as falling in love. And then Panna. She was smart, that nice Panna, and I was crying out for company. It had been so long, and it was so nice to be with her and her lovely boys, even for a short time. So nice to talk about Ocean as if she was really just a little girl I was looking after. So nice to feel a tiny bit normal.

But I should have been more careful, thought about the danger. Even though Cate had asked me to do it, even though I think anyone would have done it, I still wasn't sure what Cate might have said to cover her back. There might even be a story in the papers for all I knew. Or one of those terrible press conferences with Cate saying things like, please, whoever has her, bring her back, that kind of thing. I just want my baby back home, I couldn't help imagining Cate saying, as if she didn't know where her baby was. I understood it, there was no way she could tell the truth with that man around. If she did, Ocean would be right back in the danger zone again and all of us could be in it with her.

So I understood why Panna was slightly hostile and I made up my mind that I'd keep away, keep my distance, despite the connection I had felt. It seemed like the best thing I could do. 'I can't believe I'm so stupid,' I said to Ocean.

We were back in the flat and I was probably imagining it but I thought she looked slightly sad. She looked at the door quite often, I think in the hope that Noah would appear. I told her my best stories and drew quite a passable picture of a wombat eating toast but she didn't seem to cheer up.

I wished I'd managed the situation better. Maybe Panna would have understood, if I could only have found the right words. I'd spent months avoiding everybody and keeping myself tucked away and now, when it mattered, I blew it. For the sake of a notebook and a bit of human company. Go figure. So I wasn't surprised but I wished we could have been friends.

I left in a hurry, as soon as she talked about trouble. It was the only thing I could do, the only decent thing. I picked Ocean up before anyone had a chance to say anything else. She was still holding the fire engine, with the sheep inside it now.

'Can I?' I said.

I pointed at the fire engine. I knew if I said anything else I would burst into tears.

'Of course,' Panna said.

Ocean waved goodbye as we left.

*

I decided that I probably wouldn't bump into them if I only left the flat after dark, or very early in the morning. I would keep away, keep away properly for the sake of all of us and I was just explaining this to Ocean when the doorbell rang. I looked around the flat for somewhere to hide Ocean but of course, you can't put a baby in a cupboard and not cause them permanent damage so I sat her behind a chair and out of view. My heart was banging hard enough to escape and fly off as I opened the door.

It was the boys, and they were carrying bags full of toys and books.

'Panna knows,' Noah said. 'We are legit.'

Ocean was so pleased to see them again that she crawled out from behind the chair, grinning.

'Quack,' she said.

'Hear that?' Noah said.

He got down on the floor with her and showed her a book.

'Look,' he said while the others looked on. 'It's the great big enormous turnip, and it's so hard to get it out of the ground that everyone has to join in to pull it out, even the little dog.'

'Woof,' Ocean said.

Noah clapped and blew her a kiss. 'I reckon she's really clever, really special. She can copy anything. We could teach her French, German, all of the languages.'

'Bro,' said Jackson.

He had a warning tone to his voice, only a gentle one but a warning tone nonetheless, and Noah acknowledged it with a small salute.

'What my brother wants to say,' Jackson said, 'is that my grandma—'

'Panna,' Noah said, as if there might be some confusion.

Jackson glared at him. 'My grandma says she was pleased to meet you. She'd love to talk to you again. She's sorry that you left so quickly.'

'I think she likes you, in a way,' Noah said. 'She doesn't really like that many white people.'

'Noah be quiet,' Jackson said.

'It's fine, I get it, and I like your grandma too. Old ladies ought to stick together, didn't they?' I said. 'Tell her I think she's great. And tell her I'll pop down again soon, I promise. I think I've been lonely, but I feel much better after seeing you folks.'

I stopped there in case it was all getting too much for them. Too much emotion, too many old ladies. The worst thing was, Jackson and Noah both looked as if they really knew what I meant. They shouldn't have known lonely at their age and I certainly should not have risked making their lives any harder than they were.

I needed Jed. I wasn't sure that I had done things as well as I could have and I needed him to tell me everything would be OK. I needed his moral compass and his strengths as a fixit man. I didn't want to make a mess of things and I certainly didn't want to get other people involved. I didn't care about myself, I was probably out of here in six weeks anyway, so it was fine for me to leap in with a brave act of daring or whatever it was I'd done. I could make reckless decisions for myself, but I had no right to drag other people down with me. I think I came close to going home then. I could hand Ocean over to social services and keep my damn nose out. I could go home, leave the boys and Panna alone, shut the door and take my pills. I didn't have to wait for six weeks. Someone else could save her, it wasn't my business. It was Ocean who turned me around.

'Sheep,' she said and she held her little arms out to be picked up.

I lifted her and hugged her as hard as I could.

'I'll pop down soon,' I said.

I felt stronger when I was holding her.

I looked at them both, proper eye contact to make sure that they knew that I was being honest. I wish I could explain how much I could see that they understood. They were something else, those boys, and their grandmother. Right from the start, I knew that if I wanted to, I could talk to them more easily than I could talk to almost any of the adults I'd ever come across. Even the little one, Noah. He was such an unusual lad. He looked younger than his age until you really looked into his eyes, and then you could see that they were the eyes of an old soul. Jed would have loved him. What I had to remember was, they didn't need to be involved, however willing they were.

They nodded to show that they understood and I was pleased to see Jackson put his hand on Noah's shoulder. Just a light touch, but exactly right for a bit of brotherly reassurance.

'Let us know if there's anything we can do,' Noah said. 'I'd be happy to help. I don't know what's going on, but I'm always ace at telling who's good people and who isn't. It's one of my special skills. Don't give me that warning look or try to shut me up, big bro, you know I'm talking sense here. She's a good person and that baby likes me.'

He got a little wooden duck out of the bag of toys and held it out to her, quacking, until she quacked back.

'Noah, we've got to go now,' Jackson said. 'Really nice to meet you both.'

There was worry buried in his words and that was my fault and hard to hear. I shouldn't have spoken to them. I'd spent my life keeping myself to myself and there was absolutely no reason to have stopped that now.

'Thank you for the toys and books,' I said.

I wished I could tell them more. 'She's going to love them. And I'll return them, when things are a bit better. Please tell Panna I appreciate it.'

Noah looked accusingly at Jackson.

'See what you've done? We really are pleased you're here,' Noah said.

He sounded much younger and now definitely on the verge of tears as they went back down the stairs.

'Please, let her keep the toys,' Jackson said. 'We don't need them. Come on, Noah.'

I held Ocean's hand out and waved it at them. They were nearly at the bottom when Noah turned round.

'We go to the beach with Philip,' he said. 'If you want to come. Philip is the least scary dog ever and I think you'd be fine if we were outside, because he'd just be running around.'

'Thank you,' I said.

I had no intention of going.

As presents go, the contents of the bags were probably the best things Ocean had ever seen. There were cars, farm animals, books, the duck and a little doll in a cot.

'Sheep,' she said. She sounded like a seventeen-year-old person might sound if the car of their dreams was wrapped in ribbon outside their house on their birthday morning.

I pushed the memory of William away as Ocean crawled back across the room to me, carrying her sheep.

'Sheep,' she said.

She held it out to me and then changed her mind and held it out to the wooden pull-along duck.

'Sheep,' she said. 'Quack.'

We were waking up from an afternoon nap the next day when Annie texted to say that she had arrived in Margate. For a moment I wished that we could stay on our own, just Ocean and me, with no one else involved and no one else to worry about. Why had I let Annie come? Did I want to drag everyone down with me? It was so hard to leave the safety of the nap. I had forgotten how lovely it is to nap with a small child, feel them go loose and let go and then follow them to a place that's never quite completely asleep, in case they need you. The smell of her was amazing. She smelled of soap and flowers with a hint of sour milk, and I swear they could have marketed that smell.

I should never have let Annie come. We would have been OK, I thought, Ocean and me, we would have managed on our own. And the need for medical advice didn't seem so urgent any more. She hardly ever cried, so I didn't think she was in pain. As for company, I didn't deserve that. The more people who knew about us, the more danger we were in. The more chance there was that someone would do or say the wrong thing, and then we would not only lose Ocean and put her in danger but all these other people I'd dragged in might be in trouble as well. Panna and those lovely boys.

By the time Annie rang the bell I was ready to ask her to go home. To apologise and explain that we had got this, we didn't need help. I'd explain it was for her own good, and that we didn't want her to get caught up in any trouble. Obviously she could rest up with us before going home, but that would be all.

We opened the door, Ocean attached to me like a baby monkey.

'Oh look,' Annie said. 'Look at you, you wee beauty.'

She held out her arms and Ocean slipped easily into them, as if she knew her and had been expecting her to call. I had one moment of pure, blinding jealousy and then I laughed out loud. It was such a funny sight. Annie was tiny, with long wild hair piled on top of her head and the kind of brown tortoiseshell glasses that could either be fashionable or left over from last time they were fashionable, depending on who is wearing them.

'Who have we got here then,' she said.

'Sheep,' Ocean said.

I could hardly hear her, she was buried so deep in Annie's bosom.

'I'm sorry,' I said. 'Please come in. We seem to have lost our manners. You must be tired after such a long journey. Shall I take the little one?'

'I'm so fine,' Annie said.

Her eyes were positively glittering. 'You have no idea. I haven't left that wee place in forty years. Forty years in a tiny town where I know every pebble, every streetlight, every tree. It's a mix of heaven and hell all swooshed up together, if you ken my meaning. I knew something would get me out one day, but I wasn't at all sure whether I'd be leaving in a box or on my own two feet. Feet!'

Annie got hold of Ocean's feet and tickled them. She didn't laugh.

'That's not so fun, is it, wee angel?' Annie said.

She turned to me. 'Little children who've had to deal with a lot, they don't tend to find that funny,' she said. 'It's as though they don't think anything good can come of any attention to their bodies at all.'

I was glad to have her there, and thought I'd reconsider asking her to leave for an hour or two.

By the time we put Ocean to bed we were working as a team. I remembered how much easier bathing a baby is when there are two of you. This wasn't like any bath I had ever given before, however. Annie was calling out all of the marks on her little body, the old ones and the new, while I wrote them down. She moved Ocean's little legs in a cycling motion as she lay on her back, and she felt all over her body, noting the times she winced or tried to protect herself.

'All of that and no tears,' I said.

I could hardly believe it.

'Tricks of the trade,' Annie said. 'I'm good with the little ones. There's got to be some pay-off for damn near forty years on the trucks. It certainly wasn't worth it for the money. I learned things though, things they can't teach you in the school. And what I'd say is, there are at least two old injuries. One in her right shin, and one in that shoulder – see how she moves it quite stiffly? She'll need x-rays eventually to see what's going on but it's more important that's she stays safe for now.'

As soon as Annie pointed it out I could see it. It must have been so painful, I thought. Just thinking of it now made me want to cry, and Annie noticed.

'Hey,' she said. Her voice was always soft, but now she made it even softer.

'No wonder everyone trusts you,' I said. 'Your voice sounds like it's dipped in sugar.'

She laughed, and Ocean joined in.

'I've heard some nonsense in my time,' she said. 'Are you writing this down? More old burns on her shoulder blades, healed laceration lower back, old bruising on legs.'

'What?' I said.

I'd changed her nappy a few times and I hadn't noticed that.

Annie shook her head in a way that made me think she was tired of the world.

'I've seen a lot of these,' she said. 'More than anyone would imagine in a so-called civilised society. And this little poppet, I think she's luckier than some. She's safe now, isn't she, and I think we can look after her ourselves. I don't think there would be any benefit from taking her to hospital. The injuries she has now, they're the warning shots. The early, less significant injuries. They usually only show up once something worse has happened, but you and her poor mum, you've been very clever. You've managed to get her away before the really bad stuff starts.'

I must have made some kind of noise then, because Annie said, 'Aye, you can well be surprised. It's difficult to comprehend, isn't it, that these marks are just the beginning. There's something so nasty about cigarette burns especially, like an utter contempt for the wee soul.'

Ocean held her sheep out towards Annie and she took it, kissed it and gave it back.

I was sure that I knew what was the right thing to do.

'We've got to take her to hospital,' I said. 'Regardless of the danger for me. I don't care about that, I've had my life. She needs to be seen, and treated properly. I was trying to rescue her, not make her life worse. What if she has a limp or something when she grows up and it's all my fault?'

I could hear the catch in my voice that meant I was going to cry, and I really didn't want to do that. Annie had come all this way to help us and the least I could do was keep myself together and be a rational part of the team. I had been on my own for so long, though. So long I couldn't see straight. On my own while Jed died, on my own afterwards and now on my own in this bizarre geriatric single-parent fugitive situation.

'We don't need to take her right now,' Annie said. 'We need to keep her safe, that's the main thing.'

She had a soothing voice and I could imagine how good she had been at her work.

'I can see you're used to dealing with people in their darkest hours,' I said.

'Bless you,' she said. 'This isn't terribly dark, I can assure you. I think it's rather jolly. A bit like the first night at boarding school, only with a baby. I'm so glad that you and I have met at long last, and this wee girl is safe for the time being, and happy. Isn't that all we can ask for?'

No, I thought, no, it isn't. If asking for things was a thing, I'd ask for Jed to be alive and with us, and for William to live closer. And I'd ask that Ocean had known nothing more serious than a bruised knee, and that she lived happily with her mum. Annie must have guessed what I was thinking.

'When I was a wee girl,' she said, 'my father used to always tell me to think of people worse off than me. It never worked, so I know what you're thinking. The starving children in Biafra, people caught in the war in the Congo, poorer people – all of them on the prayer hit list. I was an obedient girl and I tried hard but the problem was I didn't know them. It was a long time before I realised that I did know them, that people are just people, all the same, even the bad eggs. So I'm not going to tell you to think of people in much worse spots of bother but I can point out that some things are OK. She's safe, this wee lassie, and I'm here to help and I think it's going to be sunny tomorrow and we've got two brains to figure things out. There. That's me done.'

Annie sat back with Ocean happily sprawled on her lap chewing on a small car.

I could see the sense in what she was saying but a part of me still longed to call the authorities. Make sure she was fine, explain what I'd done and why, and ask them to find her a better home. With her mum, if that was possible. How could two old ladies possibly look after her? What if one of us had a heart attack, or a stroke?

I've always been easy to read, Jed used to tell me that all the time. I thought that it was because we were so close, but apparently not, because Annie could read me too and we had only just met.

'If you're thinking,' she said, 'that it would be better to give her up, get the proper authorities involved, then maybe I need to tell you about some of the things I've seen. Foster parents not fit to feed a goldfish, fathers given visiting rights and then hurting children or worse, to get at the ex-wife. Women too, usually women who are being controlled by some vile person. Some of them make the headlines, and that's what could happen with this wee cherub. It would be newsworthy, because they could frame it in a way that looks bad for you. Didn't they write "paedophile" on your house? Think about it, how it could be made to look.'

I could see the sense in what she was saying, but it still didn't sit comfortably with me. I was tired, that was the truth. I was still grieving for Jed, and although I knew that I had done the right thing for Ocean, I was frightened at how out of control it had got, and how quickly. I missed the total selfishness of bereavement, and the possibility of finishing myself off without a second thought if I chose to. I hadn't even looked at my pills for ages, although I had packed them in my rucksack. There was always the sea to walk into if things got bad, but I couldn't imagine that I would be able to do that. I'd never learned to swim, and the idea of going into the water past my knees was the equivalent of skydiving from the tallest building to me. There was probably a railway line somewhere nearby but I had always worried about the train drivers in those sort of situations. It must cause them terrible, lasting damage. I wanted to lie on the sofa and turn out the lights, that's how tired I was. I remembered the feeling from when William was a toddler.

Either I looked absolutely terrible or Annie was a mind reader. I think it was a bit of both.

'Why don't you have a proper rest and let me take over for a while?' she said. 'She seems to be happy enough with me, and if she's not I could promise to wake you up. She needs to go to sleep now anyway.'

I wanted to argue, I knew that Ocean was my responsibility and I didn't mean to shirk it but there is something about being tired when you're old that is completely different from when you're young. It feels like an unbendable fact, something you just can't fight against. I think that before I fell asleep on the sofa I muttered something about, that's why old people don't have children, but maybe I just thought it instead.

CHAPTER THIRTEEN

Margate

Jackson and Panna had talked about the old lady and the baby ever since they left. He couldn't remember when he had last seen his grandmother so alert and energetic. It was as if they had woken her up, pressed some kind of a switch and animated her.

'Don't over think it, bro,' Noah said as he came back into the living room in his pyjamas, Philip close behind him as if he was on a short lead. Noah said he wanted a drink of water but Jackson could tell that he just couldn't bear to be left out.

'I don't know what you're talking about,' he said.

Jackson knew that he sounded snippy and short tempered, but living with Noah could be so emotionally exhausting. It was like being faced by a panel of experts at all times, experts who were there only to discuss how he was behaving, and what the implications of his thoughts were.

'It's OK,' Noah said, as if they were having a totally different conversation. 'It's understandable to worry whether good can come from bad. And that baby has definitely lived with bad. It's like, I don't know much about philosophy but I wouldn't be surprised if it's a thing that people have been wondering about for some time.'

'Are you for real?' Jackson said. 'I've got no idea why you think you know what I'm thinking about all the time. You're talking nonsense, and what's more you should be in bed. Not going to school doesn't mean it's not a school night.'

Noah stopped at his bedroom door and wagged his finger at Jackson.

'You can tut and steam all you want,' he said. 'But you know what I'm saying. Sometimes I think I'm the only sensible one in this place.'

Panna waited until he was back in his bedroom before she burst into laughter. Not polite laughter or forced laughter but really joyous, glad to be alive stuff. Jackson was pleased to hear it but still, he wished that sometimes he could be the funny one. He'd tried it for a while at school, and there had been some success, especially when he mimicked people. He had been good at accents and at pointing up peculiarities of speech. There was a geography teacher, for example, who said 'and things' at the end of more or less every sentence and Jackson had made such a good job of replicating it that it became the rage for everyone, and all the kids were saying it. 'Do you want to play football and things?' Or, 'I'm going for lunch and things now.' Jackson had loved it for a while, until he noticed that she seemed to be much less happy, the teacher. She had started to hang her head and she didn't speak so much, seeming hesitant when she did. Jackson never knew whether his poking fun had anything to do with it, but she left at the end of the summer term when he was sixteen.

He had been haunted by it for some time. The idea that

he could have made anyone unhappy for the amusement of other people seemed like the most terrible thing he could have done. He didn't talk about it with the other kids, that was the last thing he wanted to do. There were already enough strikes against him. One, he was Black, two, he was clever and seemed to have a knack for passing exams with top grades. Three, he was clever *and* Black, and that seemed to be quite a zany combo for some people. Four was the ever present worry that his mum might come to the school, as she had when he was in primary school. That would be the worst thing. So in terms of letting people know that he sympathised with a weird geography teacher whom he had spent almost a year mimicking, that was a no. He kept it to himself and he turned down the dial on making people laugh. Noah though, Noah was a natural. Noah made them laugh in a way that was almost instinctively kind.

'Do you think Noah could earn a living doing comedy?' Jackson asked Panna.

She stopped smiling and put on a very serious face.

'Jackson,' she said. 'That brother of yours might need a little bit of help now, because he's not grown. He's just a little boy. But he isn't going to need it forever, no, sir. So you don't have to always be thinking about what he's gonna do, how he's gonna be. He's the sort of person who is going to be responsible for his own self. And he's always gonna make people laugh because he's Noah, but I'm not sure that he could make an actual living from it.'

'I heard that,' Noah called from the bedroom. 'I'm not asleep because I'm reading, I'm reading a book about people and why they do stuff. Like the lady upstairs.'

Jackson and Panna looked at each other. You're not the only one who's wondering about that, Jackson thought.

Noah came out of the bedroom and sat on the floor at Panna's feet. He held up his book so that they could both see it. It was called *Why Do We Do It?* and had an extraordinary picture on the front of a man at the top of a ladder in the nighttime, looking as though he had captured the moon in his arms.

Jackson sighed. That was another thing no one ever said about parenting, that it was best to read the same books as the young person, watch the same programmes and films, and don't even think about the internet.

'And I'm thinking,' Noah said, 'based on what this guy says in here, that she's got more than one reason to have brought that baby with her.'

'You heard what she told Panna,' Jackson said. 'It's her granddaughter, nothing strange about that. We live with our grandma, you ridiculous boy.'

'There's more to it,' Noah said. 'You wait and see.'

'You have not got enough going on in your life, little bro,' Jackson said. 'I'm going to set you some more maths to keep you busy if you don't go back to bed right now.'

Noah skipped off happily with the dog.

'What do you think, Panna?' Jackson kept his voice low.

'I don't know,' Panna said. 'But I like her, I can't help it. I felt connected to her in some weird way, like I knew her in another life or something. I like her enough to believe that even if that boy is right, and there is more to it, then I'm on her side.'

'Plus,' Noah called from his bedroom, 'plus she kind of looks lonely. They both look lonely, or maybe I mean that

Ocean looks like a baby who used to be lonely. A baby who has known sadness. Was I like that?'

Panna nodded and Jackson remembered how Noah used to be. A scared little scrap with great big eyes, always watching doors as if he was living in a horror movie for children.

'I thought I was. I mean obviously that's why I want to help, isn't it, that's why we all want to help. Because it could be me, right?'

Bloody hell, Jackson thought, maybe not a comedian. Maybe a psychologist or something fancy like that.

'If you're thinking what I'm thinking,' Panna said. 'Then we need to go and talk it through with the lady upstairs. And I'm thinking there's no time like the present.'

There were two old ladies upstairs now, and they seemed pleased to see them, Jackson thought, despite the lateness of the hour and the fact that Noah was in his pyjamas.

'Two of you,' Noah said. 'It's like you're multiplying.'

'I'm sorry for my brother,' Jackson said. 'He says whatever pops into his head, no filter at all.'

'And isn't that the best thing,' the second old lady said. 'I'm a wee bit inclined that way myself. I'm Annie, an old friend of Virginia's.'

Annie held her hand out and Noah shook it. She then bent down and held her hand out to Phil, and Jackson could see that Noah almost exploded with pride when Phil carefully lifted his paw to her hand.

The women seemed lost, somehow, and it was difficult to work out how they knew each other, because they were so different. There was fussing over tea and biscuits and a couple of times there were soft grunts from the room where Ocean was asleep. The ladies stood still for a moment as if they were playing statues and breathed out as the baby settled back down again. Jackson wondered how two old ladies could do almost the same actions in unison and yet seem so unalike, and he resolved to talk to Noah about it later. He could imagine Noah berating him for stereotyping and it made him smile. It took him a moment or two to realise that everyone was sitting down, Panna and the other two on the sofa and Noah at Panna's feet and they were all waiting for him. Had he been asked something? He really had been away in another world.

'Classic Jackson,' Panna said. 'Jack, Virginia just asked if you're comfortable, being here.'

'Honestly,' Virginia said. 'You don't have to do anything. My daughter will come to her senses and everything will be fine. We don't need help or anything like that.'

'We're not worried,' Noah said. 'My brother is just being extra cautious, probably because we're Black.'

Jackson looked at Panna and groaned.

'I can only apologise,' he said. 'And I think we are happy to help in any way we can.'

Noah clapped his hands and this time Ocean was definitely awake and unhappy.

'Sorry, sorry,' he said in a stage whisper but Jackson could see that he was actually delighted. He had never had much interaction with younger children, and it must be nice, Jackson thought, for him not to be the baby all the time. He certainly seemed to have a knack for it.

He watched with the three women as Noah went into

Ocean's bedroom and came out carrying her. She smiled as he placed her gently on the floor and surrounded her with toys.

'It's such a lovely name, Ocean,' Noah said. 'So special. If any kids at school tease her because it's unusual, I'll talk to them. Not everyone can be called Oliver or Lucy, can they? There were four Olivers in my last class and they were all like, I'm Oliver H, and I'm Oliver Bean, so they ended up with different names anyway.'

Noah stopped for a moment and Jackson wondered what on earth he was going to say next.

'It's important, having an identity,' Noah said. 'It matters, and I'm glad she has such a great name. It will carry her through things.'

'Ocean,' he said in a soft voice.

She looked up from trying to fit the sheep in the fire engine again and smiled.

'Noah,' Jackson said.

He wasn't sure what he was cautioning his brother about and there was nothing wrong with what he'd said but Jackson couldn't read the room here. There was something sneaking along behind what was obvious and he wasn't sure what it was. There were rules and social politeness things and they were in someone else's house and needed to be careful, that's all he knew.

'It's fine,' Virginia said, 'I love her name too.'

Jackson could see from her expression that the other woman, Virginia's strange Scottish friend, had something on her mind but she didn't say anything. He wondered if it would be rude to ask how they met, and how long they had been friends. They seemed so different. Virginia had short hair, and was wearing jeans and a jumper, normal clothes really. Nothing you would notice if you walked past her. The other woman though, she was completely different. She had said her name was Annie, but Jackson was sure it must be short for something wild and unusual. She had long grey hair, and her skirt dragged on the floor like a wedding train. It seemed to be made from many different pieces of material patched together, and she had topped it with an ancient looking T-shirt bearing the name of a builders merchant on the Isle of Mull.

Jackson felt more and more worried about the women and their ability to care adequately for Ocean. He was trying to work out how he could help when Panna's voice broke into his thoughts.

'Lovely to meet you, Annie,' Panna said. 'There's a name I haven't heard for a while. Are you Irish? I had a room in a boarding house with an Irish girl named Annie, when I first came. My name is Juliana but I'm Panna to the world, thanks to these two. And we wanted to say that, if you need any help, we're just downstairs. We're not prying, don't think that, but sometimes people carry a look, a scent, I don't know what you'd call it but we've had a tiny chat and I believe you're nice grandmas, that's all. And if we can do anything we will.'

Jackson felt out of his depth. So much not being said, he thought, so many undercurrents.

'You really are kind,' Virginia said. 'And it's so nice of you all to offer but honestly we'll be fine. More than fine, in fact. We're going to have grandma seaside fun and I'm so sorry if I worried you in any way. Ocean will be fine, we'll all be fine. Thank you.'

They all stared at her but it was Noah who spoke.

'Are you OK?' he asked.

Virginia looked panicked and started to cough, and Jackson noticed that Annie immediately started talking about the weather, as if they'd agreed it beforehand. Most odd.

'The thing is,' Panna said to Jackson when they were home and Noah was finally asleep, 'I'm sure they're good people, I really am. I know it. But there's something they're not telling us, I can feel it. And that baby does not look like her grandma. Not even a whisker of a look, did you notice that?'

Jackson hadn't noticed that at all. In fact he wasn't sure that babies in general looked like anything other than each other, or a nappy advert. However, the bee that Panna had in her bonnet about the baby and the ladies seemed to be good for her so Jackson was happy to listen to her speculate for as long as she wanted.

Noah was up early the next morning, eager for a dog walk.

'I'm wearing my football T-shirt, bro,' he said before Jackson had even processed the fact that the day had started. 'I'm wearing it because if she comes, I'm going to explain to Ocean today about team sports, it's a thing that most girls don't get told about till later, I reckon.'

He should belong to a bigger family, Jackson thought. Cousins, aunts, uncles and babies all over the place. Messy spontaneous barbecues and board games at Christmas. That's what would suit him.

The boys had nearly finished their walk and were almost back home again before Virginia and Annie appeared with Ocean in a buggy. Noah clapped at the sight of them and

Jackson realised that he was much less worried about Phil the dog being seen once they were on the beach together. If the man who had owned the dog was on the beach, he would surely not be looking for such an assorted group of walkers. Virginia was still jumpy around Phil but Noah persuaded her to try a little stroke. Jackson chuckled as Noah explained that Ocean shouldn't pick up Virginia's fear. The boys turned around and they walked slowly, Noah chatting all the way about Oban with Annie. Jackson was astonished again at how many odd things Noah knew. He was talking about the nuclear submarines just off the coast of Scotland when Jackson realised that the man was there, standing farther down the beach by the seawall and looking right at them. Virginia changed her step to walk next to Jackson.

'Do you by any chance know that chap?' Virginia said.

Jackson shook his head, but he must have looked more shifty than he realised because Virginia was not convinced.

'Are you sure? Only he keeps looking at us,' she said.

Jackson dropped back a little further behind the others.

'You can tell me,' Virginia said. 'Only it would be good to know for all sorts of reasons. I would hate a scene or anything unpleasant in front of Ocean, and there's something about him I don't like at all, you know?'

Jackson was impressed. One glimpse and she'd seen how horrible that man was, she could see it even though she was scared of poor Phil. He owed it to her to tell her the whole story. Anything less would be unfair. It would be easier if she was a dog lover, but he took a deep breath and told her anyway.

When Jackson had finished, Virginia was quiet for a while.

They watched Annie and Noah, who were helping Ocean dig in the sand and pile it up into a sheep castle.

'It's so much warmer than Scotland,' Annie said.

Noah did a little victory dance, Phil at his heels. Jackson tried not to look towards the man again.

'Let's go back, we don't want Ocean getting cold, she doesn't know it's warmer than Scotland. Look, her little lips have gone blue,' said Virginia.

Virginia even bent to pat Phil unasked, which surprised Jackson.

'I believe you,' she said as they went back to the flats. 'And I believe you did a good thing, a worthwhile thing. So I'll help you if I can.'

There has to be more to that, Jackson thought. It wasn't what he was expecting, not at all, but Panna was coughing badly when they went back in so he didn't get a chance to ponder.

CHAPTER FOURTEEN

Margate

We cooked together that night, Annie and I, and we bathed Ocean and cleaned out the sand from the bath like any other grandmas at the seaside. She fell asleep quickly, and it was companionable, sitting together with only the sound of the waves and our voices, soft so that we didn't wake Ocean. We talked about the boys from downstairs and their dog, and how kind they had been.

'They're unusual,' Annie said. 'I think they recognise something in Ocean, they can see that she's special too. That child is one of the most gracious and dignified small people I have ever met.'

I agreed, and as I picked up the little lorry Ocean had left on the floor I wished I could tell Annie how scared I was, how much I realised I had built my world around the baby in the teeny time we'd been together. I didn't have anything else in my life, and that was the truth. There had been Jed, and only Jed, and then there was nothing. It hadn't always been like that, of course. I was a proper Seventies feminist, and I had been determined not to build my life around a man. Any man. I had insisted on a room of my own in the first house we bought together.

'We live together, but we don't socialise,' I used to tell people when I introduced Jed. I'd had friends, a work life, hobbies even but all of it had drifted away as Jed became more and more unwell, until my world shrank to the shape of the sickroom. I wanted to die with him, follow him wherever he was going. Until Ocean came along. Ocean had got me out of there. Only just over five weeks to go now and it seemed I might have no choice but to stay, at least for now. Ocean had saved my life, and it was definitely a mutual pact. I had to save hers too and it was my responsibility, not the lovely family downstairs or the wild woman of Oban.

'Here you are,' she said as she gave me a cup of tea, 'that's you, and it'll help. I know how you're feeling, and I think you're missing that wee lassie even though she's just asleep.'

I think I've had kinder things said or done for me in my life but at that point I couldn't think of any. It was the nicest thing anyone could have done and I was sorry I'd called her the wild woman in my head. I took the tea and burst into tears as if I was accepting an Academy Award. I felt so embarrassed.

'I'm sorry,' I said. 'I'm so sorry. It's just . . .'

I tailed off, because I couldn't think what it just was. It was everything, the whole world raged against me and no Jed, no soulmate to tell me everything would be OK. It wouldn't be OK, my whole life was about to be changed and I could feel it happening. I might go to prison or I might die, but there didn't seem to be anything else possible.

'You've probably had a really quiet life,' I said. 'But you're great at dealing with everything.'

It was a ridiculous thing to say, and I should have known that no one really has a quiet life, that life is always loud and jangling, but at that moment Annie looked so serene, and I had never been less together. I was a mess.

She sat on the floor next to me and I could see us for a moment as if I was watching from the ceiling. Two old women sitting on the floor, one crying and one in fancy dress.

'Can I tell you something, about my life?' Annie said. 'My wee quiet life, if that's how you see it? You're not completely wrong. It's been quiet for a good long time now, but it wasn't always. Och no. Not at all. Once it was full of shouting and crying and when that was over I thought, that's it. That's it for me and the noisy life. I'm staying by myself now, nice and quiet apart from work.'

I nodded and made some assumptions. I'll be honest, I didn't want to listen. I even thought, oh dear, I hope I don't have to pretend to listen to her story for too long. We've all got sad stories to tell, but now isn't the time. It's not that I didn't care, I did, but grief plays tricks like that. It makes you feel as though no one else can ever have had as much to bear, and that's without the responsibility of a baby on the run. So I wasn't completely listening when she started talking, but I liked the comforting lilt of her words. I tuned in after a sentence or two, and I think I will always wonder what the beginning of the story was.

'. . . I didn't know how on earth people got pregnant,' she was saying. 'I certainly didn't know I'd had sex. I thought it was maybe a thing everyone had to do with older male relatives. If you were a good wee girl, you know. It just wasn't a thing you talked about, that's all. So when I started to put on weight, no one noticed. That's the thing I find most strange. I was a little fourteen year old, I hadn't finished growing and although I haven't got any photographs from that time I can remember looking in the mirror and thinking, someone has to notice this. There was two of them, you see. Two babies.'

Annie shook her head as if, even now, she couldn't quite believe what had happened. I kept quiet and still. The words she was saying seemed as though they had been waiting for a long time to come out, and I didn't want to frighten them away.

'I think someone from school told my mum eventually,' she said. 'Probably the PE teacher saw it, I never knew. I never went back there. I was expelled, for immorality they said. They could do that then. Anyway, my mum had to notice then, although I only had a vague idea of what was going on. It's amazing how ignorant a person can be. Swinging Sixties and everything but I didn't live in London or even any of the big Scottish towns. Might have been different if I did. I used to collect pictures from magazines of London, Edinburgh, Sydney, anywhere far away. I knew I didn't belong in the Highlands. All sheep and religion, it was then. Who's the father? That's all anyone wanted to know and I wasn't at all sure what they meant. I was a bright wee girl, top student and never lower than A grades so I'm amazed now that I was so daft, but maybe a psychiatrist would say I was blocking it out, I don't know. Plus, how was I supposed to get my uncles in trouble? They had told me what would happen if I said anything. Lots of times. So I said I didn't know and I suppose there was truth in there somewhere because there were two of them but it didn't go down too well. I was called all manner of things, words a wee lassie shouldn't even hear. I think that hurt more than anything. That everyone went along with the easiest thing they could think. Put the blame on me and leave it there. Wouldn't you think, now, that one person, just even one, would think, maybe there's more to this than meets the eye? Maybe there's a reason we've never seen wee Annie with a boyfriend, or going out with the other ones on a Saturday night?

'I thought about that a lot over the years. I got stuck on it, really. Just one person, an auntie or my mum or grandma, and all they had to do was think, what's Annie like? Really like?'

She stopped and I thought that it made sense to me now, the missing puzzle piece of Annie. I'd been wondering, without admitting it to myself, what would make a person travel all this way to get involved in a trouble that wasn't theirs to solve. That wouldn't touch them if everything went wrong, that would leave their life alone. I realised I had been slightly suspicious of Annie and I felt bad for that. She could see the whole picture, that was all, and she wanted to make sure everything was fair this time.

'You're like a kind of truth warrior then,' I said. 'Because of what happened to you.'

Annie blushed. 'Och no, I wouldna say that at all,' she said. 'Nothing so grand.'

I thought she was pleased though, even as she denied it.

'What happened to the babies?' I said. 'I mean, if you don't mind telling me, if it's OK.'

I wished I hadn't said it as soon as the words had dropped into the little space between us.

'I thought it would be easy,' she said. 'I thought it would

be fun, the three of us living together and reading books and making tea, like any wee girl with a pack of dollies. I tried. I did my best. I wasn't old enough, but I loved them, and that's the main thing, isn't it?'

Annie was opening and closing her hands as if there ought to be something in them, as if she'd lost something or let go of it. It wasn't difficult to decide to leave it, stop pressing her for the rest of the story.

'Come on,' I said. 'You don't have to say any more if you don't want to. We'll have loads of time to talk. Let's make an actual plan. Thank you so much, it's going to be better with two.'

We talked for half the night, and in the morning we woke to a letter from Noah pushed under the door.

Dear Ladies, please could we look after baby Ocean for a little while today and you can have some me time. (You time, I mean, not actual me time because I don't need it.) We will play with her and look after her and plus, she definitely cheers Panna up.

PS, Panna would like to talk to you first.

Best wishes

Noah (from downstairs)

My first reaction was to say no. I didn't want to talk to Panna about what was going on, and I didn't want to be away from Ocean. I didn't trust anyone with her, even those lovely boys, and what's more, I still didn't want them to be dragged into my troubles.

'But it would be good to clear our heads and finalise a proper plan,' Annie said, as if she could read my mind. 'And we probably need to tell her something anyway, she's involved now, isn't she?'

'What if, what if they call the authorities?' I said.

As soon as I said it I realised that it was what I had been scared of, all along. What it they didn't understand, or couldn't be trusted, or a combination of the two?

'Do you think that's possible?' Annie said. 'Because if there's even a wee chance that they will, we've got to think hard and think quickly. And we've got to run.'

'I honestly don't think so,' I said. 'I felt a connection with her, an immediate thing, I can't really explain it. The same thing happened with you, but in a way I was expecting that. Because of the letters.'

I blushed, I think. It felt so odd to be going round emoting all over the place, so unlike me. And the thing I couldn't tell Annie, the thing I could hardly even admit to myself, was that if Panna did call the authorities, if she did manage to convince them to take some notice, then maybe she would be right. Maybe that's what was needed and then I could put this whole burden down for a few minutes. Long enough for me to keep my appointment with my pills.

'OK,' she said. 'Let's do it. We don't need to tell her too much, but I think she deserves to know what's what. And Ocean would like it. It can't be right for her to spend so much time with two old biddies.'

Speak for yourself, I wanted to say, but there was a part of me, a growing part, that agreed with her. We did need to make a plan, and it was not helpful to live from moment to moment. Ocean deserved better.

We took Ocean downstairs with her toys and blankets and a list of instructions, Ocean's user manual, Noah called it.

I knew it was wrong to involve them but I had got to a point where everything felt wrong, everything felt dangerous. So I couldn't trust myself to make the right decisions, even with Annie. We needed help.

The boys weren't there when we went downstairs, and that was odd. Panna looked different, formidable in a way. I hoped that I hadn't made a mistake in trusting her, and Annie's brow crinkled so I thought that she might be thinking the same. Panna motioned for us to sit down.

'The boys are at the shop,' she said. 'We've got about twenty minutes. Spill, please. Those boys think the world of that baby, and they've got enough to deal with. I can tell there's something off here. Don't need to smell what you can see with your own two eyes, my mum used to say. So tell me why you have this baby, and how you're related. And where her mum is.'

That was a little more than I had expected. Fiercer. I had to admire her.

'No wonder those boys are such nice young men,' I said. 'And sorry that I've caused such a stir. Are you sure you want to know everything? I could walk away now and leave you in peace, and I'm happy to do that.'

I looked at Annie, and she nodded, which was just a little bit annoying. I was managing fine without you, I thought, and then I remembered that I wasn't.

'I like you, the boys like you, and I've seen my share of troubles. I've always believed in paying it forward so I'm willing to help, but I need to know more. I think that's fair.'

She was right, and I could see that Annie thought so too, so I told her the whole sorry tale from the beginning. I tried to explain that Cate wasn't a bad person, and I may have emphasised a little too strongly that she would be OK once she had thought it through. I didn't dwell on how terrifying I found Steve because who wants to scare people? It's not like he knew where we were. Cate would make better choices, that's what I said. I picked Ocean up when I'd finished, and offered to show her some of the marks but Panna held her hand up.

'I don't need to see that, I can see it all too well in my head,' she said. 'Ocean has had more than enough of people doing things to her and I believe you.'

Panna covered her face with her hands. I could see that she was struggling to pull herself together, not burst into tears.

'I'm sorry,' I said. 'I'm sorry if I have brought any trouble at all into your lives when you didn't ask for it. And I'm sorry for making friends with your boys, I really shouldn't have. We're fine, we're sorting this and you don't need to get involved. Only one thing I want to ask. Please, please keep it to yourselves. We'll go, we'll move on, we'll be fine.'

Panna was still sitting quietly on the floor next to Ocean, holding her hand. I couldn't tell what she was thinking from her expression.

I started to speak.

'Ssh,' Panna said. 'I'm thinking.'

We sat in silence for a half minute or so. Even Ocean didn't make any noise, although she seemed very comfortable.

'I've had trouble in my own family,' Panna said. 'I want to help, and I can't walk away, but I'm trusting you not to get my boys into anything they can't handle. No police, no violence, you know what I'm saying.'

I did. And I was relieved to have her on board. But I'd spent long enough with Jed to understand that things might be harder for her. I might just be able to pull white privilege and play the 'little old confused lady' and get some kind of benefit from it. I wasn't sure but I thought it might work if it had to. But these nice people? They wouldn't have a leg to stand on. I knew that, and I should never have got them involved.

I stood up. I wanted to leave, I really did. It wasn't right and I knew that. I would go back to London and leave these people alone. I was almost at the door when the boys burst in. They cheered at the sight of Ocean, as if they had scored a goal. Ocean clapped too, and Noah swept her up and danced around the room with her. Ocean smiled and tried to clap, even though she was clinging on round Noah's neck.

I might have found it more difficult to leave her if she hadn't been so very happy but she was. She looked as though she had always wanted to be there, smiling, surrounded by toys and fuss.

'I've got this,' Panna said. 'You go, sort it all out, whatever you're doing. If she's unhappy at all I promise I'll ring you. Go on, spoil yourselves. Be ladies that lunch and next time maybe I'll come with you. She's gonna be safe and she's going to have a good time and you don't need to worry about that. You do what you have to do and then get back here and don't worry.'

It was the strangest feeling, leaving Ocean behind. She had become the main part of my life in such a short time that I kept looking behind me, sure that I'd forgotten something. This is what it would be like, I realised, if I chose to leave the whole thing behind. If I checked out completely. Five weeks more or less now until my decision and I was no nearer.

We spoke of everything, that day. Despite my fears, it was good to show Annie Margate. We knew that Ocean was happy and that she was being well looked after, and neither of us could stop talking. I guessed Annie had been very lonely, but I hadn't realised that I had too. She was easy to be with. She loved everything. She commented on the harbour, the seagulls, the old town, the clothes the young people were wearing and every single thing she saw. We ate a burger made from jackfruit at an outside table in the wind and Annie looked happy as we discussed endlessly what to do next. By the time we had finished we had the beginnings of a goodish plan. A plan, anyway. We were going to go straight to the heart of the problem, and find Ocean's mum. What else could we do if we cared about Ocean?

'If we could ask her, ask Ocean what she really wanted, she would want things sorted out with her mum,' Annie said.

I agreed. However much she was enjoying her time with us, we should try to make her life perfect. And perfect would mean her mum with her, and him, that man, out of the way. I was tired and scared and this was the only glimmer of hope I'd had since the whole thing started. Maybe now I'd be able to get back to my deadline, concentrate on what I wanted to do.

'We've got a chance, now,' I said.

'To Ocean and her mum,' Annie said and we clinked glasses.

I was still scared, lord knows there was enough to feel scared about, but I felt clearer, and less alone. I was even a tiny bit glad to be alive and helping someone.

'I don't even know if jackfruits have reached the Highlands,' Annie said. 'Or where they grow, but there's people I know at home who wouldn't dream of eating anything that didn't sail up the Clyde. I didnae sail up the Clyde on a water biscuit, my dad used to say if he thought anyone was trying to get the better of him. We had no idea what it meant.'

I loved the sound of her chatter. It seemed worlds away from the difficulties we were facing. Normal, I thought, normal, normal normal. Maybe there is a happily ever after for me.

CHAPTER FIFTEEN

Margate

Jackson was astonished at how much fun there was to be had in being with a baby, and almost equal amounts of hard work. She needed to be picked up, put down, cuddled, not cuddled, consulted, entertained, read to and fed, and that was before he had even considered her nap. Noah was a great help, and so was Panna but Jackson thought he should do most of it himself so that Panna could conserve her strength and Noah could try to do some schoolwork.

The first difficult thing was deciding what Ocean might eat. The ladies hadn't included that in the manual, which Jackson thought was strange. Panna suggested porridge with sugar but Jackson knew that sugar was bad for babies. Bad for everyone, in fact, so they gave her a snack of toast and yogurt before putting her down for a nap.

They moved the mattress from Noah's bed onto the floor of the living room and Ocean slept there quite happily. Jackson and Noah stayed on chairs in the living room and watched her.

'You don't need to,' Panna had said. 'You'll hear her quick enough if she cries,' but both boys thought that would be negligent. Noah wasn't sure why he thought it but Jackson had clear memories of a tiny baby Noah screaming for what seemed like hours and hours. He could remember being told to go away when he tried to help, and he could remember how horrible it was when the screams turned into sad hiccups. That was not going to happen to this baby, not on Jackson's watch.

Jackson must have fallen asleep. He woke up to the sound of happy gurgling, and Noah speaking quietly.

'You can't wake up big bro, not yet,' he said. 'That dude has got a lot on his plate, and he takes things hard, you know what I'm saying?'

Jackson kept his eyes closed.

'Little sister bro, I'm telling you that if there's a damn thing to worry about, that big bro will worry about it. He thinks that the minute you go outside the door, there's tigers and lions and fierce dogs and everything. But look at you and Philip.'

Jackson opened his eye just a crack, enough to see that the dog was sitting on the floor next to Ocean, while she was happily pulling on his ears. Her face was covered in pink stuff that Jackson guessed was strawberry yogurt.

'Not scary at all,' Noah said.

By early afternoon, it was as though the baby belonged with them. They fell into a kind of routine dictated by her as if they had planned it. Jackson realised that he hadn't thought about the bustling uni flat or the quiet lecture theatres even once all morning. There's other stuff you can do, he thought and it was as though someone had shouted it in his face. There really were other things he could do with his life and he was doing some of them right now.

'I need to stop thinking the grass is greener,' he said to the dog when it followed him into his bedroom.

The first cloud on Jackson's horizon appeared when he took Philip the dog out for a quick walk after lunch. They had agreed that it would be best to take Ocean out later, so they had opened the balcony doors to give her some fresh air.

'Back home,' Panna had said, 'babies didn't know what a roof was. All day out in the sunshine, never cried.'

Jackson had looked at Noah and winked. Noah smiled back, which Jackson thought was a great sign. They had stopped gently poking fun at Panna when she became so unwell, because her eulogies about back home didn't seem so funny once it looked as though she would never go back. Maybe they could go back to normal now, and maybe Panna would see her home again, Jackson thought. Maybe she really was getting better, and Ocean was a miracle baby.

The beach was a little busier than usual because the weather was getting warmer. In some ways more people was safer for the dog, because there was less chance that he would stand out. On the other hand, it meant much more stress for Jackson because he had to scour all the faces for ones that might recognise Phil and know that he didn't really belong with him. Without looking as though he was looking, which was difficult.

He was almost at the wall that runs down the beach and into the sea before he saw him. Up by the beach huts and standing very still. Still like a hunter, that was the phrase that came into Jackson's head. He looked scruffy, just as Noah had described him, and Phil the dog moved round to the other side of Jackson, still by his side but walking more slowly now and looking round a lot. Exactly as a human would behave if they were being followed by a scary person, Jackson thought. He turned back towards home, trying to look nonchalant and keep his eyes to the front. It was very difficult not to look behind him to see if he was being followed. He managed it successfully all the way to the steps up to the flat before he cracked. He turned round and waved, as if he had seen a friend far away on the beach, and the man was there, right behind him and staring. Philip the dog had shrunk in to his leg and was whimpering. The man whistled, and Jackson held his breath but Philip didn't move. He walked away towards the flat but ducked around to the side so that he couldn't be seen going in the front way. Noah did not need to know this, he thought. Not with all the excitement about the baby.

There was no knock at the door that afternoon and Jackson began to relax. Maybe it was his imagination, he thought, he had always had a reputation in the family for imagining things. Over cautious, that's what he called it. There were so many things that could go wrong after all, and surely it was better to preempt them by at least being aware. Especially after what happened in Bromley.

Jackson had been fourteen and a little lost when it happened. Lost because he didn't realise yet that he was clever, so he hadn't tapped in to friendships with the other clever kids. He was still hanging out with the crew from his estate, and they were nice enough except for a new kid had come on the scene. He didn't go to school and he seemed much older. He had a weird influence over the others, who were behaving really differently. They didn't call it a gang, not then and maybe not now for all Jackson knew. He wasn't in touch with any of them any more. But it was something, a club or a society but something that he clearly did not belong to. Fats, that's what the name of the kid with the charisma was called, and Jackson thought that was messed up right from the start. Obviously he'd never said anything about his name, but he had found it difficult to actually say it, to address him by it. Not least because he'd seen some hapless year eight kid get slamdunked to the floor for calling Fats by his name. 'Are you saying I'm fat?' Fats had said to the scared boy before he knocked him down. Which was unfair on several counts, especially as, if Fats had another name, he'd kept it to himself.

Maybe something about Jackson annoyed Fats, or maybe it was nothing more than Jackson's natural reluctance to join a tight-knit group. Maybe it was just that Jackson had picked up the year eight boy and helped him to brush himself down before he ran home in tears. Jackson thought it could even have been that Fats really did want them to be, if not friends, then comrades in some way. Comrades in petty crime. Whatever the reason, it was quite a beating. Two boys whom Jackson had known since he was at nursery held him down while Fats knocked out one of his front teeth with a screwdriver. He might have knocked out more, he certainly seemed to enjoy it, but Panna arrived back at the flats with Noah earlier than usual because he had a toothache. Jackson could see the neatness of this even as he lay in the stairwell covered in blood and spit. Even despite his poor mouth and his arm, which was broken.

'We saved you, Jax,' Noah had said.

Jackson hated more than anything that Noah had seen him like that. He didn't know how to explain it to his brother but he knew that Panna must have spoken to him about it because the awkward questions he had been expecting didn't come. In fact Noah didn't mention it at all. But, Jackson thought now, Noah had been extra thoughtful for a long time, and said almost nothing about Jackson's habit of checking stairwells and doorways. He had never made a joke about it.

Ocean was having her afternoon nap when the second cloud appeared on their horizon. A much bigger cloud this time, big and grey and terrifying. If Ocean hadn't been tired out by her happy day, Jackson thought later, if she had been up and crying, or even just whingeing a little, things could have been very different. The flat was quiet though, not even a TV on.

'I think she likes quiet when she wants to sleep,' Noah had said.

Jackson and Panna smiled at each other and Jackson felt happy, properly happy for the first time in ages. He thought that he might have imagined the man on the beach and he couldn't imagine anything better than sitting reading with Panna, Noah and Phil while Ocean snuffled in her makeshift bed. If that makes me pathetic, he thought, then so be it. So the sound of someone running up the communal stairs seemed even more shocking. Noah went immediately to stand in front of the sleeping baby, the dog by his side as if they'd made a plan earlier. He held his finger to his lips but Jackson and Panna didn't need telling. They all knew that the footsteps did not belong to Virginia or Annie.

They could hear a hammering on Virginia's door and some menacing shouting. Panna put her arms on the side of the chair as though she was going to get up, and Jackson and Noah both signalled her to stay put.

'They're not there,' Noah whispered. 'We can't do anything so just stay where you are. Let's hope Ocean stays asleep.'

Jackson felt proud of Noah for being so brave but the responsibility was on him, he knew that. Even though he hated confrontation, it was his responsibility, fair and square.

'No drama, please,' he said. 'I'm going to go and see if there's anything I can do. Don't worry, I'm not going to be in danger or anything, I'll just ask if I can help. Then at least I can see who it is, and maybe tell the ladies or something.'

The man was still shouting and banging and Jackson made a mental note to ask Noah what he thought about expectations of gender as he climbed the stairs. Truth was, his legs were shaking so either he was a gigantic coward and absolutely unmanly, or all the stuff he'd ever been told about stepping up and being brave was absolute nonsense. Maybe it was all a confidence trick to persuade men to go to war, fight each other and not the system.

Jackson tried hard not to slow down as he reached the man at the door of Virginia's flat. That would show that he was nervous, and make him vulnerable. The man was breathing heavily, and Jackson wondered if he was completely well. There weren't that many steps, after all.

'Hi,' he said. 'I live downstairs, and I heard you come up. Erm, she's not there, the lady who lives there.'

'Is she not?' the man said. 'Did I ask you that? Did I say anything at all to you, in fact? Do you even speak English? Are you some kind of crazed neighbourhood watch cadet?'

His shoulders hunched and he seemed to be poised, like one of those banned American dogs about to pounce, Jackson thought. He was so horrified at the possibility that this panting pit bull of a man was looking for the two gentle ladies that he forgot to feel scared for a moment or two. He shrugged his shoulders and turned to go back down.

'Pardon me I'm sure,' he said.

He was aware that it was not only a childish response but a risky one but the alternative was to stay and fight, and that was not an option.

'Hang on a minute,' said the man.

His face was glistening with sweat. Jackson thought he definitely looked unwell, and as if he might topple over at any minute.

'Have you seen a baby?' he said. 'Ocean, she's called, and a fucking old witch of a bitch kidnapped her. I know she did. I'm her dad.'

OK, OK, time for a reality check, Jackson thought. Missing. He doesn't know her mum asked Virginia, or he's not admitting it. And he looks crazed, Virginia never said there was a dad and I don't care if he is, he would still be the worst person to look after Ocean properly. So number one, I don't want to get any of us into trouble, but number two, I'm not letting him anywhere near that child.

'No,' he said.

'You needn't worry,' the man continued. 'Nothing to do with any of your lot, for once. So you can tell me if you've seen anything.'

My lot, thought Jackson. Brown people, Black people. My lot, people like Noah and Panna and all the other decent people I know. Nothing to do with them, for once, my arse. Jackson was determined that the baby he had left asleep downstairs was not going to have anything to do with this horrible man. He would assume it was lies for as long as he could. It was much easier that way, and he would be able to carry it off with a bit of a swagger. Keep her quiet downstairs, he thought, please stay asleep for a little while longer.

'I'm sorry, I haven't seen anything. A baby? I'd have heard if there was anything. These flats have terrible soundproofing.'

Jackson wondered if that was overdoing it slightly. He was aware that his voice sounded slightly more middle class than usual, as if his subconscious was trying to show this man that he wasn't a piece of rubbish. There's no point showing him that you're as good as he is, Panna said in a little voice inside his head, because he doesn't care and he won't listen. He's not going to suddenly realise that all his life he's thought one way about our people but gosh you're different. It doesn't happen that way. So when you meet a racist, don't hang about. Don't try and change their mind. Get.the.hell.out, that's what you gotta do.

Jackson had heard the lecture a thousand times, maybe even more, so it flashed through his head quickly and he recognised it as true. He turned to go back downstairs and the man grabbed the back of his collar. It was an odd move, and Jackson felt for a moment as if he was in a film.

'I believe you,' the man said. He spoke right up close to Jackson's ear, and Jackson could smell his breath. It smelled sour and sickly, as if the last thing he'd eaten was decaying roadkill. 'Just don't go anywhere,' he added. 'I won't be far away.'

PART IV

CHAPTER SIXTEEN

By the time Ocean woke up from her afternoon nap he'd definitely gone. Noah lay flat on the balcony for a while, watching to make sure he left and didn't come back. You could see right up the beach from underneath the balcony fence but Jackson still couldn't catch his breath. In through the nose, out through the mouth, he told himself, over and over, but it wasn't working too well. He had just about held himself together in front of Noah and Panna, but he knew he hadn't fooled either of them. He wasn't even sorry, because they needed to know. That man was bad news, and especially for Ocean. And they couldn't cover everything, that was Jackson's worry. There was always the street side of the building, although he didn't mention it in case it freaked Noah out.

'Ding dong, the nasty man is gone,' Noah sang to Ocean and she giggled.

Jackson opened his mouth to tell Noah not to make light of it, or maybe not to even mention it in front of the baby. He wasn't sure which but it only took one glare from Panna for him to change his mind about saying anything. She tapped the side of her nose as a further explanation, which infuriated Jackson. He imagined for one moment how satisfying it would be to kick a wall, or punch through a door.

'You did good,' Panna said. 'You were right to avoid any confrontation. It leaves you with feelings though, doesn't it? Do you think a run would help? I can manage here.'

A run was just what Jackson needed, he thought, but he felt ashamed of himself for wanting to get out.

'Nah,' he said. 'I'll make some tea. I've texted them and they said they'd be back soon.'

Noah was taking turns with Ocean at blowing on an old harmonica when they arrived. Jackson felt angry with them for exposing Noah and Panna to such danger, and he could tell that Panna felt the same by the set of her jaw. Panna's cross mouth, Noah used to call it when he was little. Panna stood up with her hands on her hips.

'I think we need to talk again, ladies,' she said. 'We had a visit earlier, well, you did, to be precise, but Jackson here, he's a good boy so he went to ask if he could help. And it wasn't Ocean's mum wanting to make a better choice, I can tell you that.'

Virginia turned even more pale than usual and clutched the back of the armchair. Jackson thought that she might faint. Noah opened his mouth. Jackson knew there was a strong possibility that it was going to be something inappropriate about not knowing a white lady could get whiter so he leapt in to stop him.

'It's OK,' he said. 'He's gone, we watched him walk away down the beach. But he was angry.'

'Is she really ready to leave him?' Panna asked. 'How does he know the address?'

Virginia was about to speak when Noah cut in.

'I know I'm only a kid,' he said. 'And I know I don't know much about babies, children, that sort of thing. But I'm not sure this is good for Ocean, us talking in front of her, I mean. It will go into somewhere in her brain and this article I was reading online said that she'll be trying to reach the memory and process it for the rest of her life, imagine that. So I'm gonna take her in the bedroom even though I really, really want to know everything too but I want to help her more. And that's what we all should be thinking about, like not so much about our own selves and more about her.'

Noah left the room, holding hands with Ocean who seemed willing to follow him anywhere. He shut the door carefully and Jackson wondered if they all felt as if they'd been trumped by a child, because he certainly did.

'OK,' Virginia said.

Jackson thought she was going to cry. He could see how hard it was for her to speak.

'I'm so sorry,' she said. 'I should have said more about how dangerous he might be, and how downright bad. I didn't know that he would get the address, I suppose I could have guessed. I'm so, so sorry.'

'We all underestimated him,' Panna said. 'But you are the only one who knew how bad he is.'

'I think I'd sort of blocked it out,' Virginia said.

Jackson watched Panna gearing herself up to take charge of the situation. She had been strong all his life, but especially when there was a crisis, like when he ran to her with Noah or after the Fats episode. She was still strong, even now that she was so unwell. She had never been the kind of person that you told less than the truth to, and he was sure the ladies knew that too.

'OK,' Virginia said again and this time she told them more about how scared Steve had made her feel. 'I thought it might be just me,' she said. 'I've been so caught up in the rights and wrongs, whether I should have brought her here. Plus I think I've tried not to think about him.'

'I understand that,' Jackson said. He didn't explain, but he knew he'd managed almost to block out memories in the past. Fats for one, and he was working on the policemen.

Jackson wondered why he had ever thought that adults had the whole life thing sussed. It was hard to think that Ocean had caused this amount of trouble, and to realise how much danger she was in.

Virginia's voice became louder, as if the more she said, the more she felt sure of herself and able to claim her actions.

'I'm sorry to have got you involved,' she said when she had finished. 'That's the thing I regret the most, as well as not getting involved earlier. And I'm glad I told you everything, I really am, but I definitely think it would be best for you to walk away, leave us to it. You've helped loads already, I honestly don't need anything else.'

Panna shook her head. 'That man was bad, and we want to help you,' she said. 'You're doing the right thing by that baby and I can't look away. But we have to keep these boys safe.'

'You're on,' Virginia said.

'We choose this too,' Jackson said. Noah shouted, 'Yes indeed' from the other room and Jackson felt his eyes turn damp.

'We have to help the wee girl,' Annie said and then there

was another round of hugging that made Jackson feel queasy so he went to check on Noah and Ocean.

'Jeez,' Noah said. 'Old women, bro, what are they like?'

For once, Jackson had to agree with him. Noah came out of the bedroom carrying Ocean, who looked as if it was the happiest day she could imagine.

'Old lady bros,' Noah said and Jackson winced. 'Old lady bros, we can do it, even with that man lurking around. You've got us on your side now and I have great ideas. All the time. It's like, I'm famous for it.'

'Well,' Virginia said.

Jackson had to give her credit for responding to Noah as if he was a grown man, rather than a small eleven-year-old.

'I'm afraid I'm rather stuck,' she said. 'Annie and I have talked and talked all morning but we can't think of a way out. I'm wondering whether to give up. Give her up, and explain what's happened to her. They have to believe me, I've got the lanyard she was wearing and I'll show them her scars and also they'd only need to talk to that man for five minutes to see what he's like.'

No one said anything for a moment but the silence wasn't a happy one. There was palpable tension in it and Jackson hoped that Noah wouldn't feel tempted to fill it. He tried to shoot him a warning look but Noah didn't see it. Chose not to see it, Jackson thought.

'OK,' Noah said. 'That's plan Z, giving her up and hoping for the best. I'd like to hear plan A, but also I might need to point out that at times like this, a person needs a plan B as well. At least.'

Jackson had to admit that Noah was right, but Virginia

looked worried and there was a silence after he'd spoken. Virginia twisted her hands and looked at Ocean.

'There's one thing we talked about,' Annie said.

'Well, yes,' Virginia said. 'I'm not sure, but there is one plan that might work. And we need to act quickly. If he goes to the police it might not be difficult at all for them to find out where I am. They might even be on their way now. I need to talk to her mum, that's the plan, and convince her, that's the best way and the only way.'

Everyone looked towards the door at the mention of police, except for Ocean, who was brushing the sheep's head with a tiny hairbrush. Virginia looked as though she was going to cry. Jackson didn't blame her, he couldn't see a happy ending either.

'So we need to go and see her, and I get that,' Virginia said after blowing her nose. 'But I think we are going to look so obvious travelling around. I mean, we talked about this, but do I need to disguise myself? Dress as a man or something? I don't think that would fool anybody, do you?'

Noah made a snorting noise and Jackson realised that he was laughing.

'I'm sorry I'm sorry,' Noah said, 'only I was just thinking about dressing Ocean up as a little old man too, and it was honestly funny but I know it's not appropriate.'

Just like that, Jackson thought, the tension was broken and everyone smiled.

'Do you think that the mum will speak to you?' Panna said. 'Because she's going to feel very embarrassed, ashamed even that she's got herself into this predicament.'

'She will,' Annie said. 'She'll be defensive as hell, and she'll hate us for helping her but we have to try.'

'I know her a little bit,' said Virginia. 'And the thing that gives me hope is, she really, really loves Ocean. And she's in danger herself, don't forget that. She's hardly older than your Jackson. So it could work. Do we have a choice?'

It was plain to Jackson that Virginia wasn't at all sure herself.

'When you're out of choices, you have to watch your step and keep putting one foot in front of the other,' Panna said. She sounded tired. 'Is there any other way? Talk to her first, that would be so good if it worked. Let's try that. We're here for you, the boys and me.'

'Thank you,' Virginia said.

'We'll do it right, we'll make it work,' Annie said.

Jackson wondered if Annie was completely sane. She sounded so excited, as if they were planning a holiday or a group entry to a singing competition.

'You can leave her here,' Panna said. 'The boys and I are in it now, no going back. And it will be much easier not to take her with you. And she's at home here, just look at her.'

Jackson remembered the feeling he had always had as a child when Panna came to the rescue. It had made him feel warm, as if he was being swept up in a soft blanket, and he felt that now. He hoped Ocean did too, and he could see that the ladies did. There were more meaningful glances flying around the three of them than Jackson could keep track of.

'Thank you so, so much,' Virginia said.

'It shouldn't take long to make contact with her mum, talk to her about returning Ocean home under the right conditions,' Annie said. 'Think how she must be missing her.'

Jackson thought there was a great deal wrong with trying

to take her back to the place where she had been hurt and he could see that Noah agreed, but he was also aware that the women really loved her. They wouldn't want her to be hurt so he had to trust them. They must know what they were doing. And Panna agreed, that must mean they were definitely right.

'Little people should be with their mums if they possibly can be, and that's what we have to hold on to, isn't it?' Virginia said. 'She's not a bad mum, she's just fallen in with a bad man. I think she'll be able to understand that if she thinks about it, after all, she asked me to take her baby. Look after her. Keep her safe.'

Jackson could see that although Virginia was tired, she was right. It made him feel sad for Noah. Noah would have loved a caring mum. A mum of any kind, to be honest, so the ladies were probably right. There was something else though. A twinge of excitement, if Jackson was honest. Annie wasn't the only one. He was going to have a chance to be a hero, and to help save Ocean, and that was something worth doing.

When the talking was over, Panna persuaded Virginia and Annie to bed down on the sofa bed in case the man came back to the flat upstairs. They were leaving early to catch the train.

'You know what?' Noah said. 'Having her here is a privilege, so thank you for letting us help.'

Ocean stood next to him and said, 'Ta,' when he'd finished, like his little shadow.

They were asleep in seconds.

'You sure we've done the right thing?' Panna said, when he took herbal tea in to her bedroom a little later.

It was probably the first time that she had ever asked his advice, Jackson thought. He liked it, but at the same time it made him feel unsettled. Why would he know? Did anyone ever remember that he was still a teenager? He shrugged and then realised how rude that was. What was the matter with him, for goodness' sake? This poor woman and the dear little baby were in big trouble, serious grown-up trouble, and all Jackson could think about was himself. He was ashamed.

CHAPTER SEVENTEEN

It was a plan that was fraught with difficulties and I could see that clearly, we both could but we didn't feel we had a choice. I had to do the absolute best I could to try to make Ocean's mum see sense and get them back together. Together without that damn man. Steve, such an unsuitable name for a monster. I knew Cate cared about her baby, and I was sure that the best thing for both of them was to be together. Ocean was the person who mattered most in all of this. I had to do the right thing so that I could get my life back and choose whether to live it or not, it was that stark.

I was going to offer her money, that was the beginning and the end of my plan to persuade her. It's all very well saying that money doesn't matter, we used to say that in the Seventies and I guess we really believed it but it's not true. Money makes all the difference in the world. It gives you choices, and Annie and I had agreed that was what Ocean's mum needed more than anything else. I was lucky. Jed and I had been saving our money for William for years now but the truth was, he didn't need it. He didn't need it and I suspected that he didn't want if either.

'I think he sees it as a millstone, if truth be told,' I said.

Annie dragged herself away from the flat Kent countryside unrolling outside the train window.

'Aye,' she said. 'And to be fair, you know it does come with some obligations, doesn't it? Money always does. He'd think he should stay closer, or visit more often, something like that. I mean he sounds like a nice young man, so how's he gonna take the money and run, leaving you all alone? He wants to stay where he is, from the sound of things, and I couldn't blame him. Sydney. Bondi. Kangaroos and koalas. What's not to like?'

It was harsh but it was true. So I would give William's inheritance to Ocean's mum, to try to buy a better future for the little girl. For both of them really, and for me, because I needed this to stop. It was going to be difficult to get close to her without being seen by that dreadful man, but then I had Annie to help me with that.

'Is this really London Town?' Annie said as we pulled into Bromley South. 'It's so busy and bustling, I never thought I'd really be here.'

I didn't feel it was the time to explain to her that Bromley is actually in Kent, even though it's a London borough. And that the station was rather quiet compared to a busy one like King's Cross. I'd make sure that she saw some real London after we'd done our job, I promised myself. There was something very endearing about how excited she was.

'Twelve miles to Trafalgar Square,' she said, looking at her phone as we changed platforms. 'Only a wee step and a hop. We could be there for coffee, imagine. Walking down the Strand and crossing the river Thames.'

We ran through the plan again on the train to Crofton Park. Annie was going to knock on the door and speak to Cate. She had a fail-safe plan that would definitely tempt her from her house and into a local café, where I would be waiting. I had to trust her. I was out of options, especially now that Steve had actually turned up. I trusted her, and I wanted this all to stop.

'I've been waiting all my life to start living,' she had said. 'You can be sure I'm not going to mess it up now. I feel like I've been in the wings for a very long time, and I'm going to be, well, not actually centre stage, but on the edge of the action. Helping the wee girl. Making a difference. Imagine that!'

I hoped we weren't making a mistake as we went into the café. This had to work. We chose a greasy spoon rather than any of the trendier cafés where people had more time to look about them. We had already agreed on that. I had dressed as inconspicuously as possible, in jeans and an old oversized hoodie of William's. As disguises went it was pretty good because people hearing the words, old lady, never think of trainers and jeans. Always flowery skirts and curly hair, even though hardly anyone I knew had that style. Except for Annie, obviously. Noah wanted me to wear a false moustache but we ignored him and went for an unremarkable, androgynous look instead, and I felt wonderfully invisible in the café.

I ordered a coffee and sat in the corner. There was a tabloid newspaper on the table and I opened it randomly and pretended to read. My hands were shaking too much to hold it. I don't know what I read before they returned, but I was grateful that they were back quickly.

'It's you,' Cate said as she sat down. 'It's you, I didn't know. Where is she, where's my baby?'

Cate looked as if she had aged a couple of years in the last week. Her hair was dirty and her mouth was quivering. I wanted more than anything to put my arms around her and comfort her as if she were Ocean. They really were very alike.

'Where is she?' Cate said again. 'Is she OK? Is she hurt?'

Cate's voice was rising and a large man buying toast at the counter turned to look at us.

'Sshhh,' I said. 'She's fine, she's gorgeous, she's a sweet little girl. She misses you, of course she does, but apart from that she's doing fine.'

Cate started to cry.

'Is she sleeping OK? Has she still got her lamby and her dog? Is she eating? Is she eating OK? Drinking enough fluids? Are you leaving a light on?' she said. It was impossible not to feel sorry for her. I was nearly in tears myself when Annie stepped in.

'Can you stop that right now?' she said. She spoke quietly but there was a stern note in her voice I hadn't heard before. She gave me a meaningful look and I remembered that we had agreed that I would be good cop to her bad. It seemed like the safest way round seeing as I was the baby's carer and Cate obviously trusted me a little anyway.

'Sit down,' Annie said. 'And talk to my friend here. We need to work something out. I'll get your tea, with a wee sugar in it for the shock.'

Annie went over to the counter and I think it was nerves, but I couldn't help giggling at the difference between Annie's first two sentences and the third. It was OK though, because it seemed to relax Cate a little bit.

'I don't know how long we've got,' I said. 'So I'm going to get right down to it. OK?'

She nodded.

'Ocean is fine. She's eating, she's sleeping, she has a few more words and she's happy, although she misses you like mad. But there are marks on her, Cate, she's hurt and you must be aware of that. Someone has hurt her, and hurt her badly. We can't let that happen again. I want her to be home with you, that's the right place for her but she can't come home to you while you're with him. It's not safe and it's not fair on her.'

Cate bit her lip and nodded. I felt so sorry for her that I could hardly carry on. I wanted to hug her and take her home with her baby and give them both a happy life. Do what Jed had done for me, I suppose, pass it on. Everything was riding on this conversation, though, and I knew that even good cops need to be firm sometimes.

'It's no good nodding,' I said. 'What are you going to do? You wanted me to keep her safe and I have done, she's healing up nicely and I can't go home but I don't mind that. I don't mind but I need to see where we're heading, how it's going to pan out. How we are going to move on from here in the best way for everyone. For you and Ocean mainly but for me, too. A way of her getting a happy ending. I'm old and I don't care much about myself any more, but I do care about her. Jesus, Cate, there's burn marks for fuck's sake, cigarette burns on her little hands. Her eyes are bruised and her shoulder has probably been fractured. How could you have let that happen?'

She did start to cry at that, and I wished I'd been more gentle.

'OK, OK, let's calm down,' I said. 'I know you didn't want to hurt her, and that's why you gave her to me. Lent her to me, really. I'm not trying to keep her. Lord knows I'm too old for all this. It was a good thing to do, honestly, a sensible thing to give her to me to get her out of the firing line for a bit, but jeez, Steve showed up at my place and that changed everything. Did you know he was coming? Did you tell him where we were? I didn't see him but he's a proper loose cannon and very scary for anyone he comes across. I can't take that kind of risk. I was going to leave it for a bit, let things calm down but I can't do that any more. Ocean has already been away from you for too long and we owe it to her to sort things out.'

Cate nodded and again I could see Ocean in her. They both had a way of crinkling up their eyes. It made me want to hug her again so I stirred my coffee instead.

'I want him to go, I really do,' Cate said. 'I can promise you that. He saw the address you left. He's threatened all sorts of things if I dump him though, and I've seen what he's capable of.'

She rolled up her left sleeve and put her arm on the table. It was covered in scars, old ones and new ones, all intersecting and crossing like the lines on a busy railway junction.

'He puts them there because if anyone ever saw them, if I showed anyone, he would just say I'm a self-harmer. And that I harm Ocean as well, and she shouldn't be with me.'

She started crying again and I felt as though I was rapidly losing any control I'd had over the situation. A couple of other people had looked in our direction and it was clear that shows of female emotion are not commonplace in greasy spoon cafés.

'Let's go for a wee walk,' Annie said. 'There's a cemetery across the road and no one will notice us there.'

I wondered for a moment how Annie was so on the ball when she had never even been to London before, while I was sitting like a lump in a hooded sweatshirt, trying to decide what would happen next.

It was a good call. The cemetery was the right place for us. It was empty and crumbling, and the trees and dandelions made me feel much safer. We found an old stone bench and sat down with our cardboard cups as though we were ordinary women on a morning stroll. I wished we were.

'Right,' Annie said. 'Bottom line time. We want to help you, we do. I'm sorry I had to threaten you back there, but I couldn't think of another way to persuade you to come with us. I want to help you and your wee girl, honest I do. Virginia, you take over, it's your offer.'

'OK,' I said.

I wanted to sound as purposeful as she did, but I knew my voice was shaking. 'I've got some money. It's not a bribe, I don't mean that, but it's yours if you can get away from him and make a life for yourself and Ocean. We'll help you, you don't need to be scared, we will be there all the way. I've got enough to get you a little flat somewhere out of London, and keep you going for a bit until you can get a job and a nursery. I'll help you sort things out. We can look for something in Margate if you think that would be safe. You could go anywhere, Cate.'

Cate's face was amazing. I had read about it, but I'd never actually seen so many emotions race across a person's face before. I could see them all on her. Hope, that was the biggest one. Hope and fear and longing and something else. Something I couldn't identify until Annie spoke up.

'If you're thinking about taking the money and keeping the man anyway, you'd better think again,' she said. 'Just in case you were thinking he could be cured, or go to rehab or anything like that. The stakes are too high.'

'He has got a lot of issues,' Cate said. 'He's fine until he has a drink, honestly.'

'Do you know what?' Annie said before I had a chance to speak. 'I believe you. Honest I do. You're a lovely wee girlie and I believe that you saw some good in him. But I need to tell you this, alcohol never made anyone hurt a little defenceless baby in a spiteful, calculated way. I could write it down for you if you want, you could keep it as a wee motto. Alcohol makes a person make bad choices, but we're talking about choosing a kebab over a fruit salad, not making a choice to stub your cigarette out on a tiny person who can't even talk back yet.'

It was harsh but true, and I could see that Cate knew that as well. There was silence for a few moments and then she said, 'This is so kind. Why are you doing it? Why are you even bothered with me?'

I looked at Annie, and I could see that she wasn't prepared for the question either. Why were we doing it? I could see that she wanted me to answer.

'We're old,' I said. 'We're old and some things don't work so well for us, but one thing that does work is, we still care. We still care about Ocean, and we still care about you.'

'Ocean is my wee stake in the future,' said Annie, sounding like the least bad cop in the world. 'I'm going to make sure she has a better life than I did. I want to send her forward with love.'

'And I want to keep her alive,' I said in case the whole thing was getting too soppy.

I felt more than uneasy. Something was definitely wrong.

Cate was so unhappy, and yet she hadn't fallen on our suggestions immediately like I'd imagined she might. I glanced at Annie and I could see from the way that she was biting her lip that she wasn't sure what was going on either.

'I want to get away from him,' she said, finally. 'I want to live with my Ocean and be safe and happy. But I think he is going to change. I honestly think he might. He said he would go to these anger management classes. He said he wants to be different. So if you could just hold on to her for a little bit longer, I think it will be fine.'

I really didn't know where to start with that idea. There were so many things wrong with it I couldn't even begin to explain. I was aware of the arthritis in my spine in a way that I hadn't been earlier, in the excitement, and I stared at the floor.

'I have never heard so much nonsense and wild blether in my life,' Annie said.

Her bad cop routine was picking up. It was clear that she was a force to be reckoned with.

'You're gonna die if you stay with him,' Annie said. 'You're gonna die and so is that dear girl. You know that in your heart, don't you?'

She looked at Cate with the most intent and specific stare I had ever seen. She had lived experience of something like this, I was sure of it. I was also sure that we hadn't managed to persuade Cate, and I was scared for all of us.

'Please,' I said.

She was already standing up, she had her eye on something we couldn't understand and I realised with a feeling that felt like a trickle of cold water that we had lost her.

'Ocean is so sweet,' I said.

I knew it probably wouldn't help but I wouldn't be able to live with myself if I didn't try to speak up for her. 'She can say, sheep, now and she puts the little sheep in a car and wheels it across the floor. She's made friends with a dog and she loves some Swedish picture books we've been reading to her. She can point to different things and name them, cup, dinner, window, seagull, jam and all sorts of things. She puts the little people and the cars to bed and covers them with blankets made out of tissues. What I'm trying to say is, she's a real person, with thoughts and feelings and fears. She's going to grow up into a girl who goes to school and writes stories and draws pictures and has friends. Has a whole life. And you're going to spoil that, because of this stupid, violent man. And you don't have to, you don't.'

There was silence for a moment and then Cate stood up.

'Look after her for me,' she said. 'I think you may need to move her from Margate. Give her my love, and tell her I'm sorry.'

CHAPTER EIGHTEEN

I couldn't speak for a moment after Cate left. It wasn't that I had nothing to say, I had lots, but I felt totally winded, as if someone had lifted me up by one foot and slammed me down on the floor.

'You're probably feeling a wee bit like that baby feels right now,' Annie said.

For the first time in a while, I wished I was alone. Or maybe not alone, but with Jed. Jed would have known that the best thing to do would be to give me time to mull things over. Virginia's thinking time, he used to call it. I remembered hearing him explain to William that sometimes I needed a moment to reset.

I had felt this winded before, at least twice, and afterwards the world had never completely righted itself, never gone back to an orderly spin through the galaxy. I thought of it now, of the first time it had happened. I remembered William's graduation, and being on the lawn behind Goldsmiths College with a glass of warm wine. He'd got a first in drama, and we were so damn proud. We had been talking ever since about all the things he might do with it. The world was his lobster, that's what Jed kept saying.

'He might get a part in a West End show,' Jed had said, 'and then he might want to live at home for a while, just until he's sorted.'

I could hear the hope in his voice and it nearly broke me.

'Of course', he'd said quickly, 'it would probably be better for him to live somewhere else, I just meant that he could have home as a fall-back position, in case he needed it.'

I remember squeezing his hand, and telling him that I knew what he meant. I did too. I kept thinking that even if he gets a place of his own that's nearer to his work, he could still maybe drop in for dinner now and then, or invite us over to visit sometimes so that we could meet his friends.

He didn't drop his bombshell until we were sitting down in a restaurant full of other family groups and proud people. I looked around at all the mums and dads and grandparents and I wanted to make a little observation about them being another meaning of the word pride but William could be touchy about any references to his sexuality. He'd been so sure that we would disapprove that he still believed that we did regardless of what we said. We couldn't tell him that we had always known, and that we were glad he'd finally wanted to share with us. It might have made him feel stupid and that would have been terrible. I always felt that we had been a disappointment, that he wanted nothing more than for us to scream and shout so that he could assert himself and maybe even feel hard done by. Trendy liberal empty husks, that's what William said we were later that day, and I don't think he had any idea how much that hurt. He was completely unable to see that it was coming from a good place, our acceptance, a place where he was loved more than anything.

'So I need to tell you something,' he said while we were waiting for our starter. It was something nice, I remember that, something with roasted beetroot and coriander. 'This country is rubbish. There are no opportunities here. Nothing to do, nothing to see, so I'm moving on. I've got a job in Sydney, Australia, and a visa and everything. They're very hard to get, you know. Sunshine, beaches, young people all over the place. I won't be coming back, I can tell you.'

He sounded nonchalant but I could see that his hand was shaking as he lifted his glass.

I made a noise, a little one and horribly like a whimper but he heard.

'Don't spoil it for me by getting all upset,' he said. 'You can come and visit, sometimes.'

It was the 'sometimes' that set me off, I'm sure it was. As if he was worried that we were going to be stalking him, turning up every weekend with a pie. I couldn't think what to say.

'A job?' Jed said. 'You mean, like a part in a play, right?'

William had wanted to act since he was a tiny boy, always putting on plays for us and singing songs he'd written, so it was a reasonable question to ask but William behaved as if that was the most ridiculous thing anyone had ever said to him.

'Erm, no,' he said. 'I'm through with that now. I've got a job in a finance company, they only take people with firsts and they fast-track them. I'm going to be rich!'

I suppose he thought it was a good day to tell us. A good

day to break our hearts, and there was no way we could spoil the graduation dinner by showing him how sad we were. I think I made some noises about how great it would be and I even said that koalas were my favourite animal, that's how desperate I was. He knew though, that's what I kept thinking afterwards, he knew how much we would miss him, how much we loved him and looked forward to visits and phone calls. He had chosen a safe place to tell us so that he didn't have to deal with our sadness.

I had felt the spinning, winded feeling then and I recognised it now, on the bench as Cate walked away. It was powerlessness. The absolute inability to affect the outcome in any way, only this was so much worse. Someone might die, a dear little girl with straggly hair who had recently learned to say, sheep. The worst thing that had happened when William left was two fractured hearts and an emptiness, but at least we knew that he was OK. We knew that he was having a good time and definitely living his best life, even if we did catch each other crying over some little thing or another every so often. With me it was photographs, blurry shots full of grins and ice cream, but for Jed it was always about his empty room.

Jed's death had been worse. Much worse, because he wasn't there to share it with me, but I honestly couldn't think about that. If I thought too much, I knew that the whirling wouldn't stop. It would go on and on until I felt as if I was tumbling over and over in outer space, the line to the mother ship cut. This time would be different, I promised myself. This time I was going to stay in control. Stay in control, whatever that meant, and I pushed thoughts of my escape route, my pills, out of the way. There would be time enough for them later, and I was glad they were there for back-up. Five weeks now. Annie looked worried.

'Shall I get you a cup of tea just now?' she said.

'No, no,' I said.

I took a deep breath and tried to pull myself together. 'No tea, we've got to be quick. We need to get back to Margate and pack Ocean up and get out of there.'

'I agree,' said Annie. 'And I can't find it in me to blame her. It's him. Men like that, they suck the soul out of you until you get so used to it you're offering it to them on your best plate.'

The train ride back was very different. The hope had gone, nearly all of the hope and with it the energy. It seemed ages since we'd travelled down, full of plans and genuinely believing we could make a difference. I felt as though the task we had in front of us was almost impossible, and I was sure that Annie must feel the same.

'Honestly, Annie,' I said as we reached the Medway towns, 'it's fine if you want to bow out, go back to Scotland. There's no need for you to be involved in all this. It could end up getting really unpleasant, you know. I've kind of got nothing to live for so I'm going to keep going, but you don't have to.'

I wasn't sure whether I even wanted Annie there any more. It had been good to have the company, but now part of me wanted to storm on alone without having to check any decisions or accept any help. I was full of fury and convinced I could do it. Without Annie there would be no one to stop me, no one to check me if I wanted to take an extreme decision, or a crazy one. I wasn't even sure exactly what an extreme decision would look like, not at all, but it was becoming clearer by the minute that ordinary measures were not going to work.

'There's not a great lot going on in Oban just now,' Annie said. 'I doubt if anyone has even noticed that I'm not there. So, unless you're saying that you'd rather I toddle off home, I'd like to stay for a wee while longer. Sometimes it's better to have another head.'

Is it, I thought, is it really? I wasn't sure, but I had to admit that there was something comforting about her presence. She was solid, and she was on our side, me and Ocean's, and maybe that was all I could ask for. We were going to rescue that child somehow, I was determined and I started to believe that Annie felt the same.

The train was a slow one, and by the time we got to Margate the sky was darkening. I had been so busy thinking things through that I hadn't even looked at my phone for a couple of hours, which was a mistake. I got it out as we reached the station, and my stomach flipped over. There were five messages waiting, all of them from Jackson and getting increasingly worried each time. The most recent one was from ten minutes earlier and Jackson was clearly beside himself. 'THAT MAN HAS BEEN HERE AGAIN LOOKING FOR YOU AND THE BABY,' it said. 'DO NOT, REPEAT DO NOT COME HERE. BABY IS OK. ARE YOU OK? WE NEED TO TALK.'

I showed the messages to Annie.

'OK,' she said. 'Don't panic. I mean really, there's no need, let's think. It's dark now, there are two of us, and you're not dressed like a little old lady, if you remember.'

I looked around me on the platform. There weren't many people but all of them, any of them could be him. We needed to keep hidden for everyone's sake. Those sweet boys, I couldn't stop thinking about them. We left the station by the side exit, avoiding the main station concourse where we would be lit up like Christmas trees with targets on our backs, which was a mixed metaphor but the best I could come up with.

'OK,' I said. 'We're going to need to keep moving. He could be watching the station, I've no idea. Let's saunter along by the beach for a moment, find somewhere we can stop and talk.'

We crossed the road to the seafront. Annie was amazing. She took my arm and linked it through hers and pointed things out. There was actually nothing much to point to except sea, sea, sea and sand and it took me a few seconds to catch on that she was making us look more like a couple and less, I suppose, like a pair of old women with a stolen baby at home.

'Don't worry,' she said. 'I haven't lost my marbles. Well, a wee bit I guess but I think people, and I suppose we have to class him as a people, even though he's worse than a bad animal, people don't usually observe what's around them. Especially if it involves anyone they see as old. And although we don't necessarily think it, we can be identified as old from the way we're walking. We've just got to hope that he doesn't realise you might have a friend.'

I was so glad then, glad she hadn't gone home. I was still scared, still not sure how we were going to do it but I knew that we would manage somehow.

At the other side of the beach she pointed to a pub.

'Are you sure you'll recognise him?' she said.

I nodded, but I wondered. Would I? Didn't all young people look pretty much the same these days? Then I remembered, he had a very particular scowl. A way of making his face into a grimace that looked like a mask. I couldn't possibly forget that and I described it to Annie.

'OK,' she said.

We had stopped outside a gift shop and she pointed at something as if she was showing it to me. She should have been a spy, I thought.

'This is what we are going to do. We'll go into this pub and we'll buy a drink and sit down like ordinary people. If you see him at any point let me know, just say something or pull my arm or anything. We need to talk about what to do and we are going to have to trust that our luck can't be that bad, that we would walk into the one wee pub with the bad guy in it. OK?'

I could see the sense in what she was saying. We needed to talk somewhere, and we were too old and too conspicuous to walk up and down the beach all night or sit in one of the shelters on the promenade.

The pub was fairly empty, and there was no one inside who looked remotely like him. I don't remember what we ordered, but we sat at a corner table where I could see the door and clinked glasses.

'We've got to get the wee baby out,' she said.

I felt slightly aggrieved that she had said something so obvious and wished I could say, duh, to her like a kid would but it would have been childish and ungrateful.

'Roger that,' I said. 'It isn't safe for Ocean there and it isn't fair on the boys or their grandma. They are way too close to my place, which he's going to be watching like a hawk. We just need to work out how to do it.'

'I'm thinking,' said Annie. 'I had a religious upbringing, you know.'

I honestly thought she'd lost it. What the hell had her religious upbringing got to do with anything? Perhaps she really had lost her mind, I thought, with the stress and everything.

'And one thing I remember,' she said, 'Is that they smuggled the wee baby Moses away from something or the other in a basket. A basket of rushes. I always thought it was a comfortable sounding thing, a wee basket, all filled with fluffy blankets and maybe a small bear, although I'm not sure fluffy blankets were invented just then. Whenever it was.'

Omg, I thought. I really did think it, just the letters, no words. It was that much of a lightbulb moment that there was no room for the longer version.

'I think you've got something,' I said.

We both sat there, staring at our juices and thinking. We thought so hard that we could have powered a small generator, and then Annie said, 'A shopping trolley. One of those basket on wheels things, you've got a big solid one, I saw it.'

She sounded as though she had totally solved the puzzle but all I could see were problems.

'Will she like it though? If she's not happy she'll cry and that will give the game away.'

There was a little silence, and I could see that I needed to step up.

'Sorry,' I said. 'Maybe I'm overthinking it.'

'We haven't really got a choice just now, have we?' Annie said. 'We're in a really difficult bind. This is what I think. If she has a wee practice in there first, a little play, then the boys wait till she's really tired before they pop her in with the fluffy blankets and the toys then we can get her past him and we're away. There's a chance, maybe a good chance but no guarantee, and that's better than what will happen if we do absolutely nothing. We need to think about what happens next, of course we do but the important thing is to get her out of the way of immediate harm and take her to safety.'

I loved Annie's clear thinking. And the way she knew so much about babies. About everything really. The woman was a marvel and I was lucky to have her. I was about to tell her that when there was a buzz from my phone as Jackson sent another message. He said that everyone was OK, and sent a photo of Ocean asleep on Panna's lap. Panna was smiling and she looked better than she had done earlier, so I think we relaxed for a little while.

'I only ever had William,' I said as we nursed our drinks. 'I never had brothers or sisters and I didn't mean to recreate that, for him.'

Annie had a faraway look on her face, as if she was thinking about something sad many miles away. I felt comfortable with her silence, the way I might with a sister.

'Do you know,' I said, 'My parents had a silence rule at mealtimes and I thought it was normal. What on earth does Ocean think is normal? What's she missing?'

'That's the intriguing thing about babies,' Annie said. 'You never know what they think. In the nicest way, they're all a wee bit crazy.'

'Did you love bringing up your children, even though you were young?' I said. 'You seem to know a lot about babies.'

I don't know why I asked that. I think I might have wanted to put off whatever was going to happen next, or maybe just to know more about her, why she was helping. It's always a dodgy question to ask about children for us oldies, and I should have realised that. Some people have had them and wish they hadn't, some have had them and lost them in a million different ways, more than a few have a lasting sadness and some just like to boast. I'd seen how she was with Ocean, though, and she had already mentioned the twins. Annie wasn't a boaster but I wouldn't have been surprised if her children were working on a cure for cancer or household names in tennis, something great I was sure, but I wanted to know, and this might be the only chance we had to talk.

'Yes,' she said.

She was quiet for a few moments and I thought that she wasn't going to say anything else. I started to think again about William.

'A wee girl, and a boy. Morag and Jamie. Twins.'

Each word came out with difficulty, as if she was having to spit them past a blockage. She became still. I could tell that this was not something she spoke about often, in fact I wondered when she had last said their names. They seemed rusty in her mouth.

'I'm sorry,' I said. 'I didn't mean to pry.'

It was a stupid thing to say and I knew it. Of course I had intended to pry. Why else would I have asked?

'I mean, I did kind of intend to pry but I didn't mean to cause you pain,' I said.

'Jed always said you were the most honest person he'd ever met,' she said. 'And I can see why. It's OK, it doesn't hurt to get them out now and again, dust them off and have a look. It's good to say their names, even if it hurts.'

'They're beautiful names,' I said. 'Morag is a strong name,

a lot of girls have flowery names but Morag sounds strong and clever. And Jamie sounds like a dear little chap.'

'Thank you for seeing that,' Annie said. 'I chose the right names, even though I got a lot of other things wrong. I chose the right names.'

CHAPTER NINETEEN

The boys had stayed indoors for the rest of the day. Jackson kept watch for the man while Noah played with Ocean and Phil, and Panna masterminded the whole thing from her chair. They stuffed towels under the front door for soundproofing and kept the balcony door open in the hope that the waves would drown out any noise if he was waiting on the stairs. Jackson couldn't shake off a feeling that he was nearby. He wondered what he would have been doing if they hadn't been so quick to help, but any regrets he had were banished every time he heard Ocean giggle, or watched her look at Noah with an adoring expression.

'Do you think I'll ever have kids?' Noah said when Panna and Ocean were tucked up for their naps.

Jackson had the slightly winded feeling he often got when Noah asked him a question he hadn't been expecting.

'Why not?' Jackson said. 'You'd be a good parent.'

'Ah but girls,' Noah said. 'Girls or boys my own age, none of them like me. And I don't like drama, Jax, that's what I've been thinking about. There's a lot of goings-on in personal relationships, people crying and shouting and generally being a bit messy. I don't fancy it.'

Jackson kept his face straight.

'I think there are quieter ways to have a baby than by stealing it,' he said. 'Also, with the greatest respect, Noah, you are eleven years old, however grown up you think you are. You've got a few changes and growing things to come before anyone would even suggest you should think about it.'

'I want to be ready, bro,' Noah said. He looked at Jackson with such big, serious eyes that Jackson felt as if his insides were melting.

'Come here,' he said and he held out his arms for a hug.

'When you boys have finished your mothers' meeting,' Panna called. 'Could someone make me a cup of tea?'

Jackson smiled and went to the kitchen, listening as Noah berated Panna for misogyny.

'Just because you've got an old lady gang to back you up now, it doesn't mean you can start displaying that sort of behaviour,' he said.

Jackson looked out of the window as the kettle boiled. He wasn't thinking of anything specific, he realised later. Just feeling good, and more or less happy. Safe even. He might even have been smiling, he wasn't sure but if he was, the smile was wiped off instantly. He was there, the man who had knocked on the door upstairs, sitting in a camping chair down by the sea. The tide was on its way out, so he couldn't have been there for long. He was facing away from the waves and back towards the flat, staring directly towards their windows. He looked nasty, unpleasant, even from this distance, and Jackson wondered what on earth they had got themselves into.

'It's OK, bro,' Noah said as he came into the kitchen. 'I've seen him out of the window too. I'm not scared, I've got bigger fish to fry. Well, the fish aren't actually bigger, but they're different fish and that's important.'

Jackson stirred the tea and stared at his brother.

'What fish?' he said.

'Poo, bro,' Noah said. 'I don't care if that stupid bully man is out there or not, Phil the dog has to wee. And he is embarrassed on the balcony. Couldn't I just slip outside for a moment or two? If anyone speaks to me I'll just act like the most gormless kid ever. Look.'

Noah stuck his finger in his mouth and hung his head slightly. It was subtle, but there was a remarkable difference. He looked like a younger boy, and a less intelligent one. Jackson wondered where on earth he had learned such a trick, and more to the point, why.

'School,' Noah said as though he had read Jackson's mind. 'Did no one ever tell you that nobody likes a smart arse? I guess they can't have done.'

Jackson had the familiar feeling that Noah was way smarter than him, but he still had to refuse his request to go out. It wasn't safe out there, not at all. Jackson had a big future planned for Noah, sunny quads and people carrying books and talking about the big questions. It was his job to keep him safe until he could get to it. Meanwhile, though, Jackson had to concentrate on the rather more important job of keeping the baby away from that man and all of them alive and out of prison.

'You're a little troublemaker and you've got no idea, have you?' he said to Ocean when she woke up.

'Bah,' she said.

She was holding the sheep and Jackson felt an enormous surge of pride.

'Wow, baby face,' he said. 'You are a smart smart baby. Sheep do say baa. I want to call you a clever girl but Noah says that's praising your gender not your own self, and I get that. And also, I need to say, Ocean, none of this is your fault.'

'Amen,' said Noah, high-fiving Phil the dog.

Jackson wasn't embarrassed about talking to Ocean any more. They had all agreed that she was just as good a conversationalist as anyone else they knew. And she was calm and quiet, and Jackson knew that was going to be important. However they got her out, there could be no noise at all, no crying that would give the game away. The man might be capable of anything and they had to be ready.

'I was so sure he wouldn't be back,' Jackson had said to Panna. 'He seemed like he was in such a hurry to be somewhere else.'

'Men like that, who knows,' Panna said, which didn't help at all.

Jackson told Noah again that he couldn't risk taking Phil out. Whatever happened they could deal with it indoors. He sent increasingly desperate messages to Virginia and her friend asking them to come back, and it was more than maddening that they didn't answer. In the meantime, he had to keep the baby safe. The consequences if he didn't manage were unthinkable for everyone. Ocean would be in danger and Jackson had no doubt that everyone would be delighted to have a Black family to scapegoat for her disappearance. They would never be believed, no matter what the nice old ladies upstairs said.

'One minute at a time,' Panna said.

Jackson let his head drop onto his hands as he watched Ocean and tried to think of a way out of their predicament.

'I'm sorry,' he said. 'It'll be fine, honestly, I'm just tired.'

'I'm old and doctors say I'm sick but no one has said that I'm crazy. Yet,' Panna said. 'I can see how bad you're hurting and I know how much you want to do the right thing. But I've been around long enough to know that sometimes, the right thing hides its face. You can look and look but it just isn't there. Those times, you've got to step really close, a little bit at a time until you can see clearly again.'

Jackson sighed. Sometimes living with Panna and Noah was like living with the two most irritating motivational speakers in the world.

By the late afternoon, everyone except the baby was starting to feel cooped up. Phil had finally managed to use a puppy pad in the kitchen but he sat with his back to everyone to show he was offended. Jackson felt stir crazy.

'Imagine,' Noah said. 'If there was some like, plague thing that was really infectious and with no cure or anything and they made everyone stay at home all the time. Like a lockdown. Imagine what it would be like.'

'Too much imagination,' Panna said. 'Way too much imagination and not enough common sense. Why would that happen? Now that we've got antibiotics and everything? Isn't it enough to worry about the things we have to worry about now instead of conjuring up new ones out of thin air?'

Jackson and Noah smiled at each other while Panna huffed and puffed and danced slowly round the sofa with the baby in her arms. She was so different from the weak, sick old lady they were used to. It had started with the dog, Jackson thought, and then she seemed to get better in leaps and bounds once they had the baby. Maybe some people just needed to be needed, he thought, although that didn't make complete sense. There was Noah and him, for a start. They needed her, and they always had done. Jackson wished for the zillionth time that he didn't have so much responsibility. The list was too long. A small boy who was too clever by half, an old woman who sometimes seemed as though she was going to die any minute and now an illegal dog and a baby in danger from a weird stalker man. It was too much for anyone and Jackson wondered for a moment what would happen if he just slipped his trainers on and left. Best-case scenario, the women return and find a way to rescue the baby without him, Panna gets better and goes back to looking after Noah, who returns to school and makes friends, happily looking after his dog in the evenings. Worst case, Panna dies, baby is snatched and killed, dog is taken back and beaten to death, Noah is forced back to school and is so unhappy he kills himself. Jackson decided to stay home.

By the time Virginia and Annie saw their messages and got back to him, Jackson was very anxious. He couldn't rationalise his way out of it this time. Of course not all of them would die, he knew that, but he couldn't shake the thought that at least one of them would, and that it would be his fault. He put the call on loudspeaker for Noah and Panna to hear too.

'We've seen your messages now, sorry, Jackson, sorry, all of you. It didn't go well in London, and we should have looked at our phones. We're not used to it, I guess. So sorry we didn't look at them sooner.'

'It's OK,' Panna said. 'No time for that now. We need a plan, and quickly.'

'You're right,' Virginia said. 'And we've got one. You did the right thing by staying put and we are going to take over now. We're in Margate, but we're not coming back to the flat because we agree, he's obviously watching the place. But we have to act quickly. We need to get the baby out so that we stand a chance of getting her to social services, see what they can do. We don't really have a choice. I know it didn't work before, but they've got to pay attention now, and once they see her injuries it'll be different. If we explain, and show them the scars and the photographs of the scars, and tell them about him they'll have to listen, won't they?'

'I don't know,' Panna said. 'I've got other experiences of social workers. They don't always act in the child's best interest and these boys are living proof of that.'

There was silence at the other end and Jackson wished that Panna could have said something more encouraging. Virginia sounded confident as she talked them through their new plan, and Jackson felt a stirring of hope, even though it was so crazy. He was absolutely sure that Panna would reject it out of hand but to his amazement she got more and more animated as the conversation went on, until she was grinning and clapping and dancing like a teenager. Noah looked at Jackson and shrugged as if he was enjoying the spectacle. Jackson made a mental note to do some research, to check whether old people could develop some kind of collective madness when they were overexcited. The energy of them was exhausting.

'One last thing,' Virginia said when they'd finished. 'I haven't even told Annie this yet and I'm sorry, I really am but I looked online on my phone and I did see something about Ocean. It's just a little story in the local paper so far, but it's possible that other papers might pick it up, I don't know. And I'm so sorry.'

Jackson heard Noah gasp but Panna shrugged and said, 'It was only a matter of time.' Bloody hell, he thought.

'You can back out, I know that changes things,' Virginia said.

'I think we should,' said Jackson. He could feel the little flutter of hope take flight and leave the building. 'Sorry, Panna, sorry, everyone, but there's too much at risk here. We can give you Ocean but that's it. It's not fair on Noah.'

There was silence after he spoke and then everyone began to talk at once. Virginia and Annie were reassuring him that everything was OK and it was fine for them to stop helping, and Panna was explaining why they had to help but all Jackson could hear was Noah.

'Bro,' he said and his eyes were brimming over with tears. 'Bro, we've got the chance to help someone here, like you helped me.'

Disappointment, that's what Jackson could hear. Disappointment that his big brother wanted to cut and run at the first sign of trouble, that he wasn't the hero Noah had always believed him to be.

Once the plan was set the baby slept peacefully while they waited for the right time to act. She was probably tired out by all the fuss of the last few days, Jackson thought, and she wasn't the only one. He was pleased to be back in Noah's good books, and he wanted to help but boy, he was so tired.

'We've got to assume he's watching,' Panna said. 'And that

makes it really difficult. But he's got to sleep sometime, or at least lose focus. He's probably a drinker, and that's gonna help. Noah, for once I'm going to let you stay up but you've got to lie on that couch and close your eyes. When it's time, we are going to need you.'

Jackson had noticed Noah's eyes growing even more huge as he digested the whole thing. Panna declared a ban on looking at anything online or on TV just in case, and Jackson fully agreed. He kept a careful eye on Noah to make sure. He seemed OK, but Jackson could tell that he was worried, so he was glad when the boy finally fell asleep. Panna dozed in her chair too, and it was the first time the three of them had slept in the same room for ages. Camping in Devon, somewhere around 2013, he thought. They'd gone to one of those places where the tent is already up and in place, so all they had to do was turn up and marvel at life under canvas. Jackson had absolutely loved it. The freedom of spending all day in the swimming pool, the way Panna had relaxed and best of all, the sound of Noah laughing. It had seemed as though Noah was laughing all the time. At night, he could hear both of them breathing through the zipped-up canvas of the little bedrooms. It seemed similar now as they snoozed on the sofas. Everyone present and correct, that's what Jackson liked, although how that fitted in with his plans for uni and travelling and possibly a jet-setting career, he wasn't sure. Two more people breathing too, Ocean with her soft baby snores and Philip with his strange dream barks.

Jackson thought of the scene in *Romeo and Juliet* where Romeo talks about not wanting the night to end, and determined that he would never tell anyone that he felt the same kind of feelings listening to his grandma, little brother, a stolen dog and a stolen baby. Even if they were rescued rather than stolen, it wasn't the kind of thing he would ever be able to share. Jackson went to sleep dreaming of a family of his own. Babies, dogs, they were easy to imagine. It got more difficult when he tried to visualise a special partner, and he went to sleep thinking of his brother instead.

The alarm on Panna's phone went off when it was still dark. She shut it down quickly.

'This will be the hardest time for him to stay awake,' she said. 'The darkest hour is just before dawn. He's probably in a car if he stayed down here, and I'm gonna bet he's dropped off. The tide is high too, and that's going to help. No one can stay awake long with that whooshing and watery wave-crashing stuff.'

Jackson could hear the fear in her voice even though she was determined to pretend everything was fine. He was sure that even Noah could hear it, but for once he didn't say a word.

'I've got an add-on to the plan,' Jackson said. 'I've been thinking.'

He paused for a moment for Noah to make some kind of quip about Jackson thinking too much, or wearing his brain out or any one of a hundred joshes Jackson had heard before, but the boy remained oddly quiet.

'So we'll still go with the shopping trolley thing, but we need to think how he thinks, her stepdad, we're not going to outwit him otherwise. We will look much more suspicious if we're all together, I can see you shaking your head, Panna, but you know I'm right. What I suggest is this, you two pop her in the trolley with blankets and toys, etc, and I'll carry something,

I was thinking of Noah's big monkey. I can wrap it in a shawl or a blanket so that it looks like I'm carrying a child, then I'll go a different way from you. You two walk along the seafront and up the slope to the cliffs like we agreed with Virginia and Annie, and I'll go towards the station and double back. He can only follow one of us and I'm going to bet it'll be me. And I'm fast, I can run and weave and dodge. You go on slowly up the cliffs, meet up with them, go along with whatever they've worked out next within reason, and I'll draw the heat. That's what they call it in cop shows, I've seen it a hundred times.'

Noah and Panna both seemed to be lost for words. Jackson knew it was because his idea was a good one, but he still couldn't help wishing they would stop him, explain to him why it made no sense, maybe even persuade him to go back to bed. Instead Panna nodded.

'I'm proud of you,' she said. 'Very proud, but what are you going to do when he catches up with you? If he does, I mean.'

'Nah, you're right,' Jackson said. 'I really think he will. I mean I have to keep him busy as long as possible, don't I? So I need to have a really plausible story.'

'Bro,' said Noah. 'I haven't watched that many cop shows but I cannot imagine one where the plot involves someone carrying a large stuffed monkey across town, whatever it's wrapped in.'

Jackson privately agreed with Noah but he also knew that it was vital that he didn't let them see how worried he was. If they knew, they might insist on all going together and he was sure that they wouldn't stand a chance if they did that.

'Desperate times call for desperate measures,' he said. 'I've got the gift of the gab, remember?'

Jackson couldn't remember a time when he'd been so glad

to use clichés. That's what they were for, he realised. To cover up the times when people had absolutely no idea what they were talking about.

Getting the shopping trolley from the flat upstairs was easy. Virginia had told them that she left a key on a string hanging inside the door, so that all they had to do was to reach a hand through and pull it back. Jackson made the other two wait downstairs while he got it. There was one moment when he was sure he could hear someone breathing behind him on the staircase, but it was the sea, the sound it makes when the tide is coming in. He was sure of it.

Inside the upstairs flat, all Jackson wanted to do was leave. He couldn't risk putting the lights on, so he used the light on his torch, which made everything look otherworldly. Every object seemed to send shadows by torchlight, even things that were usually inoffensive, like bookcases and chairs. The shopping trolley was by the door where Virginia had said it would be. Jackson grabbed it and left, closing the door behind him as quietly as he could. He ran back down the stairs as if the devil was on his tail. Which he quite possibly was, Jackson thought.

Panna carried the sleepy baby from her mattress on the floor. They had padded the bottom of the trolley, and the base was big enough for her to lie curled up in comfort. She wasn't a big toddler, and she looked even smaller in the trolley.

'We've made lots of little holes, for the air,' Noah said. 'You know, like with cat boxes. You wouldn't see them, especially in the dark, but you'll be fine, little Ocean.'

It was almost as though she knew what they were doing, Jackson thought, as if she knew they were trying their best to help her and her mum. She clutched her sheep and closed her eyes again, which made it much easier to snuggle her up and loosely tie the cord at the top. Noah had wrapped Big Monkey in a flowery sheet and as he gave him to Jackson, Jackson could see what a little boy he was really.

'Wish him luck,' Jackson said.

Noah looked grateful that it was Jackson's idea and that he hadn't had to say anything. He saluted the toy and said, 'May the force be with you.'

'I'll leave now, and you two, I mean three, better wait five minutes then leave. You can call me if you need me, otherwise I'll keep going and run this guy round for a bit before I join you.'

'One more time, are you sure?' Panna said.

Jackson nodded and danced a few steps with the swaddled monkey to make Noah laugh, only he didn't.

It was colder than Jackson had expected and darker too, although he would never have admitted it. Not even to himself. How pathetic, he thought, being nearly nineteen and so unused to leaving the house in the evening that I'm not prepared for it to be dark.

'It's literally nighttime,' he said under his breath. 'What the actual fuck.'

He had an urge to explain to Big Monkey that he wasn't actually talking to him, and resolved to talk to someone, his GP perhaps or a counsellor, when this was all over. He needed to get his head straight.

By the time he got to the clock tower Jackson was having to force himself to put one foot in front of the other. The town was so damn quiet, that was what Jackson didn't understand.

All the nights he had stayed home with Noah and Panna he had assumed that the middle of town would be buzzing, full of people living their best lives, drinking beer and cider and smoking cannabis. It turns out that everyone was home watching box sets like he was, he thought. Fancy that. He held Big Monkey close and tried to concentrate on noticing all the streets he was passing without constantly looking around to check if he was being followed. That would mark him out more than anything else. Look confident, he thought, stride it out and look as though you know what you're doing. If he is watching, he'll be less likely to attack. He was a coward, Jackson knew that much. Only a desperate coward would attack a teeny little baby like that. The thought made his back a little straighter, and his step a little lighter. I can do this, he thought, I can do this for Ocean.

Jackson was almost at the art gallery by the harbour before he knew for sure that someone was behind him. He had heard the steps for a while but thought his imagination was working overtime. Almost sure, and then there was no mistaking them. They matched his almost exactly and he could hear breathing as well. Heavy breathing, as if the breather was not used to any kind of exercise at all. It had to be him, Jackson took a deep breath, paused on the slipway that led down to the sea and turned around.

It was like the defining moment in a film, Jackson thought afterwards. Everything seemed to slow down and every move seemed exaggerated. The man was standing a few feet from Jackson and seemed suddenly impossibly tall. Every moment I keep him talking, he thought, is an extra minute for them to get to the sunken garden.

251

'Why you following me, dude?' Jackson said.

He tried to make himself look as menacing as possible, and to copy a swagger he had seen on TV. He thought it looked pretty stupid, as if he was Noah's age and playing a game, but the man stepped back. Jackson made himself stand a little straighter. He remembered something he'd read about posture being important in self-defence and pushed his shoulders back.

'Give me my daughter,' the man said, gesturing towards Big Monkey.

Jackson held the toy closer and pretended to pull the shawl back a little to check the baby.

'She's asleep,' he said. 'She's asleep and she's comfortable. I don't want to wake her.'

'You're chatting rubbish,' the man said. 'Just hand her over now or I'm gonna come and get her.'

The man took a step forward and Jackson wanted to run, oh so badly he wanted to run, but he stood his ground and tried to puff himself up even more. Every second he managed was a second longer for the baby, a second longer for his sweet brother and sick old gran to get away. He had to stand his ground.

'Where's her mum?' Jackson said.

It was the first question he could think of.

'What do you want to know that for, Black boy? You think she's gonna look at you?'

Jackson breathed deeply and concentrated on keeping his nerve.

'No, that's not it at all,' he said. 'I'm asking because babies should be with their mums, that's all.'

'Babies should be with their mums,' the man said in a falsetto voice. 'That's funny, seeing as it was you or one of your mates who kidnapped her in the first place. Come on now, Black boy, or do you mind if I call you blackie, for short?'

Jackson felt a wild desire to giggle. 'Black boy' was about the least offensive thing he had ever been called, and yet this guy obviously thought it was a terrible cuss. He stayed still for a moment or two trying to weigh up his options. He had every chance of getting away, if he was careful, he thought. He had local knowledge, he was young and he used to be a damn good runner, even though he was out of practice now.

'So where is she?' Jackson said, trying to stall for a few more seconds. 'I mean is she nearby? Can I give the baby to her?'

'I tell you what, you're really getting on my nerves now. Really winding me up. Give her to me, or you're gonna be more than sorry.'

The man moved a couple of steps closer and Jackson saw something in his hand catch the light. He was sure it was a knife.

'Stop,' he said, in the most commanding tone he could muster. 'Stay where you are. You can't come any nearer the baby when you're carrying that, bro, it could hurt her.'

Jackson tensed, prepared for the man to jump him but for some reason he stopped, and stood quite still as if he couldn't make up his mind. Jackson had a fleeting thought of how impressed Noah would be if he could see him and then his brain started moving again. He could practically hear it crank up.

'Drop the knife. Drop it now and I'll put her over in the shelter, on the bench. When I say and not before, you can go and get her, OK?'

'You don't get to tell me what to do, Black boy,' the man said.

He sounded slightly less frightening, Jackson thought. Perhaps he was nothing more than a typical bully, picking on vulnerable women and children. Jackson tightened his grip on Big Monkey as if he really was trying to protect him.

'I do,' Jackson said.

He walked backwards slowly towards the shelter. It was one of Noah's favourite things to do, walking backwards. He often persuaded Jackson to race backwards with him and even though Noah usually won, Jackson was grateful now for the many hours of practice he had put in. The man had dropped the knife, although it was clear to Jackson that he had some other form of weapon from the way he kept his hand on his pocket.

A what-if thought flashed into Jackson's head. What if he really was the baby's father or stepfather, it didn't matter which if he honestly loved her and had her best interests at heart? What if Virginia was crazy and the marks had been made some other way, if she had never been hurt at all? It would have been so nice to believe that, to tell him where she was and go back to worrying about Noah and Panna instead, so nice that for one moment as Jackson walked steadily back towards the shelter he was tempted. Tempted for the smallest of nanoseconds, until he heard what the man was chanting.

'Little girl, little girl, daddy's gonna get you,' over and over again in the most scary voice Jackson had ever heard. It made him think of a film he'd seen once where a man with a terrifying face chased a little boy on a tricycle down endless hotel corridors. He thought of Ocean's sweet smile and the way

254

she slept holding her little sheep and he gripped Big Monkey more tightly.

'Stay there,' he shouted as he got to the shelter.

He was glad now that there was no one else around to get involved. The man stood still and Jackson put the monkey carefully on the bench, patting it gently and fussing with how it was lying.

'OK,' he said and then it all happened so quickly.

Jackson ran as fast as he could, as fast as he ever had up the beach and out of sight, but he was still near enough to hear the roar as the man discovered the trick.

CHAPTER TWENTY

The Sunken Garden
Clifftop

It was a long night, and when I think about it now it's hard to say what happened when. There was so much going on and I'm not sure if I could have made it play out any differently. Looking back, it seems like a different version of me, more sure, clearer and full of energy. We'd been up early, of course, been to London, met poor Cate and come away again but somehow we were still buzzing. It was cold and dark and we had to wait, two old ladies who needed their beds. We had to pass the time and make sure our plans were watertight until it was safe for the boys to bring us the baby. We sat in a shelter at the other end of town and we talked a lot, about anything and everything in our lives.

When the time came we left, keeping to the backstreets until we got to Westbrook. We didn't go anywhere near the flat in case he was there. Instead we followed the path up onto the cliffs. It was a walk Jed and I had done dozens of times, although never before at nighttime, and I was surprised by the spooky shadowiness of the clifftop shelters. No one was in them, or no one that we could see, but they looked purpose built for ghosts and ghouls if there had been any around. We kept to the path along the edge of the cliff, which was lined with benches in memory of people. 'Beloved dad,' one of them said and I felt bad that I hadn't made any kind of memorial for Jed.

'I should do something like this, for Jed,' I said.

We sat down on it for a moment and it felt good to stop walking.

'There's time enough for that,' Annie said. 'Don't beat yourself up. You've had a lot to deal with and besides, I bet you want to choose the exact right thing, don't you? These things take time.'

It was true, I did want to make sure I made the right choice, and I wondered again how she could be so understanding when so many other people were not.

'I thought about a tree,' I said. 'He loved trees. Every so often he used to say to me, "I need to see some trees," and off we would go to a forest or an arboretum or the local park, even if it was the middle of winter.'

I hadn't thought of that for a while, and it was good to remember. It made me feel stronger, in a way.

'I wanted a wee bench, for Jamie and Morag,' Annie said. 'I was going to paint it in bright colours, decorate it and leave toys, you know, so that any passing children could take them home. Like a magic bench, that's what I was hoping for.'

I was shocked, and glad it was too dark for her to see my face. She was quiet for a moment and I could see even in the moonlight that she was fighting tears. I wanted to know what had happened to the twins but I wasn't sure that this was the right time.

'We could talk about something else?' I said.

It wasn't that I wanted to shut her down, I didn't, but I also didn't want to hug her or anything clumsy like that. Such an intimate situation to be in and I hardly even knew her. She might go to pieces completely for all I knew. Jed always used to poke fun at me about my discomfort with intimacy, and I got cross with him but he was right. I wasn't good at it except for with babies. Annie didn't respond, so I felt I ought to plough on. Even if you get it wrong, I remembered Jed saying, it's always better to try.

'You're living your actual life as a testament to them, though,' I said. 'That's way better than any bench. What you're doing, what we are doing to try to make things OK for that baby, don't you think Jamie and Morag would be proud of you?'

For a second I thought she was going to hug me anyway, even though I'd sent out my best aloof signals with my body language, but the moment passed and I was so grateful that I put my hand on her arm as a consolation.

'Sorry,' I said. 'I didn't mean to upset you.'

'You didn't, oh no you didn't,' she said. 'I don't know how many years it's been since anyone other than me mentioned their names, and it's the best thing in the world. I've been on my own so much I'd started to wonder if they were ever real, or whether I'm such a mad old lady I've made them up. Being alone does that kind of thing, it messes with reality because you haven't got a sounding board, or anything to ground you.'

I nodded. She was right. When I was back at home I'd wondered over and over whether I had made up the whole thing about Ocean, and I'd even been starting to believe that I had until I saw all the scars and marks on her little body.

'The minute I heard you say their names, Jamie and Morag, I could see them again. How they looked when they were sleeping, and how they looked when they opened their wee eyes and looked at me, or at each other. I can even imagine how they might have looked when they were crawling around, following each other across the room and giving each other toys. I haven't been able to see that for years but you sort of unlocked it and I'm grateful. They looked so similar, same dimples, same puckered little mouths, only Jamie was second and so much smaller. Morag was bigger and I thought that maybe she would do everything first, smiling, teething, reaching for things. I wondered which of them would be first to sleep through the night. People obsess over that, don't they, when they have little babies. I just had this one thought in my head, after they'd gone. I kept thinking, if I'd known, if I'd really known that they would be here for such a short time, I would never have let them sleep at all. They could have just stayed up, you know? We could have spent the nights playing.'

I felt so sorry for her then. What a sad thing to think, and how come I had never realised that people might be thinking that sad thing when I was sleep-training William, exhausted and moaning?

'Do you want to talk about what happened?' I said. I owed it to her, I thought.

I looked at my phone. It was going to be a while before they came and I was getting more and more jittery, so we had to do something to pass the time. 'Only we could go over there, we'd be way more hidden then and ready for the others.'

If they come, I wanted to add but I think Annie could hear it anyway.

'They'll come,' she said. 'Not long now.'

We went to the sunken garden. It's totally amazing, the sunken garden. Those Victorians had some great ideas. Or whoever it was. It's exactly what it says on the tin, a garden on the clifftop but sunken down to the level of a few steps, maybe ten or fifteen feet deep so that anyone visiting is totally out of the wind. There are plants and flowers in the summer, and grass in the middle. Like a floral swimming pool with no water, only much bigger. Almost like a church, or a sacred place. We sat on a bench on the lower level and it was remarkable how cosy it was.

'Go on, if you want to,' I said. 'I would love to hear.'

'It wouldn't happen now,' she said. 'The whole sorry story. Things have got better for women, only sometimes nowadays there's a glimpse of how it could be if we slid backwards.' She shuddered.

'I was fifteen,' she said. 'I didn't think I was so young then, I thought I was grown up and in some ways I was. I was ignorant though, and like I said before, I hadn't realised I was having sex. I wasn't sure what it was and I didn't like it but it was never named, you know. I didn't like it at all so I kept away from the boys after that. I was sure it was my fault for being on my own with the uncles. That's what we all believed then, us girls. That it was up to us to help them control their urges somehow, can you imagine that?'

I knew that it still happened, that kind of thinking, but I didn't want to depress her and I wanted to hear the story, so I just shook my head.

'I knew what it was when my period didn't come. I knew that much but I couldn't believe it. They were my uncles after all, and it was all so quick, and dark. There were usually other people around, but downstairs making lunch or washing up. How could something so big happen in such a wee while?'

Annie shook her head, and I could see that it still perplexed her, so many years later. For a moment, in the dark, she looked like the teenager she had been then, dealing with the thing all teenagers dreaded.

'I was born in 1950, so it was the Swinging Sixties but the permissive society hadn't reached Scotland, and certainly not the Highlands. I wanted to have an abortion, I really did. Everyone talked about ways you could do it back then, and always they would know someone who knew someone who would swear by gin, or nutmeg in yogurt, or pills you could nick from bathroom cabinets that people's mums took for high blood pressure. I tried the lot, and I got nothing but sicker and sicker. Someone gave me an old envelope with the name written on it of a doctor in Edinburgh who would do it for seventy-five pounds, but it might as well have been a million. I couldn't even imagine how to raise that kind of sum so I thought I'd go anyway and explain to him that I couldn't have a baby, that it would ruin my life and all that. It's mad looking back, but at the time I was so desperate I thought it might work, and that maybe he'd be sympathetic and do it anyway when I explained I had a great career lined up. A doctor, that's what I wanted to be then so I thought this chap might have a wee bit of sympathy. I was going to promise to pay him back.

'They noticed at school though, like I told you, and they told my parents, who were Catholic, and old. My wee mammy was nearly fifty when she had me, so I was a miracle and her views were from another century. All anyone wanted to know was who was the father but I never told.'

Annie was quiet for a while then, and I thought that it was all maybe too much for her.

'You honestly don't need to go on,' I said. 'I didn't mean to upset you. Maybe it's best not to bring it all up.'

Especially now, I was thinking, when we've got a big job on and I need you to be on top of your game, not falling apart. Also, I was getting more and more worried that I wouldn't know what to say. I'd opened the tin but I really wanted to put the lid back on it now. There was no chance. I don't think she even heard what I was saying.

'I haven't talked about this for more than half a century,' she said. 'Thank you so much for listening. They sent me to a home, you see, a home for unmarried mothers. They had those everywhere. Horrible, horrible places. They treated you like dirt, and they wouldn't give you any pain relief in labour. I was three days with the twins. No scans then, so we didn't know there was more than one baby until wee Jamie popped out. I got such a surprise, although as soon as I saw him it felt right that we were a family of three now. Like it was meant.'

I thought of how terrifying that must have been for a girl of fifteen. Having William was scary enough, and I was stuffed with pain relief and had my mum there holding my hand. Plus I wasn't a teenager.

'No wonder you're such a strong woman,' I said.

I meant it as well, there was something about her that emanated strength and calm. She would have made a great parent.

'What happened after they were born?' I said.

I could hear the wind rising outside the sunken garden, and I was glad she was there with me.

'They'd always told me I couldn't keep the baby, but it wasn't real until I saw them. The twins. In a second I was ready, you know? I thought I could manage, I'd change my life, we could grow up together, all that sort of stuff. I would have managed.'

'You would,' I said. 'I'm sure you would.'

'They absolutely refused. Apparently I'd signed something, when I first arrived, I didn't remember signing it and I certainly didn't read it but I was a good girl, I did what I was told. I'd have signed anything. They told me the twins would be going to good families, they wouldn't even promise that they'd be kept together. I so wanted them to have each other, you know, especially when they didn't have me. They were in the same cot, and for a few days they were allowed to stay with me. Some girls had their babies taken as soon as they were born, you could hear them crying for their weans all night. But they didn't have anyone ready for the two of them, you see, so they had to stay with me and somehow that gave me a crazy surge of hope. I'll be a writer instead, I thought, that's a job I can do from home. I even started writing something, a novel, it was going to be, while the wee babies were dozing or lying in the cot staring at each other. I'd honestly told myself that my parents would be coming to pick me up soon, with the twins, and that we'd be going home to start a new life together. I'd even convinced the other girls, and one or two of them had started saying that they were going to keep their babies too. There was a wee lassie in the next bed to me who had a little girl the same day as the twins, Rosemary, she called her, although we all knew the adopters could change the names, then.

'I'll come and see you every year so I can know what wee Rosie would be doing,' she said. 'I can't take her home because my dad will be having sex with her before she can even walk.'

Just matter of fact like that, she was, I'll never forget it. She cried more when my twins were taken than she did when wee Rosemary went. She'd already given up on her, you see. It was such a bleak, hopeless place. All of us young, and with our lives in front of us, and all of us crying, nearly all the time. Some of the lasses tried to take their own lives, you know, and a few of them succeeded. I've been to hospices since then and do you know, they're like holiday camps in comparison.'

'What happened?' I said. 'I mean, I know what actually happened but how did they get away with it? If you'd said you wanted the babies, wanted to keep them and bring them up? Surely it must have been your choice, even in those days?'

The moon lit up Annie's face as she turned towards me, and I could see a mixture of pity and anger.

'Women had no choices then, unless they were very lucky, do you not remember? Especially the young ones. My parents didn't want the shame of it, and I think they might have genuinely believed that the babies would be better off with a two-parent family with a house and a dog. They didn't even see them, and they tried not to ever mention them but when they did, it was always singular. He'll be fine, they said, as if they hadn't heard that Morag was in the world too. I held on to Morag for the longest when they came for them. It was hard holding both and there were three of them trying to get the babies. I was frightened that Jamie might get hurt, he was so much smaller, you know? Then I hung on to Morag with both hands, I was like a cornered animal. Let me kiss them goodbye, I kept shouting, let me explain to them. I think I thought that if they brought him back for me to kiss I could grab him and run, and I genuinely think I might have jumped out of the window with both of them, even though we were on the third floor. They got me on the bed though, pinned me down and took her. I just hope she wasn't ever troubled by the memories, I mean it had to go somewhere in her brain, didn't it? I didn't realise that my finger was broken for a couple of days – I've never been able to bend it properly but I have always loved that. A physical reminder, every day, of saying goodbye to them.'

She held her finger out for me to see and for once I broke all my own anti-intimacy rules and I reached out to hold her hand.

'I was so glad when The Abortion Act came in soon after,' she said. 'Glad and sad all at the same time. Talk about bad timing. It could all have been so different.'

I held on to her hand as if someone was coming to tear us apart too, and I tried to imagine how terrible she must have felt. There were no words that would help, so we sat quietly like that for a while. Until we heard the noise of someone, it had to be a person, panting. Panting, and steps, too, the sound of someone running up above the sunken garden on the clifftop. I motioned to Annie to come with me and we slipped behind a bush. Not a great hiding place but good enough to hide us while we worked out whether it was friend or foe.

CHAPTER TWENTY-ONE

The Sunken Garden

Jackson ran three times around the top of the sunken garden before he went down the steps, in order to be absolutely certain that he wasn't being followed. He thought he'd left the guy behind shortly after running off from the harbour, but being quite sure wasn't good enough. He had to be one hundred per cent cast iron, no doubt sure or nobody was safe. All of Jackson's anxieties had been running wild since he left the flat with the monkey, and although the run had been good to clear his head slightly it got worse again as soon as he stopped.

It was bleak on the clifftop but Jackson could see clearly in all directions. There were hardly any cars at this end of town, and the nearest houses had only an occasional light shining behind curtains. He could see nothing, no running man, no one lurking by the bushes, nothing, so he took several deep breaths and jogged down the steps and into the calm of the garden. He'd been here before with Noah but on a hot day, a day when people were sunbathing on the grass and playing games with their children and dogs.

This was different. There were dark places everywhere

where trees and shrubs grew, and moon shadows like looming giants in every direction. Focus, Jackson said to himself. It'll all be over soon, and you're not doing it for yourself. It's not all about you, as Noah would say. He thought of Ocean and the way she had looked at him when he had played with her earlier that day. So trusting, as if other adults in her life hadn't abused her trust all the way along the line. She was willing to give him a chance, that was the thing, and he wasn't going to let her down now, even though every cell in his body was desperate to take the flight option and run like the devil until he was somewhere far away. No baddies here, he muttered, it's all for Ocean, all for Ocean.

Jackson stood in the middle of the garden and turned round slowly. They had to be here somewhere, he thought, one of those shadows had to be exactly in the shape of two old women. The sunken garden, that's what they had said. Why on earth didn't they narrow it down more?

'Hello,' he said.

He said it very quietly but the air was still down here out of the wind and the noise seemed enormous, as if it was bouncing off the sides of the garden. He tried again, a little more loudly but still keeping his voice down, in case. He heard some rustling after he said it the second time. He turned in the direction of the sound and two figures stepped out from behind a row of hedges. One was smaller than he remembered and one taller, but he recognised them anyway.

'We're so pleased you're here,' Virginia said. 'Where's the baby?'

Good question, Jackson thought. He would have expected Noah and Panna to be here by now. His anxiety went into overdrive. What if Panna had become more ill? What if Noah had tripped on the way up the cliff and Panna couldn't leave his unconscious body? What if they'd encountered the man, the man who had made those terrible marks on a little person who couldn't fight back? If he could do that to Ocean, what would he be able to do to Panna, or to Noah, who looked younger than he was?

Jackson looked at the stairs up to the top. Maybe he could just run up, see where they were and get back again. He knew roughly which path they would have taken.

'So pleased,' Annie said. 'Why just you though? Do you know where they are? The others?'

Jackson could hear a wobble in her voice. He wanted to tell her how worried he was, but this was clearly no time for him to fall apart. He felt a twinge of resentment. Why was it, he wondered, that every time he felt like cracking up, someone else got there first?

'They'll be here any minute,' he said. 'My gran will be obeying the plan to the absolute letter, and if anything she'll be overcautious. She's really not well, though. She walks quite slowly and she'll be looking in every direction to make sure.'

He explained the monkey ruse and Virginia clapped her hands.

'That's such a great idea,' she said. 'You should be a spy or something, when you're older. You've obviously got exactly the kind of brain they need, able to think on the spot and come up with solutions.'

Jackson shrugged in an awkward way. He wasn't used to praise, or if he was, it was only from Panna. For one second he entertained an idea of being a spy and imagined himself sitting by a pool with a cocktail, until his sensible head kicked in and reminded him that James Bond probably wasn't much of a template. Real spying would involve dangerous things, shady deals, nighttime assignations like this one and never being able to tell family what you were doing, or where you were.

'Thanks,' he said. 'I'd rather be a teacher.'

Jackson stepped back in surprise. Since when had he wanted to be a teacher, he wondered. He recognised it as soon as he said it. He did want to be a teacher, it was true, and yet he really had never said it before, not even to himself.

'You'd be great,' Virginia said, although Jackson couldn't think why on earth she might say that.

'I'll tell you why,' she said. 'You've got a natural way of being with little ones. I saw it with Ocean and with your brother. You talk to them on their level, and that's rare. I don't think you even realise it because it's so much a part of you. I can see you maybe working with real high-flyers.'

'Or the troubled ones,' Annie said. 'Maybe the wee kiddies with special needs.'

'Hang on a minute,' Jackson said. 'You're going too fast for me. I'm going to be all kinds of special teacher now?'

Even in the dark he could see the women were smiling, and he couldn't help feeling a little bit pleased.

'Maybe I'll get my degree first. When this is all sorted. If I don't end up in prison, of course.'

There was a sharp intake of breath from one of the women and Jackson realised that it was not a subject to joke about. It helped him, though, and he felt a flash of irritation at these women who didn't seem to realise that he had to make a joke of it, and that if he didn't he might turn and run, run to London, to Oxford, to Scotland, anywhere but here.

'No one is going to end up in prison,' Annie said. 'I've got a sixth sense going on here, I've always had it and I'm going to predict that the only one in prison will be that man, for the things he's done to the wee lassie.'

They all nodded. Jackson tried to distract himself. Dawn in the sunken garden, he thought, there's a poem here somewhere. He had got as far as trying to think of a way to describe the moon when he heard them. Heard Panna, huffing and puffing her way down the steps and into the sunken garden, holding hard to the side rails. Noah was carrying the shopping trolley rather than pulling it, and he was carrying it so gently that Jackson felt a little crack widen in his heart. It must have been heavy for him, but Jackson guessed he was trying to make the journey as smooth as possible for Ocean. At the bottom of the steps Noah reached in and lifted her out. She put a tiny arm around his neck and looked in every direction with interest, as if she was perfectly used to finding herself in strange places in the middle of the night. Noah looked pleased with himself and Jackson gave him an awkward one-armed hug as he placed Ocean gently on the ground.

'Oh dear,' she said and immediately the atmosphere changed.

It was as if the tiny girl had cut through the tension and fear and said just the right thing. Everyone said 'oh dear' back to Ocean and then to one another and Jackson helped Panna to a bench so that she could sit down. Virginia and Annie sat with her while Jackson and Noah squatted on the floor with Ocean. She was clearly thrilled to have got such a good response and was now oh-dearing at a rate of knots.

'Sshhh,' Jackson said, putting his finger to his lips.

Ocean reached out and pulled his finger away, chuckling.

'I'm serious,' he whispered to the others. 'She's got to be quiet, that's a piercing little voice and it's just the kind of thing that could travel on the wind. We still don't know where he is, don't forget.'

Jackson hoped he hadn't scared them too much.

'I may be the youngest apart from the littley,' Noah said. 'But I might have watched the most TV. You know, shows about criminals and true crime stuff, that kind of thing.'

He looked at Panna. 'I'm not allowed to but I do, on my iPad. Anyway, the point is, like I said before, there always has to be a plan B. And a plan A, really. I'm not clear what ours is from here.'

Noah looked down and stroked Ocean's hair to cover his embarrassment. Virginia clapped. It was a soft clap, hardly louder than the rustling of the trees, but Jackson could still hear the admiration for his little brother. He felt completely torn between pride and jealousy, and wondered if that was a thing proper parents felt. Say if your kid got to be a great footballer, for example, and you'd always dreamed of that for yourself but never made it. Would a person perhaps feel a sudden cold shock that it wasn't about them any more, the narrative, it was about the child now, the great footballer, and they would be nothing but a walk-on part in the story of his life? He supposed it didn't even have to be a big thing, like being a famous singer or sportsperson. Maybe the jealousy and pride mix could turn up anywhere, just at the idea that your child was living a better life, with a career you might have liked or a woman or man you could have loved. It was complicated but he was glad that Noah had spoken up.

271

'I've been thinking,' he said. 'It might be difficult to run with her, because there's so many of us, and . . .'

Jackson tailed off. He couldn't think how to say that they were old and slow without causing any offence, but Panna laughed and then the other two joined in.

'We're old, Jax, is that what you're trying to say?' Panna said. 'Only it's OK, it's not a secret. We kind of know we're old because guess what – we've been around for a long time.'

The other two women nodded and smiled and Jackson felt foolish.

'It's true though, he's talking sense,' Virginia said. 'I can see that it would be easier for you and Noah to scoot with her, or even just you, but we can't let that happen and you know why.'

'Last time I looked, Jackson,' Panna said. 'Last time I looked, you were definitely Black. This is Thanet, and even though people are the same wherever you go, sometimes they're a bit worse and sometimes they're a little bit better. There's lovely people here, I don't doubt it, including our new friends. But the systems, the way it all works here, that's not so good for anyone who ain't white.'

They stood in silence for a moment, digesting what Panna had said. There was a great deal of common sense in it but Jackson knew that however right she might be and whatever the risks were, they had to act fast. Whatever might happen for him, he had to get the baby away from that man. His voice was echoing in Jackson's ears, and it was the scariest thing he'd ever heard. Worse by far than the two policemen, so he was prepared to take his chances.

'I think,' he said but he didn't get any further before Panna spoke.

'I've been thinking,' she said. 'And we've done well up until now, we're here, we're all safe, but this isn't Kansas, we're not home and dry yet. I don't think he's around here, but we don't know. There's something been niggling at my slowpoke brain, and I've got it now.'

Panna's voice was quiet but firm.

'I was in Broadstairs,' she said. 'About a year ago, and before these two came to live with me. I wasn't feeling too well, and I stopped at one of the benches overlooking the sea. It's so pretty there. It's very English, and for some reason that makes me think of home, I'm not sure why.'

Jackson was alarmed. Here they were in the middle of the night on a clifftop absolutely heaving with old women plus a stolen baby, and Panna appeared to have chosen this time to lose her grip on both her marbles and her tongue. Why was she telling a story? Where was it going? Jackson looked at Noah to see if he was feeling worried as well but Noah grinned and gave him a thumbs up so there was no solidarity there.

'I can see Jackson is worried that I've gone crazy,' Panna said. 'He's always been too sensible for his own good but I'm gonna get to the damn point nonetheless. I appreciate we haven't got all the time in the world. So I was sitting on this bench and another woman nearly my age but much more glam came to sit next to me. She had a boy with her, a boy in a wheelchair. It was one of those electric ones that a person can drive themselves and not need to be pushed along. Very high tech. He wanted to look at the sea, he said. I think he'd been ill and stuck indoors.'

Jackson tried to stop himself jiggling from one foot to the

other, and instead went to look at all the entrances to the sunken garden, to check there was no one lurking. It was all clear, and as he came back he heard Panna finishing off the story.

'So I shouted at them,' she said. 'I told them they should be ashamed of themselves. But I could see that the boy was embarrassed so I didn't let rip as much as I would have liked to. They looked stupid in front of the girls they were with, though, and that's a harsh punishment at that age. She thanked me, the mum, said she would have said something but the boy hated it when she got involved. Such a nice woman, and she made me take her number. "If ever you need me," she said, "I've got a big van and a broad back." I thought that was such a funny thing to say. I've thought about it a lot.'

Panna got her phone out of her pocket.

'We can't take a bus or a cab, and we can't walk far together,' she said. 'I'm feeling rather tired. What have we got to lose?'

Everything, thought Jackson, but it was true that he didn't have a better idea.

'What about the long game?' said Virginia. 'It sounds great and Panna, I trust your intuition but we need to think ahead.'

Jackson admired the determination in her voice. She was as strong as Panna in her own way, he thought.

'I mean, even if the woman with the van comes and we get away today, we're still running, aren't we? We're fugitives and we think the local press might already be aware of the story. For all I know, by now my face could be all over the news. Maybe even more of our faces, who knows? And we need to think about Ocean's poor mum, we need to rescue her too.'

Jackson imagined a poster, with a picture of Noah's face

and 'WANTED' written underneath. Or Panna, even more terrifying. Maybe it wasn't too late to cut and run, he thought. He looked towards the exit.

It was Annie who spoke, but Jackson knew that Panna would have said the same.

'One bridge at a time,' Annie said. 'Our feet aren't big enough to cross them all at once, so we can only go bit by bit. We'll keep her safe today, and each day we do, we will all be a wee bit stronger.'

Jackson could see that Virginia wasn't content with that and he didn't blame her. It was an act of faith, what they were doing, an act of faith and an act of desperation. One look at Ocean, though, one look at her sitting on the grass in the moonlight picking up stones and he knew they had no choice.

'Come on,' Jackson said. 'Make the phone call and let's get going. I'm frightened that he'll find us if we fanny around too long. I think that only the locals know this garden is here, but we don't know who he's spoken to.'

For a moment Jackson wished he'd gone in a little softer because all of them started looking around them then, as if the man might be standing just behind them.

'It's OK, people,' Noah said. 'My big bro, he like, lives every emotion he feels to the max. It's good to be cautious, but if I tell you that he told me if I ever chew gum I should keep my head hanging down towards my feet while I'm chewing in case I choke, you'll know what we are dealing with here.'

The women smiled, even Virginia, and Jackson shrugged. How does he know how to do that? Jackson thought. To lighten the atmosphere and make people feel safer?

'You'll need to check that the van is big enough,' he said.

Panna made the phone call. Virginia went with her and they were behind a tree, so Jackson couldn't hear everything but he heard the last part.

'Thank you,' Panna said. 'I'll explain everything when I see you. Thanks for trusting us and I'm sorry to put you out.'

Panna clapped her hands quietly and Virginia bowed towards the others.

'Yes!' she said.

He could see that Panna hadn't been at all sure that this woman would help, that it was as much of a surprise to her when the woman said yes as it was to everyone else. She was brave, his grandmother, and he wished he was more like her.

Noah came and stood by him as if he knew what his brother was thinking, knew that he needed support.

'This is going to be the difficult part,' said Panna. 'Am I right, Virginia? Are you happy for me to explain?'

Virginia nodded.

'We need to get out of here and to the bus shelter on the nearest road. That's where she's meeting us. We'll go in stages, and we will leave the babe till last. Jackson, she's going to be your job. Noah, you and Annie are going to go first, and stand in the shelter as if you were saying goodbye after a night out. Noah, pull your hat down a bit so that no one can see how young you are. Virginia, I think you and I should go next and then Jackson with the trolley baby.'

'We'll leave a couple of minutes between each of us,' Panna said, 'and we'll be really quiet and really careful.'

'What if we see something?' Noah said.

Jackson marvelled at how normal it seemed for everyone to be accepting that Panna was in joint charge with Virginia, even though a few days ago she had been so unwell. You'd think, now, he thought, that she had spent her life in command of a crack troop unit or an entire high school.

'Can you whistle?' Panna asked.

Annie and Noah nodded.

'Excellent,' Panna said. 'Jackson – listen out for them. You'll be going down last, and getting straight in the car. I'm timing it, she said she'll be here in just over ten minutes.'

'What does he look like, Jax?' Noah said. 'I didn't see him up close. Is there anything we should be looking out for in particular?'

Jackson tried to think, but there was nothing really distinguishing him.

'He's just horrible,' Virginia said. 'He's got hate in his eyes.'

Noah stood a little closer to his big brother and Jackson could see his hand twitching as he tried not to put his thumb in his mouth, a habit there hadn't been a trace of for years. Jackson wondered for the millionth time whether they were doing the right thing, but he knew there was no way they could back out now.

CHAPTER TWENTY-TWO

People talk about difficult times as being the 'longest ten minutes' of their lives, or 'the longest half hour', etc, and I suppose
that until it happens to you, that might sound like nonsense. It
isn't. When I'm extremely stressed, there's a feeling that takes
me over and it's like one of those drugs they use to paralyse
a person on the operating table. Every movement seems like
the dial has been moved to slow motion, and every word that
comes out of anyone's mouth takes forever to complete, like
shouting in an echo chamber. I was in charge, but directing
the play in slow motion, that's how it felt.

Noah and Annie were the first to leave the sunken gardens,
and they were so cheery a person would have been forgiven
for thinking they were slightly deranged. I hadn't been sure
they were the right combo but when they went off waving
and smiling and blowing kisses I could see that Panna and
I were right, they were perfectly matched. Their optimism was
meant to be a boost for the rest of us and it may have worked
for the others but of course, it didn't work for me. It was all
my fault, that was the difference. If I hadn't done what I did

and especially if I hadn't got the others involved then any consequences would have fallen fairly and squarely on my head, and that would have been my choice and totally fair. But that nice woman from Scotland had seen enough trouble in her life, and that little boy should have been tucked up in bed with a superhero comic on the bedside table.

I was miles away and biting my nails when Panna spoke, up close and softly so that Jackson couldn't hear. He was on the floor despite the damp and playing with Ocean. The baby.

'Hey,' she said. 'They'll be OK, Noah and Annie. I know the town a bit, and from what we know of him, he doesn't, and it would be so unlikely that he'll hit on this end. And she's smart, Annie, I could tell that straight away. Not to mention young Noah. That boy is the dictionary definition of thinking outside the box, I swear. He's seen a lot in his life and in some ways he's got an old, old head. And he loves that baby.'

'I know,' I said.

I felt better just talking to her. There was something about her. A peace, or a calm acceptance of her fate or something. Or maybe I just wanted there to be something bigger than me, if that makes sense.

'You did right, you know,' said Panna. 'You did absolutely, unequivocally right. You couldn't have left her there, and if you had, she would have been dead. These things escalate so quickly, I'm afraid I've seen it before.'

It meant a lot to me, her vindication. She and her grandsons were up to their neck in it, so without their consent it would have been appalling. She didn't seem well though. I saw her grimace and hold her side, and then look towards Jackson.

'It's OK,' I whispered. 'He didn't see anything. Are you OK?'

I could see the pain play across her face and I knew she was holding it close so that the boys weren't worried. I made a mental note to ask her about it later.

'I'm fine,' she said. 'Just a twinge.'

I knew it was more. I wanted to be with her when things got difficult, so I was glad that we were a pair. She winced again at the pain and smiled at me as she caught me noticing. She trusts me, I thought. She trusts me and I wanted to be there in case she needed me. I hoped that I was up to the job.

It was Jackson I was worried about. Jackson who seemed so weighed down by the cares of the world, and who looked worried all the time, even when he was smiling.

'Do you think it's fair?' I said quietly, gesturing towards Jackson.

'Absolutely not,' Panna said. 'It's not fair, and it's not right, but we don't have any choice. He's got to be the one who brings her. He's the only one who can run, and we might need that. He can run fast.'

Jackson looked up from where he was tucking Ocean into her shopping trolley.

'I'm on it, Panna,' he said. 'No one is going to get her, not while I'm with her. If the worst happens, she doesn't weigh very much. I can tuck her under my arm and run.'

'Do you know, I think she'd like that,' I said. 'And when this is all over, I'd love to see that, for fun.'

As if on cue, I could hear Ocean giggle.

'You keep snuggling that sheep,' Jackson said.

'Right,' said Panna. 'We're going to go, Jax, but we won't

be far away. Like I said to Noah, whistle if you need anything – you know how to whistle, don't you?'

Jackson smiled at that, and I had a moment of pure envy. What would William have done, I thought, if I'd tossed out a film reference in the middle of a conversation? He would have looked around, that's what he would have done, first thing. He would have looked around to check that no one could see how embarrassing his mum was. If no one was watching, he might have given me a little nod, but a smile? That wouldn't have happened. And yet here this young man was, on a morning so early the light was only just starting to creep across the sky, and with a bunch of old women and a baby in a basket. And he could still smile.

'You're a good chap,' I said. I hoped it didn't sound too old ladyish.

'He's the best ever,' Panna said and then he did start to squirm.

We all laughed and it was good to leave on a happy note. I held my arm out to Panna and she took it and leaned on it quite heavily.

'Are you sure,' I said. 'Sure that you don't want to go on home and leave this to us?'

She stopped walking for a moment and I stopped with her. We would have been great friends, I thought, if we had met earlier.

'I like you, you're my kind of gal,' she said as if she had read my thoughts. 'But listen. I haven't got long. I can feel it coming. I've had my time. But this is one thing I want to do, I need to do, before I go. I need to know that baby is safe, even if it means my grandsons might be in difficulty. She can't fight back, can she? She's only a wee baby. My Noah, he had a difficult start. Such a difficult start, and every time I look at Ocean I know that could have been Noah. He got lucky. He got out. This little one has got a feeling of bad luck around her, have you noticed?'

I had, but I thought it was just my overactive imagination.

'No,' I said.

I wanted to reassure her, I think, but it was pretty clear that she could see right through me.

She asked to stop a couple of times on the walk from the sunken garden to the road so that she could catch her breath. I saw what an effort it was for her and how heroic she had been in disguising that effort until we were alone.

'Tell me something about yourself,' she said.

It was the second time we had stopped and she was gasping for breath. 'Give me something else to think about.'

It was impossible to ignore a request like that so I told her the first thing that came to my mind, the uppermost thing I'd been thinking which was how much I wanted this to be over and Ocean safe so that I could die. Less than five weeks to go now and I still wanted that option. Quietly, no fuss, just getting the hell out of here so that I didn't have to hurt so much any more. What a thing to throw at someone as unwell as Panna was. I thought then and I still think now, I must be one of the most self-centred people on the planet.

'I'm sorry,' I said. 'I didn't mean . . .'

Panna waved me away with a tutting noise. 'None of that,' she said. 'I've been there. But I'm gonna give you a big ask right now. Please don't do it here, and don't do it until the boys are over me. On their way. You may think you're just a bit part player . . .'

That was exactly what I thought. A tiny walk-on part, that was me now Jed was gone.

'. . . but those boys are going to lose me soon and that baby as well and they've taken a shine to you so don't you dare.'

Great, I thought. A binding promise to a dying woman, just what I needed. I couldn't bring myself to say the words, and I knew that was really childish but I couldn't.

'It doesn't matter if you don't say it. I know you're going to listen to me,' Panna said. 'Because I know I'm right. And I know you know that too. You're sensible, so we can stop talking about it and work out how the hell I'm going to get from here,' she pointed to the tree she was leaning against, 'to there.'

She gestured towards the road and I could see the bus shelter lit up by the streetlight next to it. Annie and Noah were standing by it and Noah saw us looking and waved. Panna straightened in front of my eyes, as though there was a string attached to her spinal column and someone was pulling it from above.

'Shall we?' Panna said and she held her arm out as if we were at an old-fashioned dance. I'm pretty sure that the touch at those sort of affairs was supposed to be a light one but Panna held on to me with every bit of strength she had and it was all I could do not to stumble or sink to the floor. I waved back to Noah and Panna managed to lift her hand a little.

'Should you be in hospital?' I said.

She made a movement as though she was brushing away a fly.

'Nah,' she said. 'We've got work to do.' She squeezed my arm, just lightly but enough to show me that she meant business.

When we got to the shelter, Noah was desperate to give us a blow by blow account of all the moments we had missed, even though nothing had happened.

'I looked around,' he whispered. 'I looked to all sides and then back again. No one has been past. Nothing to see here.'

'Well done, Noah,' I said.

Panna hadn't caught her breath yet. She looked at her watch.

'Let's just be quiet for a moment,' she said eventually. 'The last thing we want is for anyone to hear us in the houses.'

We sat there quietly as the sun rose.

CHAPTER TWENTY-THREE

Jackson was terrified as Panna and Virginia left the sunken garden. He wondered for a moment whether he could tell them how scared he was but Panna knew, he was sure of that. Panna had known everything about him since he was a baby. She must know how frightened he was but she still believed they were doing the right thing. Jackson squatted down next to the shopping trolley containing Ocean.

'Are you OK, little tiny?' he said.

He said it quietly in case she was asleep.

'Star,' she said.

It was crystal clear, Jackson was sure she'd said it.

'There are stars, you're right,' he said and he pointed up to the sky that she could see through the open top of the shopping trolley. Ocean clapped and Jackson felt better, stronger.

He wondered for one mad moment whether it would be wise to call the police, explain the whole thing to them and hope that they understood. He even reached for his phone but as he held it their faces flashed through his head again, the two policemen who had been so concerned about him going for a run. What if it was them? What if they put the whole lot of them in prison, sent Noah to a school for young offenders and sent Ocean back to her awful stepdad? The thought of anything happening to Noah and Ocean was ten times worse than anything that might happen to him. He put his phone back in his pocket.

Ocean looked really sleepy now. She was curled up on the cushions in the bottom of the shopping trolley, and somehow she made it seem like the most comfortable place ever.

'Here's your sheep,' Jackson said, handing it to her. 'I'm just going to pull the sides of the bag up so it will be a bit dark for a while, and you'll be able to go to sleep. When you wake up again everything will be lovely.'

'Sheep,' Ocean said in a tired little voice.

Jackson tucked her in and pulled up the sides of the bag so that she couldn't be seen. It was as if she knew, he thought. As if she knew what a danger she was in.

'I promise you,' he whispered into the shopping trolley. 'I promise you that when this is all over, we will try to let you be as noisy as any other toddler. I'd like to take you to a place where there are echoes, and we will shout together until the noise bounces off the walls. We could splash in the sea that's got the same name as you, and we won't mind if you splash us. This is the annoying bit, that's all.'

Ocean fell asleep quickly, her thumb in her mouth and her sheep in her hand. Jackson set off towards the meeting place, ready to fight wolves or demons for her. The trolley was noisy so Jackson picked it up like Noah had and held it gently in both arms.

Leaving the sunken gardens was terrifying. It seemed crazy

to break cover, and the surrounding clifftop was as alien and dangerous as the landscape of the moon. The few trees that had managed to survive clifftop life were bent over like very old people on a windy day out, and the shelters looked like the only safe places. What if Ocean's stepdad was watching from one of the clifftop shelters? Maybe with binoculars? He could be watching right now, Jackson thought, and here they were, Jackson and Ocean, in the middle of a moonlit, windswept open plain.

He had to keep moving, stick with the plan. He couldn't leave Ocean, or Panna and the women, or Noah. He couldn't stay in the sunken garden. He had no choice. All he could do was hold the shopping trolley carefully and keep moving forwards. Jackson stood tall. If he hunched over, he knew he would look suspicious and guilty. He tried to make his steps not too hurried, and to look relaxed, as though it was the most normal thing in the world to be walking across a clifftop carrying a stolen baby as the dawn rose in the east.

On a good day Jackson could have covered the ground between the sunken garden and the shelter at the side of the road where the others were waiting in about thirty seconds. Now though, with the trolley and the baby and the thundering noise of his heartbeat, it seemed to take forever. He stumbled once and almost dropped her but he held on tight. So tightly that his arms seemed to remember holding Noah that day and how scary that had been for him, how much he had wanted a grown-up to come and help. Nothing changes, Jackson thought.

He put the trolley down gently as he reached the shelter. They were all there waiting for him, and he noticed how tired and drawn the women looked, especially Panna. They all needed to be in bed, and somehow the thought gave him a kind of energy. No choice but to step up, and Noah high-fived him silently as if he could read Jackson's mind.

Jackson gestured to the others to show that Ocean was asleep, but a tiny movement made him stop still, like in a children's game of statues. He wasn't sure whether he saw something out of the corner of his eye, that was the problem. A flitting, a brief movement, could have been a bat or a seagull. Did seagulls flit around at night? He wasn't sure that they did. Could it be Ocean's step dad? He looked at the women to see if they had noticed anything but he didn't think that they had, until he caught Virginia's eye. An understanding flashed between them, he was sure of it, and that must mean that she had seen something too. He didn't dare to peer round again, but he readied himself for some kind of attack. He picked up the trolley again and did some knee lifts on the spot, so that he could run if he needed to. One minute, two minutes crawled by and just when Jackson thought he couldn't wait another second in this kind of limbo agony, he heard a car approaching down the silent road. A van, in fact, a large black van with a woman at the wheel. She looked younger than Virginia and Panna, but not by much. Jackson didn't know much about women's ages, and it was not fully light, but she looked strong and capable and that was what they needed. She jumped out of the driving seat and swung the side door open.

'Hi,' she said. 'I'm Ellen, get in the back.'

Jackson motioned for the women to get in first, and they got in more quickly than Jackson would have thought possible.

He put the shopping trolley on the floor at their feet and turned to look for Noah.

Noah. Jackson looked around and couldn't see him anywhere.

'Noah,' he whispered. 'Come here now.'

There was no answer. Panna caught his eye and it was clear that she had also realised that he wasn't there. For a moment it looked to Jackson as if she was going to get out of the car so he motioned for her to stay where she was. He looked up and down the empty road and then turned to run back towards the sunken gardens. As soon as Jackson was behind the shelter he could see them. Noah, and the damn dog.

'I thought he was shut in,' Noah said. 'I'm sure I left it closed, absolutely certain. You saw me. I don't know how he got out, Jax, honest. But he's so clever, aren't you, boy? He knew where we were and he knew to follow us and everything. We can't leave him here, bro, we have to take him with us.'

Noah picked up the dog and Jackson tried to gather his thoughts. He was sure they had locked up, Panna had specifically said so. It wasn't something they were likely to have forgotten, especially in their heightened state of anxiety. Noah had left puppy pads everywhere and enough water for at least twelve hours. Neither of them had envisaged being away for longer than that. They had left dried food and fed him lots before they left. Noah had said that he heard the dog whine as the key turned in the lock. Jackson believed him, and that meant that the only way he could have got out is if someone had gone in there and let him out. Noah seemed to draw the same conclusion at the same time.

'Run,' Jackson said in what he hoped was a calm voice.

Noah scooped the dog up and ran towards the van, and Jackson ran behind him. He knew there was someone following them now and he wished he could let rip and run faster but he had to cover Noah, and Noah was just a little boy. They managed to get to the van and Noah threw the dog in and jumped in himself, with Jackson right behind him, slamming the door. They sat on the floor at the feet of the women and Panna shouted, 'Go, go go.'

Ellen started the van before Panna had even said the last 'go,' and they drove off at a speed Jackson had seen before only in the movies. Virginia, Annie and Panna were all clapping and Jackson felt slightly hysterical. Virginia turned round to look out of the window as they left.

'I can see him, he's standing in the road but he's not running after us,' she said.

'Number plates,' Jackson said. 'What if he's noted your number and he's going to call the police? They'd listen to him, you know. They definitely would.'

Ellen turned around and grinned, and for a moment Jackson wished he hadn't said anything. Surely she should keep her eyes on the road, driving so fast and swinging round corners?

'That's where we're in luck,' she said. 'Someone knocked it off, or maybe it was me driving a bit carelessly, I'm not sure which.'

Jackson tightened his grip on Noah, who was sitting on the floor with his legs either side of the trolley, and Virginia reached into the trolley and pulled out a snuggly, sleepy Ocean.

'Either which,' Ellen said. 'It means all he's going to see is a big old black van with a poke of people in it. I don't think he'll be going to the police with that, do you?'

The women seemed happy with that but Jackson wasn't at all sure. How many big black vans were there round here? It could be easy to find her for all he knew. She might even be known to them, which was actually quite likely if she made a habit of driving around without number plates.

It took about ten minutes to get to Broadstairs, and it was a wild ride.

'My son says I'm a terrible driver,' Ellen called over her shoulder. 'He says I should keep my eyes on the road and indicate more but I think it's just mother/son sparring, I'm sure he doesn't mean it.'

I'm sure he bloody well does, Jackson thought, and as he thought it he looked at Noah, who was clearly struggling not to laugh. Jackson had always been prone to getting infected with laughter or tears and also, it was funny. Outlandish, dangerous, mad – and funny. Jackson started to laugh too, quietly at first and then big, hiccupping snorts of laughter that he couldn't control. Noah joined in with a shrill laugh that made him sound much younger and soon the women were giggling too. Except for Panna, who was smiling but holding her side as if she was holding herself together. Jackson noticed and tried to stop. He breathed as deeply as he could and counted each breath, a trick that Panna had taught him. He could see that she was watching.

'Well done,' she said when he had finally stopped, and she patted his head, the nearest part of him that she could reach. She probably would have preferred to give him a good natured thump or a hug, but the pat worked just as well to pull him back to his senses.

By the time the car stopped in Broadstairs Jackson was completely calm.

'We need to be careful here,' he said. 'It's almost fully light now and we might look a bit noticeable all piling out of the car.'

'I've parked right in my driveway,' Ellen said. 'It's a moment or two to the front door, and there's a care home next door where the old folk won't be up yet. We are facing the sea, so no one to look over us in that direction. I'll go first and I'll leave the door open, then come in quickly and quietly.'

Jackson hoped she was right as they got out of the van. Panna needed a lot of help, and Jackson thought that she looked an unpleasant grey colour that reminded him of when she first got ill. She had kept the details of her illness secret for weeks, months probably, and told Jackson that she just needed some space. The boys had lived alone in her flat in London for a while until Noah got really distressed after school one day. He wouldn't tell Jackson what the problem was, but he kept saying that he needed to see Panna so Jackson took him on the coach the next morning. She had been putting them off, not encouraging them to visit, and when they got there Jackson could see why. Panna had been in a terrible state, and it was obvious from the moment they let themselves in. She couldn't get up to answer the door, that's how bad it was. She was lying on the sofa with no water or food to hand and she looked much thinner than she had only a few weeks ago, when the boys had seen her last.

They hadn't gone home, of course, they had stayed and cleaned and cooked and found a new school for Noah and Panna had been brighter and happier with their company and she had had some good days. Really good days, and this last part with the dog and then the baby had been the best of all. Jackson knew what stage four meant, but she had been so perky and he had seen online that some people could live for years with it so he had begun to hope, he really had. Seeing her hold on to Virginia's arm so tightly as she got out of the van made Jackson feel as though the ground beneath his feet was shaking. As if a crack might actually open up and swallow him whole, or as if it already had and now he was hurtling towards the centre of the earth. Jackson looked at Noah, and realised that he must feel the same. Some kids of his age wouldn't have noticed, but you could never pull the wool over Noah's eyes.

CHAPTER TWENTY-FOUR

I imagined for one crazy moment that we'd thought of every-thing, that we'd be able to relax and plan and make the right decision. I even spared a guilty thought for my pills, and imagined them lined up in a quiet place waiting for me. No such luck. Life moves on when you're not looking, Jed used to say, and as usual, he was right. It turned out that while we had been planning and running and keeping her safe, Ocean had turned into big news. I should have known the story would take off. Missing babies, crying parents, what's not to worry about? Anyone would want a happy ending. It's just that it was hard to see her as missing when she was so very present, happy, well fed and sound asleep on Ellen's sofa clutching her sheep.

The television news told a different story. They had a picture of her mum looking sad and interviews with police officers with stern faces. Poor Cate was definitely crying in the picture. I felt sorry for her, I really did, and I had to keep reminding myself that she had asked me to take Ocean. She had known that she couldn't protect her. Why was she saying all this?

I could see that everyone felt uneasy. We watched the rolling news channels on our phones and tablets while Ocean slept. Noah was sitting on the floor by her head.

'If I say "off", you need to turn it off, straight away,' he said. 'Split second reflex or she might hear something that will scar her. Or scare her.'

I looked at the photo of me they were showing on the news. 'Person we'd like to interview,' I heard and of course, 'Virginia,' in a tone that showed the presenter didn't really believe it could be my name. It was a terrible photograph too. I couldn't imagine where they'd got it from, but I thought I remembered when it had been taken. On a day out, when Jed had been very ill, one of our last days out in fact. We'd sort of known that and so we asked a passer by to take a photo, but it was pointless because it was such an extraordinarily bad picture that we never looked at it again. I looked old, really old, and there was a horrible scowl on my face. I think I was braced against the wind but I was also worried about Jed, who I knew was in pain that day. They'd cut him out of the picture on the news, and on my own I looked like the kind of old woman they used to call a witch. I knew that was what everyone watching the TV would be thinking. That I was some kind of evil old crone, enticing babies away and eating them or something like that. I couldn't listen to what they were saying because my brain closed off and started whirring round. I couldn't think, for a moment, how I'd got myself here. Number one fugitive, hiding in the house of a woman I didn't know, mug shot on TV, unable to go outside and what's more, with a baby and a band of helpers to worry about.

'I think I've got the wrong life,' I said. 'I just wanted to help.'

'Listen,' Annie said. 'You did the right thing. Her mum wanted you to, she wouldn't have left her in your garden otherwise. And I've looked at her now, examined her, and I'm sure of it. Sure that you did the absolute right thing. It was a brave thing to do, there's a lot of people, especially folk of our age, who would have turned away and thought it was nothing to do with them. Everyone here agrees.'

I looked around at their faces, my new friends, and they were all nodding. And I knew I'd be able to justify what I'd done if I could explain myself to the authorities, only I knew they would make assumptions. That they might not listen to me and I would be the bad guy. As if to underline that, a picture of the most well known female child-killer of the twentieth century flashed on the screen. Even Annie gasped. The woman was seen as the embodiment of all evil, the vileness of her crimes somehow enhanced by her out of date bleached bouffant hairstyle. Everyone knew who she was.

'You can go if you want to,' I said. 'Panna – take the boys home. Annie – go back to Scotland and forget all about us. Ellen, thank you for what you've done. I'll be fine, honestly. You've helped me this far and Ocean is safe and well. But I don't see why any of you should be involved any further, you're putting yourself in danger and you don't need to.'

I remembered what I'd said to Panna a couple of days and a million years ago. I'd said I was going so that I could keep them safe, and I needed to punch on with that.

'I'm leaving as soon as I can,' I said. 'I'm really grateful for all your help, honestly I am. I've learned so much from all of you. I think I have to do this on my own, though, and it's probably hopeless but I'm going to try and make them listen.

Maybe I'll be sent to prison but maybe, just maybe I can make them listen and her mum will be able to sort herself out and get rid of that man. And I'll be fine. It's my fight, and believe me, I don't have much else going on at the moment. I don't really care about myself, I've had my life.'

It was weird. As soon as I said that I had a flash of realisation that it wasn't true. I wanted to stay out of prison for lots of reasons, and I knew at once that I was going to fight for my freedom, and for Ocean's life, and one thing I wasn't going to do yet was to take the pills I'd squirrelled away. I had work to do, and a purpose. I had almost promised Panna and there were new things to be taken into consideration. I patted Annie's shoulder and she looked alarmed.

'You'll need help,' she said. 'We just saw your face on TV and everyone who watched today's news will have seen it too. And where are you going to stay? Anyone who sees you will put two and two together and shazam. There you are, scuppered.'

I knew there was sense in what she said, but my feeling of impending danger was stronger. I felt trapped, and unable to make the right decision.

'Surely if I explain,' I said.

No one answered. I was worried sick, mainly about Ocean and her mum and whether I was doing the right thing, but I have to admit, there was also a bit of concern about whether I would end my days in a prison. I'd have to be in solitary confinement because of being thought of as a paedophile. There would be people waiting for me in the shower with sharpened toothbrushes and my food would be full of spit, but none of that mattered compared with what might happen to Ocean if no one was looking out for her.

I couldn't understand how quickly life had gone from my husband and I waving to a neighbour's baby out of my window, to being all alone with no husband and wanting to die, to loving a stolen baby and a bunch of other people. And as if that wasn't enough, I was Britain's most wanted woman. I looked around the room. Not alone any more, I thought, but somehow that didn't help. It was all my fault, that was the difficult part. The part I was alone with. They were so great, my merry band of supporters. They didn't deserve to get into trouble with me.

'I'm so sorry,' I said and I'll admit it, I was sniffing a little.

Of course, everyone began to speak and I knew they would all be saying the nicest things and I felt bad about that, too. So I was pleased when Noah held up his hand as if he was stopping traffic.

'I read this thing,' he said.

Jackson winced and groaned.

'And this bro, I think he was a psycho something or the other, he was saying how like people are programmed to think it's all about them. It's a survival thing or something like that. So if you ask a person who's been in say a bombing, if you ask them when it happened they'll say, the minute I opened the door it went off. Or, as soon as I looked up. There was one dude who was in a fire in a restaurant and he thought it happened when he cut into his potato. So I'm just saying, Virginia Panna, it's not anything you made happen, if that makes sense.'

Jackson smiled, and Panna patted Noah on the head.

'Well said,' she said.

I could see that she was still feeling bad. I tuned out of the conversation for a few moments then, to try to think things through again. I had to get it right. When I looked again, Ocean was in her favourite place, on the floor with Noah.

'Look,' Noah said. 'Look what she's learned. She's so clever.'

We were in Ellen's front room, which was restful, like something out of a magazine. Muted, earthy colours, comfortable furniture and real pictures on the walls. The dog sat between Ocean and Noah like a storybook dog and I realised that I wasn't even the teeniest bit scared of him any more. Noah was teaching Ocean a clapping rhyme and I wished I could freeze time. I don't think she had much of a clue about what she was doing, but she was enjoying it anyway. I had given her some hot milk in a cup and she had managed it well. We were resting, that's what it felt like. A group rest, with something terrible waiting for us round the corner. Or in Panna's case, probably closer. She looked grim. She had been so strong, such a rock for the last couple of days but the strain was starting to show in the way she held herself. Jackson was sitting next to her on the sofa and she had her head on his shoulder.

'Isn't this lovely?' Annie said. 'I never knew it could be so good, having friends and all that.'

I was shocked. There were literally lives at stake here and although I agreed with her it seemed wrong to mention it. As if it might jinx it, I guess. She was relaxed though, and she looked as if she was having the time of her life.

I looked at Jackson and he smiled.

'It doesn't always help to make the right decisions, panicking,' Panna said. 'We've got to do the right thing now, in a world where there are so many wrong things. And it's OK to like each other's company, while we wait.'

Ellen produced cups of coffee that were strong but not

bitter and no one spoke except for Noah as we all tried to process what was going on. I was tired, I'll admit it, and feeling every one of my years and months and days. I kept trying to think what to do next. I wanted to come up with a plan that would make everything OK, and I didn't know where to start. I was so deep in worry and panic that I almost didn't notice when Ellen's son wheeled himself into the room. It was an electric wheelchair and almost completely silent until he was close.

'I've seen your picture on the TV,' he said. 'I don't think it's right, stealing babies.'

'Daniel,' his mum said. 'Not everything is black and white. You're fifteen, and you don't always know everything.'

'I'm prepared to listen,' he said. 'And if you're talking rubbish I'll ring the police.'

'Fair enough,' I said.

To be honest, I was glad of a chance to spell things out, see how they sounded when I said them out loud, and glad too that I could stop being stuck in my own head, with my thoughts spinning round on a loop. Not to mention the fact that this young man deserved this. He deserved to hear why we had turned up so early in the morning, bringing danger and mayhem with us. What if his mum got into trouble for helping us? Who would look after him then? I opened my mouth to speak but Annie got there first.

'I just want to say,' she said. 'I just want to say that I've had a wee idea, and it's a good one. I'm thinking that if the worst happens, and we get arrested, I could easily, easily say that we forced your lovely mammy to stop. We like, pulled her over pretending to need assistance and then we made her take us. So we are kind of holding you hostage, you know, like in the films.'

'Oh,' Daniel said. He looked around the room. 'I'm not sure if that's going to do my street cred any good, being held hostage by three old ladies.'

'Daniel,' said Ellen. 'That's rude.'

Daniel shrugged. 'It's true though,' he said. 'Can we not say it's him,' he pointed at Jackson, 'him that's holding us hostage?'

I opened my mouth to say something, and I could see that Annie and Ellen did too but Daniel beat us to it.

'No,' he said. 'That wouldn't be fair.'

Noah jumped up and held his fist out for Daniel to bump. It was difficult for Daniel to move his arm but they made it work.

'Way to go, bro,' Noah said. 'One for all and all for one. It's like that story that Ocean likes, you know, with the turnip. No one can pull it on their own but when they all get together they can. The great big enormous rescue, that's what we've got here.'

Bloody hell, I thought. Another person getting involved. What on earth have I done?

I explained to Daniel as clearly as I could what was going on, and it was good to straighten it out in my own head, voice what we were doing and why. Luckily he didn't ask what would happen next and he and Noah went off to play on his PlayStation, taking the dog with them. I could see that Jackson would have liked to go too but he knew that his place was with the grown-ups, and my heart went out to him. I had a sudden, clear lit flash about William. That's why he never really grew up, I thought. That's why he's never been able to take responsibility, or to hang around when things get difficult.

Because I've never asked him to, never expected him to be with the grown-ups. I wonder, I thought, if he would have been different if I had had another child?

'There's something about the way those two boys have just gone off together to play their games that makes me wish I'd had a whole pack of children,' I said.

Ellen laughed. 'You and me both,' she said. 'I always imagined I'd have a house full.'

Panna took a few deep breaths and sat up straight.

'Jackson,' she said. 'You need a break. A break from old ladies and babies and young boys. I know you well, and I know that you need some time to be you, on your own, even if it's just for an hour.'

Jackson looked embarrassed and started to argue but it was obvious that Panna was telling the truth. Ellen explained that the upstairs rooms were usually rented out for bed and breakfast but no one was staying there at the moment so Jackson could go and have a rest.

'Right,' she said when she came back from showing him where to go. 'Spill, ladies. I trust you enough to have you here, but I need to know the exact story, in more detail than you gave Daniel. And we need to make a plan, a proper plan about where to go next.'

I had Ocean on my lap, we had been singing nursery rhymes and she was at her sweetest and most snuggly. I buried my face in her hair for a moment, so that no one would see me tear up. It was so wonderful to have someone else say that sort of thing, to suggest a plan, rather than leave it to me. Panna would have done it, I could see that, she would have taken charge in an instant and sorted us all out but she wasn't well enough and Annie? Annie had her own stuff going on and it couldn't be expected of her either. I pulled myself together and gave her a full account of everything that had happened. I put my hands over Ocean's ears when I got to the parts about the terrible things that had been done to her, and I rolled up her little sleeve to show some of the fading bruises and burn scars.

'There's ones like that all over her body,' I said. 'She doesn't flinch so much now but still sometimes if you make a sudden movement. She guards her little face if you bend too close to her unexpectedly. It's horrible to see.'

'I had twins,' Annie said.

Jeez, I thought, this isn't the time, mate. But the others were all looking at her as if they were fine with it and I didn't want to be the mean girl in the group. I've been that too often in my life.

'I had twins, tiny wee lovelies, when I was a teen. Not much older than your Daniel.' Annie looked at me. 'Honestly, Virginia, this is relevant, I promise,' she said.

I blushed, I think. I couldn't believe I was that transparent and I was ashamed that she felt she had to justify herself.

'They wouldn't let me keep them. They had to be sent to foster parents and I won't tell you about that, or about how it felt when they took them away, because you can probably imagine. It's not relevant, that part, but the next bit is. Because they died, my wee twins, you probably read about it at the time. It was in all the papers. Morag was dead when they got to her, bless her wee heart, but Jamie lived for a few days and they let me see him in the hospital. I couldn't hold him because of the tubes and the drips but I could put my hand on his little leg, and hope that he knew I was there. But it's why I'm here

303

really, to help this wee one. Because what they did.' Annie swallowed and we could all see that she hadn't said anything to anyone about this in a long time, possibly never.

'What they did, and we never knew whether it was the foster mum or the dad and it doesn't matter, the other one let it happen, whichever one of them did it. They banged their heads together, their tiny wee heads. Can you imagine that? They were nine months old, not even crawling yet but just sitting up. They banged their heads together to stop them from crying. There were other, older injuries too and that's probably why they were crying so much. And I wasn't there.'

Annie was crying now and Panna and Ellen both produced tissues and patted her.

'Morag died within minutes, they think, because she was on the floor so she got the harder impact. She was lying on a rug, and someone must have picked Jamie up and slammed him into her. There was blood round their wee ears.'

She shuddered and I couldn't help hoping that she would stop now. The images were just too terrible, and everything about her made sense. Why she had worked for the ambulance service, why she had never been able to settle, why she hadn't left Oban before – the whole lot. Even why she wore bright swirly skirts dating from 1974. I imagined someone doing that to little babies and then I stopped, couldn't think about it any more. It was too much.

'We're not going to let that happen here,' Ellen said. 'This one was born under a semi lucky star, because she has all of us and we won't let it happen any more. We'll get her out like Noah's turnip.'

We all nodded and agreed and I wanted to shout, yes, and

high-five someone. Of course we needed to protect her and I was going to do that or die trying, but I didn't want to drag them all down with me. There was no need. I held Ocean a little more tightly and she put her hand on my arm as if she wanted to reassure me.

'Hickory dickory snack,' she said.

'And it's OK,' Annie said. 'I know you're thinking about us but you don't need to, we're all here voluntarily.'

'Amen,' Panna said and Ellen gave me a thumbs up.

I was grateful to them for their support but I was still determined to protect them all if I could. I needed a separate plan of my own, the Captain Scott version. I needed to be able to walk off into the metaphorical snow with her, keep her safe and take the blame. The trouble was, my mind had gone blank. I mean completely whiteout blank, and I didn't think I could do it. I couldn't catch my breath for a moment and Annie noticed.

She scooted over so that she was sitting on the floor next to my chair, and held out her arms for Ocean. I felt conflicted, because I didn't really want to let her go but on the other hand I could hardly claim exclusive rights, most especially after the horror story I had just heard. Also I was still panting a bit, trying to get my breath back on an even keel, so to hand the little bundle of baby over would be sensible on every level. I didn't want to but I straightened her cardigan and held her out. She seemed very happy to go to Annie, who had a reper-toire of nursery rhymes that far outnumbered mine.

'I think you're all exhausted,' Ellen said. 'There are lots of beds, I promise to wake you in an hour. You need to rest, if we are going to make a coherent plan.'

I wanted that more than anything, but I knew I couldn't do it. Panna, though, Panna was looking worse by the moment. It was the right thing for her, so I helped her to Ellen's bed on the ground floor so that she wouldn't have to climb any steps, and made sure she drank some water.

Annie was still singing nursery rhymes when I returned and to look at her, you would think that nothing had ever been wrong in her life. I thought of William at nine months and wondered how she could function, how she could have lived her life since her babies were killed and how it would be to move from minute to minute with the weight of all that sadness.

I think I dozed in the chair while I was watching them, or maybe I fell fully asleep again, I'm not sure. The minutes ran away from me though and it was afternoon before I properly surfaced. Ellen was putting out bread and cheese for lunch, and Ocean was sitting in an ordinary chair, kept from falling by brightly coloured scarves which wrapped round her and tied at the back.

'Sheep,' she said, holding out a chewed piece of toast.

'We've been talking, while you were asleep,' Annie said. 'There really is no choice, Virginia. We have to come clean to someone, or else it will look as if we're just as bad, d'you see? Just as bad as the other people in her wee life.'

Of course she was right, I'd always known it, I just couldn't think who it would be safe for us to talk to. Safe for Ocean, it didn't matter about me. I wondered for a moment whether I would be able to take her and run, maybe when everyone was asleep.

'I think I know what you're thinking,' Annie said. 'I know you want things to be OK for her, we all do. But where could we go? Where could you go if you tried to make a break for it on your own?'

She was right, I knew she was. I couldn't live in a cave with Ocean, or get to another country where we could be anonymous. I couldn't do anything, and I suddenly thought of Jed, and what he used to say when I got upset about the world. Dogs being eaten in countries far away, babies separated from their parents at borders or children bombed in occupied zones. It's not about you, he used to say, it's not your fight. You can't make everything better and there's no point trying.

I think that was my lowest point, despite the camaraderie and the support I was getting from everyone. Despite the fact that I knew Ocean was better off away from that man. I knew that her own mum had believed she was better off with me, whatever they were saying in the news. I still wanted to make things better and I still believed that somehow I did have the power to do it, regardless of logic. It was mad to imagine living off-grid in a forest or a tent. What on earth would happen to Ocean if I died? What even would happen if I didn't die, I still wouldn't be able to provide her with everything she needed.

'OK,' I said. 'This is the part in the film where someone says it's curtains, right?'

'That would be me,' Panna said.

Jackson had an arm around her and she was walking slowly but she looked better than she had done before she went for a rest.

'I think we need to call it quits,' I said. I surprised myself, but as soon as I said the words I knew it was the right thing.

'I think Ocean has had such a high profile that he wouldn't dare to do anything else, and whatever happens they're gonna keep an eye on her.'

There was silence as we all weighed up what I had said. What I hadn't said, of course, was that Panna's lovely boys were probably in more danger than any of us if we kept hold of Ocean. They might think I'm a witch while I've got her, but no one really expects little old ladies to transgress. Once I've said sorry and talked about being a lonely widow it would be easy for the transgressions to be explained away. Dementia even, or an insane desire to be needed. The only hope was to hand myself in. Not ourselves, not the others, because I didn't want any of the others to be implicated in any way. No, it had to be just me, on my own.

'I'll go,' I said. 'I'm going to take her to the social services office, before they close. I'll sit down and talk to whoever it is on duty there and explain it all. You're right to call curtains, Panna. We can't keep her forever and I've got to face that.'

I was going to say more but I couldn't. Just the sight of her on the floor made me cry again. That darling baby was so happy with Noah. She had changed in a few days, from a wary, watchful, scared little dot to a strong and funny girl. The very idea that anyone would harm even a tiny piece of her little body made me want to tear out my own hair and wail, but I couldn't do that for a million reasons, not least because she would be scared. So would everyone else, for that matter. I'd brought them all here, got them all involved in this and now I had to do the right thing.

I explained what I was thinking to the others and they were relieved, I could see that. There was some muttering, especially from Annie, but I couldn't afford to listen. I'd just got to the part where I was going to offer to have Ocean for weekends sometimes when Cate was busy, and that we could all get together for a meal with her then, when Ellen's son Daniel glided in. He stopped his wheelchair right in front of me and I could tell from his face that he was going to say something serious. Noah was right behind him and his eyes looked very bright, as if he was about to cry. He tapped Daniel on his arm.

'Don't say anything yet,' he said and bent down to where Ocean was playing on the floor. Noah picked her up and danced across the room with her, away from the grown-ups. Everyone except Noah had stopped talking, and we were all looking at Daniel. Jed's big friendly face swam across my vision as I waited.

'Noah, are her ears covered?' Daniel said.

Noah nodded and held her to him more closely, so that one of her ears was against his chest and one covered by his hand. She looked snug, I did have time to think that but everything else was drowned out. I knew he was going to say something that changed the game, and I could see that Annie felt the same. She reached for my hand and I let her hold it. I think Jackson and Panna were holding hands too.

'For goodness' sake, say it, Daniel, whatever it is,' Ellen said. 'We could do without the drama.'

'OK,' Daniel said. 'I had the news on, in the background, while Noah and I were on the PlayStation. It's easy to do, if anyone wants me to show them. It's all about her, the news.' He pointed to Ocean. 'Anyway, I'm afraid they've found a body and they think it's Ocean's mum. It's all over the news. They're not actually saying you did it but . . .'

I heard Annie gasp and I held on to her hand so tightly I must have hurt her.

'Oh no,' she said. 'That poor wee girlie. I'm going to guess she did it herself, god bless her.'

'It must have been just after we went to see her,' I said. 'If we had managed to persuade her we would have saved her life.'

We shouldn't have let her walk away, I thought. We should have grabbed her, made her see somehow. We had blood on our hands, that's what I thought then and I still think now.

'That poor wee girl,' Annie said. 'She loved that baby, I believe she did.'

Annie put her head in her hands and sobbed.

'Hang on,' said Panna. 'I'm not sure that she killed herself. It doesn't ring true, from what you've told me. Didn't you say she was planning to sort him out, make it better?'

There was a silence for a moment as we all tried to take it in, make it rational. I thought about how Cate had been when Ocean was little. So excited, so loving. Annie was right, it didn't make sense, but I felt so sad and so responsible I couldn't see straight.

'It's him,' Noah said. 'The last time we saw him was in the afternoon, yes? Late afternoon. And the next time was early this morning? He's got a car, right? And I'm sorry, sorry that it happened and sorry that everyone is sad. I'll look after Ocean for a little while, with Daniel.'

Noah put Ocean on Daniel's knee in the wheelchair and they moved off towards his bedroom.

Everyone was crying. I wanted to say something that might help but I couldn't think of anything except Cate, and how sad she had looked when she gave me Ocean. How happy she had been in those early days, when Jed was still alive. I felt as though I had been winded. That poor woman. Could things have gone differently? And poor little Ocean. She would never see her mum again.

'I never meant for this,' I said. It just burst out of me somehow, I couldn't keep it in.

'I did it,' I said. 'They're right on that one, I'm so sorry, Ocean. So sorry, Cate. She tried her best to keep Ocean safe, and she loved her, I know that. She really did.'

I couldn't say anything else. I couldn't speak. I wished so hard that Jed was with me and I felt a tide of grief wash over me, for Cate and Jed and Ocean and even a little for myself. I slunk off to the bathroom, where I could be on my own. I washed my face with cold water and I thought things through. Social services would be closed shortly, and if I wanted to speak to anyone I needed to go now.

'There won't be anyone to give you an alibi if you go on your own,' Annie said. 'You're going to need to prove to them that you couldn't have killed Cate, I'm afraid. Someone is going to have to go with you.'

I felt panic sweep over me. Was she right? Was I going to have to prove I didn't actually kill anyone? I couldn't think straight but Ellen could.

'Annie,' she said.

She said it gently and I thought what a great mum she must be.

'Annie, Virginia doesn't need an alibi at the moment, because it said on the news that Cate's body was found at her home. Virginia hasn't got a car and she couldn't have been there and here at the same time.'

Annie nodded but I knew we were missing something. I tried to figure out what it was while I packed a few things for Ocean but it was Noah, of course, who figured it out.

'Miss Virginia,' he said.

It was clear that he was agitated by the way he hopped from one foot to the other, and it was heartbreakingly cute to see that Ocean was trying to copy him from a seated position.

'Sorry, Miss bro, but I've seen that one on TV, it doesn't work. Just because you're here now, right, that doesn't mean you were here when it happened. It's a rookie mistake, like, you can't walk into a police station and say, oh, obviously I didn't do it because it happened seventy miles away, because you could have travelled. Basically what I'm saying is, you don't know how long she's been dead. You went to see her yesterday morning. We don't know when she died. I'm sorry to be blunt but hey, you've got to start thinking like a lawyer.'

Or a criminal, I thought, but he had an unarguable point. I couldn't just rock up to the police or social services with no idea of what I was walking into. Not to mention the fact that I had actually been to London and met with her. We might have been seen, and I was on the suspect list for murder now as well.

'It's going to have to be me,' Annie said. 'Panna and the boys have got enough going on. Ellen has only just met you but I've been with you the whole time, and they've got no beef with me. I'll come with you.'

I couldn't bear the idea. It was my trouble, my responsibility.

'I'm going on my own regardless,' I said. 'I have to. No arguments. Annie – I'll keep you in reserve and I'll call on you immediately if I need you.'

I had never thought of myself as a particularly strong person but for some reason it worked, and I was only slightly sorry. I changed Ocean's nappy, and Noah sat by her the whole time, talking in a soft voice about sheep and books she might like.

'There's books with every kind of story,' he said. 'Ducks, turnips, dogs, pigs, all the animals and little people too, little people like you. We're gonna keep in touch and I'm going to try to come and see you, when you're in your new home.'

He broke off, and looked at Panna. 'I will be able to, won't I, Panna? You should never lie to children. I can see her again, can't I?'

Noah sounded panicky and his voice was full of tears. Panna was crying too.

'Tell her you'll try, boy,' Panna said. 'That won't be a lie.'

'I will try, I will,' Noah said to Ocean.

'Sheep,' she said and held her sheep out towards him, for all the world as if she wanted to comfort him.

That finished us all off, I think. There were sniffles and sobs coming from everyone. I wanted to join them, cry and shout, talk about how terrible it all was but I had to pull myself together. I had to do at least this part well, even if I'd screwed up the rest of it. I owed it to Cate. I took her from Noah and let everyone give her a kiss goodbye. They took a cue from me, bless them, and all of them tried hard to smile and see her off in the right way. Noah helped me to pop her in the buggy Ellen lent us and I walked out of there with my head held high.

'Let's do this,' I said to her.

'Thissssss,' she said.

CHAPTER TWENTY-FIVE

Broadstairs

It was terrifying being on my own again. We had become so close, all of us, that it was all I could do to keep walking, not run back and beg them to come with me. I had avoided any kind of group activities all my life but this little gang was different, and no sooner had I got used to them than I had to go solo again. Or solo apart from Ocean. She had been on the verge of tears when we said goodbye, I knew she had been about to cry but she was a happy little soul, with an underlying sunniness that I hoped would stand her in good stead. Instead I cried for her as I thought about Cate, and we sang 'Old Macdonald' as we walked along the seafront. In different circumstances it could have been a lovely walk, and I tried to pretend for a moment that everything was good. There were no animals except sheep in Ocean's version of the song, and she clutched her little lamby as we went.

I thought through the plan we had agreed on again. I was going to walk to the local social services office. Ellen had explained to me where it was and I had the directions firmly in my mind. I would tell them the whole story, starting with the part where Cate had asked me to look after Ocean. If I explained it properly they would certainly understand why I had taken the action I had, we had all been certain of that. I was aware of the power of the media but I hoped and believed that they would listen to me rather than jumping to conclusions. I had the lanyard Ocean had been wearing and talking had always been one of my strong points. I was sure I could explain the situation properly. Plus, I was an old woman. Could anyone really believe I was also an evil kidnapper?

I stopped for a moment to show Ocean the ocean. We were walking along a cliff path on the seafront with the beach far below us. Everything was as pretty as a summer postcard. There were railings that obscured her view so I stopped by a broken one. It was buckled as if something had crashed into it but her view from the buggy was much clearer, less obscured.

'Look, Ocean,' I said. 'See down there?'

I pointed down to the beach, and she followed my finger.

'Sheep,' she said and I supposed she meant the dogs we could see down there so I agreed.

When I first left Ellen's house I had walked quickly, aware of the possible danger of being recognised, but there was hardly anyone around now and the few people there were didn't seem to look at me twice. It was good to unwind a little and enjoy Ocean for probably the very last time. She was at such a wonderful stage – interested in everything and keen to communicate. She seemed to love me for myself, and she trusted me, and even though I was so sad about saying goodbye, and about her mum, it was still a good feeling. So good, in fact, that I forgot to be a trustworthy adult. I started to relax and that was a huge mistake. I should never have dropped my guard even for a moment. I owed her that. She trusted me with her whole heart, despite all the things that had been done to her that could have and should have made her suspicious. So there we were by the seafront, for all the world as though we belonged together, a grandma and her granddaughter just hanging out and having fun. I will never forgive myself for that, and for what could have happened. What almost happened.

He tapped me on the shoulder. Such an odd thing, a tap on the shoulder. I guess in a perfect world a tap on the shoulder could mean something nice, like, 'Is this your wallet? It just dropped out of your pocket.' Or, 'What a lovely baby, do you mind if I say hello to her?' Only it doesn't, does it? It means, 'I've clocked you, mate, and for whatever reason I feel entitled to not only touch you but to make you feel intimidated.' And intimidated is exactly what I felt. Intimidated as fuck, if I may use a bad word. He was certainly a bad man, so I'm thinking that's OK.

He touched me on the shoulder and I spun around. It was Steve, of course, the ultimate horror show for Ocean and for me. I've read a lot of horror books in my time, and I would have preferred a cackling clown in a gutter or a grey man in a long overcoat to this one very ordinary-looking person. That's what evil is, I realised, it's not dressed up in recognisable masks like a Halloween ghoul. It's young men who look like they might live next door to you, maybe someone who looks like they could be your friend, and always, always a smile on their face. He had a smile, Steve, a horrible smile that would have terrified anyone and it certainly terrified Ocean. She was so scared she didn't even cry. She went silent at the sound of his voice, Old Macdonald silenced and forgotten in an instant and she seemed to shrink in on herself, clutching her sheep as though someone had let the air out of her.

'Keep away,' I said but my voice sounded broken, weak.

I wanted to reach down, stroke Ocean, tell her that everything was all right even if it wasn't, but his grip on my shoulder was firm and I was frozen. He spoke quietly and directly into my ear so that I could feel his rancid breath.

'Don't try anything clever, old lady,' he said. 'I'm afraid you haven't got a leg to stand on, you disgusting old paedophile. One word from me and I could get the police, raise a mob, anything I wanted to. I've got you and you'd better do exactly what I say. Even her stupid mother,' and he pointed at Ocean, 'understood that. Until she thought she'd try to be clever.'

I tried to think about how clichéd the words were, how I must have heard them many times on bad crime shows and films at the cinema with Jed, but somehow I couldn't get the thought going. I was too scared, that was why, and my head was full of that. Fear, that's all I could experience, a blinding white light of fear that drowned out any rational action. I don't know how other people in terrifying situations manage to make smart decisions but my brain was mush. My brain was mush and my fingers and feet felt as though the power supply to them had been turned off. If I had even tried to push him away at that point, I think it would have been like a push from a small and sickly child. A laughable push, and besides, he was right about one thing. He was holding all the cards.

'Don't hurt her,' I said.

Pretty pathetic really, but that's all I could come up with. He laughed, and it was a horrible sound. Quite the match for any cackling villain or underworld demon, and that's probably what he modelled it on.

'Me? Nice normal daddy me? As if I would. She loves me to bits, and I'm all she's got now. Isn't that right?' he said to her. 'Mummy's gone away, but you've got me.'

He made a sad face and if it was possible, I think Ocean shrank back further.

'Don't upset her, please,' I said.

I hated how weak I sounded but I had to say something.

'Oh don't worry,' he said. 'I won't let them see anything. They'll let me have her. I know they will. Who's gonna believe you?'

He closed his eyes briefly and when he opened them and spoke, his voice sounded completely different.

'Come to Daddy,' he said, the cartoon horror gone from his voice.

It didn't reassure Ocean, I could see her tremble.

'Money,' I said, quietly at first and then more loudly as I thought I might have the answer. 'Can I pay you to stay away from her?'

It was a mad idea, I know that now and I knew it then but I was desperate.

He laughed.

'Don't worry about me,' he said. 'They'll pay me for my story and there's all sorts of things I can do to earn money, you sick saddo. I'll take that, thank you.'

He pointed at Ocean and she whimpered. I felt angry, furious that this little person should be subjected to even one moment of fear. I breathed in deeply and let the bolt of anger at the fake sadness clear everything out of my head. I could almost see the anger, and I concentrated on clearing away all of the other stuff in there, even the terror. I stood a little taller, I think, and I reached down and touched her little head.

It was only a soft touch, a stroke, but it surprised him and I realised that despite all the panic, I had been thinking about what to do. Somewhere in the back room of my brain, I had been calculating how to get away from him. There weren't many people around, that was one thing I had noticed. He wouldn't actually be able to summon a mob, which I thought he had been hoping for. So that was the first glimmer of hope. Second, just from his response to my touching Ocean's head I could see that he had been expecting to scare me into submission, first go. He had thought I would be a quivering wreck and to be fair, I almost was. Almost. What he hadn't taken into account was that my fear would all be about her, Ocean. For myself, I didn't care at all. I didn't care what happened to me. What I had to do, though, was convince him that I was scared for me. I knew it instinctively. He'd behave totally differently if he knew I didn't give a damn what happened to me.

'Please don't hurt me,' I said.

He laughed and I pushed the buggy slightly towards him. I know it was a dangerous move but it also enabled me to grab hold of the handle more tightly.

'Here, take her,' I said. 'Go on, you can have her.'

He stared at me for a moment and I could see right into his soul. He was angry, there was no mistake. He didn't want Ocean, he only wanted a fight and to have some fun baiting me. OK, I thought, I'll give you that. It would buy me some more time to work out what to do.

'I'm going to tell the police,' I said. 'Just so that you know,

Cate told me everything and I'm going to tell them all of it. Do you know what happens to people like you in prison?'

His eyes flashed a storm warning and I thought about how terrifying that must have been for Cate, and for Ocean. He hardly looked human, he was so angry. Ocean tucked her sheep in behind her as she sat in the buggy and the simple, tiny movement almost finished me off. She's protecting her sheep again, I realised. She knows what's coming, and what he is capable of, and she wants to keep her sheep safe. That was it for me.

He reached towards her and that's when I did it. I pushed him, and it wasn't premeditated at all but in some ways it was, it was like a dance on the TV, building up to a crescendo where the man lays the cloak at the woman's feet or lies on the floor or holds his partner in the air. A dramatic climax, that's what it was, and for a moment it felt smooth and choreographed. He fell back and I swear I had not realised how near to the edge we were, or how off balance he was, and I certainly hadn't completely clocked how alone we were, and that there was no one around. He fell back, and he lost his footing and scrabbled, sort of reaching out to me so obviously, I stepped away and out of his reach. I had my hand on the buggy anyway, so if he had pulled me over I might have pulled Ocean with me and that wouldn't have done at all. It was bad enough that she had to watch the whole thing. I turned her slightly so that she couldn't see so much, and I tried to sing to cover up the noises he was making but I couldn't get any sound out. He was making so much noise, shouting and swearing and trying to hold on to clumps of grass but it had been raining and they were either not deeply rooted enough or too slippery and he couldn't do it.

I could see that he would be fine if he just stopped panicking and looked for a toehold, then put his hands flat and heaved himself up. I started to call out some instructions, but I only got as far as, 'put your hands . . .' before I thought, really thought, about where else those hands had been. And what he had done to Ocean.

I stopped speaking. I watched instead as he flailed and grabbed and slid out of sight. It's only a small drop, I thought, we need to run before he gets back up and starts chasing us again, only I didn't move, I couldn't. And another thing I couldn't do was see the drop clearly. It looked like a small drop because there was a bush growing out of the rock a little farther down, but it was actually a long drop. That's what they used to call state execution by hanging, I think, the long drop, and that's kind of what happened, only without the rope. Not the state-sanctioned part, that would be cruel. This way was a mistake, pure and simple. A fortuitous mistake but it must have been dreadful for him. There was no screaming on the way down, although obviously I needed to get to the social services office as soon as possible so I didn't stick around but I did hear a kind of 'oof' noise as he hit the bottom, a bit like the sound it might make if you pushed a very large sack of potatoes off a cliff. Or maybe the noise a fat person might make if a big swinging weight swung right into their stomach in a slapstick comedy film. A silent movie with a soundtrack of noises dubbed on, in black and white.

It was really amazing that there was still no one around, although I couldn't stop to check that too thoroughly. Either someone had seen what had happened or they hadn't, and there wasn't much I could do about it either way. Best to act as if it hadn't been seen, hadn't even happened in fact, and as soon as I walked away that's what it felt like. As if it hadn't happened. I didn't feel anything except for a smattering of pure elation, joy that I'd protected Ocean. On my own, with no one else around, I'd kept her safe. Oh Jed, I thought, I wish you could see me now. Maybe I could go to see William, I thought and for one mad moment I could see the three of us, William and Ocean and I, on the beach and picnicking in the sunshine.

I had to keep going though, and we went to the social services office, me and my dear little friend. I would probably have been a lot more scared if what had just happened (the long drop) hadn't happened but somehow it gave me strength. Looking back, I wonder if I would have been able to get away with it, if I hadn't taken her to social services, I mean. Could we have lived together happily ever after anywhere? Only in a story, I thought. And there was Cate's family too, who must have been worried out of their minds. I knew I didn't have the right to keep her.

'I need to talk to someone, and I need them to listen,' I said to the receptionist.

She seemed surprised, but she did find me an experienced social worker and I was grateful for that. I needed to sound normal, believable with no drama and no histrionics, and it's hard to explain how difficult that was when I'd just pushed a man off a cliff, however inadvertently.

'My name is Virginia,' I said. 'And I know you've seen my name on the news. This is Ocean.'

I knew I was probably holding Ocean on my lap for the last time, and I kissed her head.

'You don't look dangerous to me,' the social worker said.

'So I'm going to level with you that I will call the police but I want to talk first.'

I explained the whole thing to her then, starting with Jed and the window.

'I'm not a nosy neighbour,' I said. 'I mean I've never taken more than a passing interest but there was something about this one, she was so smiley and friendly and then so different, honestly anyone would have been worried.'

The social worker smiled, but it was a tight smile.

'You'd be surprised,' she said.

Ocean snuggled in to me and fell asleep.

'Her mum,' I said and I couldn't help crying at the thought of poor Cate. 'Her mum asked me to hide her, it's like she was under his influence so much but she was a good mum, or she tried to be, at least.'

I got out the lanyard. The social worker nodded as if she knew exactly what I meant and I began to feel some hope.

'Why on earth didn't you come to us sooner?' she asked.

I told her about the London office where they'd told me to join a club for lonely old people and she put her head in her hands and groaned.

I even told her about my plan to buy Ocean a happier life.

'Everything escalated so fast,' I said. 'One minute I was taking a baby to the seaside because her mum asked me to, and the next I was a fugitive on the run. And look.'

I held out parts of Ocean's body as she slept and showed the social worker some of the scars. I even said that I had had an inkling that Steve had followed me to Broadstairs, but said that I was probably wrong. She agreed with me on that, and explained that fear can make us see all sorts of things and I was grateful for that. I even started to think that she might be right. After all, how would he know I'd gone to Broadstairs and not anywhere else? Noah had been sure that he had a car and had followed us at a distance, and I suppose he must have been right, but I was never sure.

Sarah, the social worker's name was, and when the time came she didn't grab the baby away from me straight away. I thought of Annie saying goodbye to her twins and although I tried not to cry, I really did, I knew there were tears pouring down my face. I didn't care that we weren't alone, I sang her some of her favourite nursery rhymes and I rocked her gently.

'Don't worry,' Sarah said. 'I can see you care about her. We're going to take good care, I promise.'

'Will you?' I said. It was the first time my composure had really slipped, but I couldn't let that go.

'Will she go to a children's home or a mean foster parent? She deserves the best, this child.'

'All children deserve the best, Virginia,' Sarah said. 'And I'll try, I promise. But you know I'm going to need to take her in a moment and I'd hate for her to be upset, for both of you. Can we make this an easy transition?'

'Of course,' I said.

I stopped crying, or I tried to, and I looked at her little face.

'You're clever and you are strong,' I said. 'Never forget that. Go and live a happy life, Ocean.'

I'll always be grateful for that last cuddle, and even though I knew she wouldn't remember me I whispered as many lucky charm things as I could into her ears and every day now I hope they've stayed in there somewhere. The kind of things fairy godmothers might wish for.

'Tell me that man won't get custody,' I said. 'Please tell me there are family members who can step in.'

Sarah looked at the recording device on the table and I realised that was something she couldn't tell me. 'We'll try,' she whispered. It had to be enough.

'You're going to a lovely new home,' I whispered in Ocean's ear. 'Bye bye, my darling.'

She waved her hand as we had been teaching her, my little darling, and I thought Sarah might have a tear in her eye too.

The police came as I knew they would. Sarah hadn't told me they were waiting outside but by then I didn't care. They checked the window was locked as soon as they came in, and I wondered who exactly they thought I was. It had been hard enough climbing a few steps on the way in, never mind scaling a wall to leap out of a high window. I was absolutely exhausted.

There were two policemen, one tall and one short, and I wondered for a moment whether they always came in opposing pairs. The short one was definitely in charge.

'I hope you understand that you are in very serious trouble,' he said as soon as Sarah had left with Ocean.

I couldn't say anything for a moment as the sheer loss of her winded me like a punch in the gut. She had looked at me and smiled as Sarah stood up holding her and I had that at least, the fact that we had let her smile and trust again. I managed somehow to wave and smile back and say goodbye and then they were gone, and I wanted to pull out my hair, scream, grab her back and punch someone but I didn't. I sat there and cried while PC Short explained to me in jaunty tones how much trouble I was in. He was thrilled when he realised I didn't have an alibi for the day that Cate was killed.

325

'Of course I don't have an alibi,' I said. 'I was looking after the baby, in Margate. How would I have had time to go on a murder mission?'

Annie had said she would be my alibi, and the boys too, but I wanted to manage this on my own. I had to. It had all been my idea, my project, and I didn't want to drag them into trouble with me. I tried not to think about the irony of being questioned about a murder I didn't do, and I shut the thought of the noise he made (oomph) as he hit the stone walkway below entirely out of my head so that I could concentrate. My secret weapon was this, I'm a middle-class old white woman and we are never to blame for anything more important than a lost pair of glasses. How can we be, when we are invisible?

It wasn't enough this time, and I realised it wasn't as the questioning went on and on and the police (especially PC Tall) became louder and more angry sounding. What I didn't realise at the time was that it was fake, their anger, and they were probably playing parts that had been written for them by a thousand poorly scripted police shows. Good cop, bad cop, shouty cop, quiet cop. All that kind of nonsense. It was effective, I'll say that for it. I was almost worn down after an hour or two, and I could understand why people confessed to crimes they hadn't committed. I wanted to cry again but I thought that if I did it would look as though I was guilty. I don't know why I thought that, it didn't make sense but one thing I know about men is this, most of them hate women's tears. They hate them so much that they'd ban them if they could but the next best thing is to twist them. Make them mean something they don't, so that you're only crying because you're guilty, or scared, or trying to cover up that you don't care. So I didn't cry, and I tried to breathe deeply without it being obvious. Secret deep breathing, and lots of women do it all the time, I'd guess. They said they were going to take me to the station and I tried to think how much worse those words were for people with a genuine and well-founded fear of the police, or in brutal regimes where people disappear, but I was scared anyway. Who knew a person could still be scared even with a broken heart?

I think we were nearly ready to move to the station when PC Tall got a message. He looked at it, then at me before gesturing to his colleague that they should go outside. I was sure they had found Steve and I wondered for a mad moment whether I should own up, explain that I hadn't meant it and take what was coming. It would be worth it to be left alone to think about Ocean, and hope that she was OK. I wondered why I hadn't given more thought to jumping out of the window and I considered standing on a chair to get out but I couldn't remember what floor we were on and I wasn't convinced that it was high enough to do more than break my ankle.

'So it seems we can let you go, for now,' PC Short said when they returned. 'Don't leave town, as they say. We're going to want to talk to you again.'

They started to pack up their things. I felt as if I'd been body slammed. I didn't know what game they were playing but it made me feel very insecure. I'd seen the movies, they were going to let me get just outside the door and then they'd arrest me again. It was a well known tactic in films so I walked out slowly, expecting something terrible at every step. My back felt as though someone had a dagger hovering between my shoulder blades and every nerve was tingling but nothing happened, and I was outside in the street. It was dark and I was grateful for that. I didn't want to see anyone, and I certainly didn't want anyone to see me. I looked up at the windows, hoping to see Ocean one more time, although I knew she would have gone by now, and I wished on the stars I couldn't see that she would be happy with her grandmother or auntie or anyone kind, and that she wouldn't miss me.

By the time I got back to Ellen's house I had prepared a story about Ocean leaving that made it sound much happier than it really had been. I didn't want to go near the seafront and I was glad of the longer walk back through the streets, so that I had time to get it right. I had decided to say that her grandma was coming immediately and that she waved bye bye happily but I couldn't do it. I couldn't get any words out and I was so glad to see them that it was all I could do not to cry.

It was late, very late, and everyone except Annie was in bed. I sat with her, and it was obvious that she had something that she wanted to say. I wanted to talk to her, too. I wanted to explain how hard it was to give up Ocean to someone who would understand. Someone who had been there, only worse.

'It was hard,' I said.

'I know,' she said. 'I've never been able to explain how difficult it was handing over the twins, because I've never had the words. I'm sure it's the same for you. You don't have to give birth to a baby to love it completely and unconditionally.'

The thought of how truly terrible it must have been for Annie when they took the twins away made it hard to catch my breath. She was amazing. At no point did she say, well you've only known Ocean for five minutes so obviously it wasn't that bad, and she could have done. She just listened, and held on to Ocean's little tractor while I spoke. She gave me tissues and water and when I'd finished there was silence for a few minutes.

'I followed you,' she said eventually. 'When you left with the baby. I'm really good at stealth following. I used to trail around behind the family who adopted the twins, not so much when they had them because I couldn't always bear to see them. But afterwards until they went to prison and even a bit since they've been released. So I'm good at it and you wouldn't have noticed but I followed you.'

I stopped crying and looked at her and I could tell straight away that she had seen him fall.

'I went down the cliff,' she said. 'And I did a bit of tidying.'

'Thank you,' I said.

I didn't ask any questions and I had no idea exactly what she had done, but I was grateful.

CHAPTER TWENTY-SIX

Jackson was never sure whether the excitement had been the last straw for Panna. She had been so steady and strong all through the rescue of Ocean that he had stopped thinking about how sick she was. She had adored that baby, and for a day or two Jackson had been able to see her as he never had before. He saw her as an equal, a teammate, a leader and a strong person with determination and ideas. She was funny and smart and he wished he had known her when she was young and starry-eyed with thoughts of the future, arriving at Tilbury docks in her best dress. There was no photograph from that time, but Panna had found some other people's photographs of the docks online one day, and her eyes had shone.

'That's what it was like,' she said. 'People everywhere and the noise was coming from every corner and over my head. Jangling and clanking and shouting, babies crying and one poor woman was so overcome she just sat on the floor and sobbed, surrounded by bags and boxes. We couldn't leave her there so she came with us.'

Panna had lingered over the photos for longer than Jackson would have thought possible, looking for anyone she knew. She stretched them out as he had shown her, and muttered to herself, listing names he had never heard before as if saying them might invoke their presence. So many things he didn't know about her, he thought.

He had thought it often, and he thought it again as he looked at her sleeping in Ellen's bed. He could tell from her breathing that Panna wasn't doing well. She huffed and puffed and thrashed around on the pillow as if she was looking for something and Jackson sat with her and held her hand for most of the night. In the morning she rallied again, and got up to listen to Virginia's story of what had happened. Jackson noticed that she was crying through most of it although everyone else was upset too so it was possible that no one else noticed, or realised how unusual this was for Panna. She had the dog on her lap and Jackson was pleased that she had him for comfort. Noah sat by Panna's chair, holding her hand and occasionally stroking Philip.

'You're a hero,' Noah said. 'An actual, real-life superhero.'

Jackson was surprised at how much Virginia bristled at that.

'I'm absolutely not,' she said. 'Nothing of the kind. Anyone would have helped her and you all did.'

Noah looked up, and Jackson could see that he was surprised at the steely tone. He looked over at his brother and shrugged. Old women, what are they like, he could hear Noah thinking.

'Where will Ocean go?' Noah said. 'I mean, no one knew her except for us and her mum. Who would know that she likes to play that game with her sheep, or which songs she likes to sing?'

Virginia took a deep breath and Jackson could see that this was what she had been waiting for.

'Oh Noah, that's the best bit,' she said. 'She's got an auntie who loves her, and a grandma and grandpa. They will have collected her by now, and I reckon they're going to be really happy.'

Jackson could tell from the way Virginia looked off to her left that the story wasn't completely true, but as long as Noah was happy he didn't mind. There was something more, too, he could tell. Something about the man. Something the women knew and hadn't said, otherwise there would have been more talk of watching out for him, being careful. He didn't care. He couldn't think about anything else and he didn't want to know. He had had enough drama, and he could see that there was more coming, probably in his own home. If he could get Panna home, that was. He knew that was where she wanted to be, though, so he had to try. The other women picked it up quickly and Jackson was grateful.

'Let's get you home,' Ellen said. 'All of you. I can take you in my van.'

Jackson had never been more pleased to get back to the flat, although he could see that Noah was sad to be leaving Daniel.

'You can go back,' Jackson said. 'If they'll have you.'

'We'd love it,' said Ellen. 'Any time.'

Jackson thought later that it was the last slightly normal conversation he had for some time.

The women left as soon as Panna had been put to bed in her own bed. They offered to stay, and Jackson knew that he could call on them, but this was family business. Panna was too tired to eat or drink and by the afternoon, he knew it was time to call the hospital and take her in. He held on to Noah as the paramedics carried her downstairs.

'Don't come with me, Jax,' she said. 'You can't leave Noah on his own and it's not right for him to come yet. Come and see me later, when they've settled me in.'

Jackson could have ignored her and for the rest of his life he wished that he had but he kissed her goodbye and stayed home with Noah.

The phone call came at about eight o'clock, and Jackson thought at first that it would be Panna, ringing from the hospice phone to say that she was settled, and that they could come in. He picked up his wallet and keys before he answered.

CHAPTER TWENTY-SEVEN

I could hear the boys crying as they left their flat to go to the hospice where their lovely grandma had died. I remembered how private my own immediate grief had felt so I didn't go out to them at first and I wonder now how I could have got that so wrong but Noah saved the day. He has an emotional intelligence far beyond his years and that day it was on display for everyone to see. I thought they must have gone and then I heard a banging on my door. It was Noah, with Jackson right behind him.

'Virginia,' he said and he barrelled into me for a hug.

He held on to me so tightly it was hard to catch my breath.

'Noah,' Jackson said. 'Leave her, come on, we've got to go.'

Jackson had been crying too and at that moment he was about the most miserable, embarrassed young man I had ever seen. I wasn't sure what to do but Annie was there, and she stood on tiptoe to put her arms round him and let him snuffle into her shoulders for a while.

We made our way to the living room like a strange, many-legged and wounded animal, stumbling and rocking so that we didn't disturb the hugs these boys needed.

'She liked you,' Noah said. 'I mean, for a white woman she said you had guts.'

'Noah,' Jackson said. 'For goodness' sake.' And suddenly it was so funny, so normal, and the exasperation in poor Jackson's voice was just what we needed.

'It's OK,' I said. 'Jackson, your brother can't do anything wrong as far as I'm concerned so don't worry.'

I tumbled into a chair as my legs threatened to give way. It wasn't just the weight of Noah, it was something else, something I wouldn't be able to say to anyone, not even Annie. It was what I didn't say, what I would never be able to say again for any reason. He could get away with murder, that's what I nearly said about Noah. And I'd never say it again about anyone.

'What do you two have to do today?' Annie said. 'Maybe we can help you.'

'We have to get her things,' Noah wailed. 'I mean her watch and her phone and stuff, and I keep thinking she might need them even though I know she won't. Not really.'

'Oh I get that,' Annie said in her lovely soft voice. 'That's a wee bit hard, isn't it?'

She sat on the sofa next to Jackson, who was screwing his fists into his eyes as if he wanted to rub them out.

'Two things,' Annie said. 'Number one, some things are easier with pals. We'll come with you, we'd be honoured. No arguments. You were there for us and we'll be there for you. Number two, if it's too hard to look at a thing in one way, turn it around and look at it from another angle, so I'm wondering if you can think of Panna's things as things you've been trusted to look after, for the time being. Just to start off with.'

They're bright, these lads, and I wasn't at all sure they'd buy it but she's bright too, lovely Annie, and she judged it right. Noah sat up, still sniffling but smiling too.

'That's a great idea. I mean, two great ideas,' he said. 'Jax, can we make a special place to put her stuff, so it stays safe? Like a really special place?'

'We can, No, of course we can. You can help me sort that out. There's another thing, though, No, which I haven't mentioned so far, and maybe I can talk to you about it while the ladies are here.'

'Shoot,' I said and Annie nodded.

'Well, Noah, I know we said goodbye to Panna last night, at the hospice, and maybe that's enough, but we could see her today at the other place if we want to. It's just something they offer, that's all.'

'The other place?' Noah said. He sounded shocked and I worked it out.

'Jackson means the funeral parlour, No,' I said. 'Nothing metaphysical.'

I thought that might go over his head but it didn't, and he even managed a giggle.

We went with them that day, and we skipped the 'other place' after a few words from Annie about souls, and what Panna would want. She can be very persuasive. We cooked for them that night and we've eaten together quite a few times since then. We walk the dog with them sometimes, the dog I've grown to love, and we've all learned to avoid the man who hurt him. I think he's given up.

Annie has been a rock to me too. She has a light touch, that's the thing I value. She doesn't bustle around and produce tissues or tell me that there's light at the end of the tunnel or any of those sorts of things. She listens, and that's something most people can't do. She helped me manage all those interviews afterwards, with the police and endless social workers. They knew he'd done it fairly quickly, because not only did an actual police officer see him nearby but his DNA was everywhere. All over the place. He'd strangled her apparently. The part that made me cry (again) was that she was holding on to one of Ocean's little baby cardigans as she died. She did love her, and I told the social workers that at every chance I got. They suggested I write Ocean a letter and I did, although I'm not sure she'll ever see it.

She won't remember me or Noah or Annie or Jackson or any of the nice memories we tried to make with her, but I have to hope that they will be there in the background, like a theatre set. We tried to change her life from a horror story to one full of nursery rhymes and porridge, and we succeeded for a few days. A few days that saved her life.

I saved my own life too, or Annie and Panna did, or the boys, or maybe it was Ocean all the time. Someone rescued me anyway and all the pills went into the bin on bin day, so that I couldn't change my mind. Panna was right. It would have been terrible for the boys. They had had a hard enough time.

Some days I spend more time in the boys' flat than I do my own, and they seem to like my cooking. I've even started to wonder whether Noah could live with me when Jax goes off to uni, but it's early days. Annie has gone back to Oban for a while – I think she wants to sort things out, say goodbye to the twins where they were, where she knew them. She says she's coming back though, and she's going to take up painting, find an art class. I miss her but I know she'll come back. I'll never stop missing Jed, but most days I'm proud of what I achieved without him. I miss Panna and William too. And Ocean, my lovely girl. Sometimes I think I miss her most of all.

ACKNOWLEDGEMENTS

Thank you to everyone at HQ for their advice, wisdom and belief in me, especially my editor, Manpreet.

Thank you Julia, for being such a great agent and friend.

Thank you to all the babies I have loved, including Samuel, Anna, Charlie, Georgia, Molly, Joey, David, Bella, Matilda, Arthur, Elsie and Iona. And the ones I have yet to meet.

Thanks as ever to Dom, my constant companion who puts up with my endless 'what ifs'.

I also want to acknowledge all the babies and children who have not been as lucky as Ocean. Their stories inspired me, but I wish it had not been so.

If you enjoyed *Virginia Lane is Not a Hero*, then don't miss the debut novel from Rosalind Stopps, *The Stranger She Knew*, shortlisted for the Paul Torday Prize 2020.

As a young woman, May found that sometimes it was easier to say nothing and cope with what life threw at her in silence. Now, decades later, May has suffered a stroke and has lost her ability to speak. She is still as sharp as ever, but only her daughter and a new friend from the care home, see this.

When May discovers that someone very familiar, from long ago, is living in the room opposite hers she is haunted by scenes from her earlier life. May is determined to protect everyone from this new threat, but how can she warn them without her voice? And who really is this man charming everyone in May's life?

Available to buy now!

Don't miss another gripping, sharply written novel from Rosalind Stopps.

Grace, Meg and Daphne, all in their seventies, are minding their own business while enjoying a cup of tea in a café, when seventeen-year-old Nina stumbles in. She's clearly distraught and running from someone, so the three women think nothing of hiding her when a suspicious-looking man starts asking if they've seen her.

Once alone, Nina tells the women a little of what she's running from. The need to protect her is immediate, and Grace, Meg and Daphne vow to do just this. But how? They soon realise there really is only one answer: murder.

And so begins the tale of the three most unlikely murderers-in-the-making, and may hell protect anyone who underestimates them.

Available to buy now!

ONE PLACE. MANY STORIES

Bold, innovative and
empowering publishing.

FOLLOW US ON:

@HQStories